WILD LOVE

REBECCA JENSHAK

Wild Love
Copyright © 2021 by Rebecca Jenshak

Rebecca Jenshak, *www.rebeccajenshak.com*

Cover Design by Emily Wittig Designs
Editing by Edits in Blue and Ellie McLove at My Brother's Editor

All rights reserved. Except as permitted under the US Copyright Act of 1976, no part of this book may be reproduced, distributed, transmitted in any form or by any means, or stored in a database or retrieval system, without written permission from the author.

The characters and events in this book are fictitious. Names, characters, places, and plots are a product of the author's imagination. Any similarity to real persons, living or dead, is coincidental and not intended by the author.

ALSO BY REBECCA JENSHAK

Campus Nights Series
Secret Puck

Bad Crush

Broken Hearts

Wild Love

Smart Jocks Series
The Assist

The Fadeaway

The Tip-Off

The Fake

The Pass

Standalone Novels
Sweet Spot

Electric Blue Love

PLAYLIST

"Twerkin in the Mirror" by Ying Yang Twins
"If I Were U" by Blackbear feat. Lauv
"Slow Motion" by Charlotte Lawrence
"Let it Go" by DJ Khaled feat. 21 Savage and Justin Bieber
"Sure Thing" by Miguel
"Heartbreak Hotel" by Abigail Barlow
"No Scrubs" by Sam Robs, Kelvin Wood
"Wow" by Zara Larsson
"Fuck Up the Friendship" by Leah Kate
"Play with Me" by Bailey Bryan
"Sweater Weather" by The Neighbourhood
"Obsessed" by Mariah Carey
"I Wanna Be Your Girlfriend" by Girl in Red
"You & Jennifer" by bülow
"We Belong" by Dove Cameron
"Problems" by DeathbyRomy
"Time of Our Lives" by Pitbull feat. Ne-Yo
"Vices" by Mothica
"Angels Like You" by Miley Cyrus
"Alone in My Car" by Niki Demar
"Champagne & Sunshine" by PLVTINUM feat. Tarro
"Frustrated" by Lauren Sanderson

Chapter One

DAKOTA

He's ridiculous.

I'm getting back from my morning run when I spot him. The apartment complex is just starting to wake up. It's the last week of the spring semester, and between finals and the nightly end-of-year parties, everyone is exhausted and ready for summer break. Me included.

I slow my run to a jog as I cut through the parking lot of my apartment. It's hard to tear my eyes away from him, but I do as I navigate around cars and people. I pass a couple of fellow Valley U students heading out to their cars; backpacks slung over their shoulders, coffee in hand, eyes still bleary.

"Morning," I chirp and receive mumbled greetings back.

At the sidewalk in front of my building, I let my gaze return to the walk of shame in progress from his first-floor apartment.

Johnny Maverick is shirtless, athletic shorts hanging low on trim hips, tattoos covering his chest and arms. Ridiculous, but undeniably hot.

The girls, because yes, there are two of them, cling to him

like their rumpled dresses from last night hug their curves—one blonde, the other black, both stunning.

I bite back a smile at the three of them. Since he scored a hat trick in the final game of the Frozen Four, Maverick has been the center of attention at Valley U, and by the look on his face, he's very much enjoying it.

I hang back as he says goodbye to his guests.

"Call us later?" the blonde asks after she kisses him on the cheek.

He says something I don't catch, and the girls walk hand in hand away from his front door. His gaze lifts as he stares after them. When he spots me watching him, a sheepish grin pulls at his lips.

"Good morning, Kota," he says, sounding far more awake than the people I tried to offer the same sentiment to in the parking lot.

I laugh. Yeah, I'll bet he's having a good morning. I wait until his guests are out of earshot. "Have fun last night?"

"Always. Missed you, though. I was looking for you."

I ignore that remark. I see how much he missed me. Hey, I'm not blaming him. Johnny and I have a complicated relationship. Complicated but easily summed up as he hits on me, and I turn him down. Because clearly, he isn't that serious.

"You're up early," he says, and his gaze rakes over my sweaty body. "Out for a run?"

I nod, feeling the sweat pool at my lower back. Despite having just rolled out of bed, he looks as handsome as always. His dark hair is messy, but his hazel eyes are bright, and his smile playful.

His French bulldog, Charli, races out of his apartment and circles my feet.

I lean down to stroke her soft fur and scratch behind her ears. "Hey, pretty girl. Did you have to avert your eyes all night long?"

Mav chuckles and runs a hand through his hair. The movement makes his abs contract and his bicep pop.

I scoop her up to distract myself from checking out her owner. She's small but heavy. Her coat is white with splotches of black. She's adorable. Charli licks my face, and I laugh and hand her over to her owner. Up this close, I can smell him, or rather the girls he was with.

"You smell like sex and vanilla."

"Vanilla." He snaps his fingers. "I was trying to place the smell all night. She smelled like vanilla!"

"Which one?" I glance back at the parking lot, but they've already disappeared from view.

"Blonde."

"Does Blondie have a name?"

He squints one eye and smirks. "Do you really care if she does?"

"Good point." I'm still standing close, and Charli rests a paw on my arm, looking for attention, which I absolutely give to her.

"Maybe you should let Charli stay with me when you're entertaining."

"Or maybe we cut the other girls, and you could stay at my place and keep us both company."

I roll my eyes. See what I mean? Not serious. "I can't believe any line that comes out of your mouth actually works."

"I don't usually have to run lines. I mean, look at me. All this could be yours." He grins as if he knows how absurd he sounds.

"At least shower off the last girl... I'm sorry, *girls*, before you hit on me."

He smiles at me, which always makes me feel a little off balance. Not just because he's totally hot. Maverick has this way about him that, despite all reasoning, he makes people feel important and seen. Or he does me, anyway.

Our attention is drawn upstairs as the apartment door above his opens, and my best friend and roommate, Reagan, and her boyfriend Adam tumble out. Arms around her waist, Adam walks her backward toward our apartment across the breezeway. He presses her against it, devouring her mouth.

"I gotta go," he says but keeps kissing her. Mav and I are frozen, staring at them. The air crackles with the chemistry between them. A flight of stairs separates us, but I can *feel* how desperate they are for each other.

"Just ten more minutes." Reagan opens our door, and they disappear into it, slamming the door behind them.

Mav's deep chuckle sounds beside me. "Want to come in for a few minutes?"

"Not really," I mumble but follow him.

"What is it with everyone this week? They're…" I pause, searching for words.

Mav drops Charli in the living room and continues into the kitchen. "Fucking like the world is ending?"

"Yeah, that." I scan his living area for evidence from last night. I don't want to sit anywhere that he had sex in the past twenty-four hours.

"It's the end of an era. People are graduating, moving on…" He holds out a Powerade and a bottle of water. I take the first, and he motions toward the couch.

"I think I'd rather sit outside."

He cackles like he knows what I'm thinking. If he did, he'd be repulsed with himself and not smiling like a guy... well, like a guy who just had a threesome. To be clear, I'm not anti-threesomes. I'm not really anti-anything when it comes to sex. I'm just so over all of it right now. All of my friends are deliriously in love, and I feel like I'm the last single person. I might not be ready for my own happily ever after, but can't a girl find a decent guy to date?

The last few guys I've met think foreplay is sexting, and dating is meeting up when it's convenient for them to get drunk and then go back to their place.

"How far did you run this morning?" he asks, holding the door open for me.

I push past him and sit on the second step leading up to my apartment. He falls into the narrow space beside me.

"Just two miles. I have a tour at the Hall of Fame this morning. Some hockey guy named Toby Russo."

"Oh, right. Coach is salivating over that kid."

"Not you?"

He takes a long drink from the bottle in his hands and then leans forward so that his elbows rest on his thighs. "He'll be an asset wherever he goes, but something about him rubs me the wrong way."

"You've met him?"

"Yeah, he was at the Frozen Four. He came up to me after our first game and gave me some tips."

I snort. "He gave you tips? Seriously?" Maverick is one of the best college hockey players. I'm not just saying that because we're friends, there's a list.

"Yeah." He nods his dark head.

"What'd you do?"

"I told him thanks and walked off."

"That's it?"

"I've gotten really good at letting criticism and condescending assholes roll off my back."

I think he means his father. I don't know a lot about John Maverick Sr., but I know that the few times Mav has talked about him, he lost a little of the playful, fun demeanor that he's known for.

"Well, I think you're doing okay. Plenty of people are waiting in line to ease the burden of your success and celebrate by getting naked. In pairs, apparently."

He grins. "Could have been you. We all hung out upstairs and then went to The Hideout. I was looking for you. Where were you?"

"I went out for a little while, then crashed so I could get up early and run before work."

"Date?"

"Yeah." A guy I met online—total waste of time. I knew within seconds we weren't compatible. I sigh. "I cannot tell one more guy my favorite color or pretend to care about the places he wants to travel to someday. I'm so over it. I need a change of scenery." I spent twenty dollars on drinks last night, and for what?

"What are you doing this summer?" He leans back on one elbow.

"I applied for some internships, but so far, nothing. It looks like I'll be staying in Valley and working at the Hall of Fame." I bump my shoulder against his. "Maybe I could start a coffee and dry-cleaning service for the chicks that come out of your apartment in the morning."

"Not unless you're moving to Minnesota."

"What?" I pause, bottle to my lips.

"That's why I was looking for you last night. I wanted to talk to you."

I stare at him, trying to make sense of the words coming out of his mouth. "Talk to me about what?"

"I, uh, signed with the Wildcats," he says.

Maverick came to Valley already drafted by the NHL team, the Wildcats. This isn't news. Except. "Oh my gosh! *Signed* as in…"

His eyes hold mine. "I'm not coming back next year."

I TEXT THE GIRLS FOR AN EMERGENCY GROUP LUNCH, AND WE meet up on my hour break between work and classes so that I can fill them in on the Maverick news.

"I can't believe it." Reagan digs through her purse for gum and then offers it around the table. "When did this happen?"

"I'm not sure," I say, pushing away my plate. My stomach is a ball of knots. "He told me this morning. None of you knew?"

Ginny raises a hand. "Heath told me after the championship game. I would have said something, but he made me promise not to until Maverick announced it."

Her boyfriend and Maverick are best friends, so it makes sense he knew before the rest of us. Still, I hate that I'm just now finding out. The championship game was weeks ago.

"Did anyone else know?" Reagan asks. "I don't think Adam did because he's terrible at keeping secrets from me."

"I did." Sienna raises her hand from the table the same way Ginny did. She's dating Rhett and the newest addition to our friend group. Newest, but no less important. I don't know what I'd do without these three.

"That's why he went to Minnesota," she adds, and the pieces start to fall in place as I think back to Maverick's actions over the past month. If he were anyone else, the signs would have been obvious. The trip to Minnesota, the extra partying, doubling up on girls.

I can't imagine him not living downstairs from me or hanging out with all of us upstairs. He routinely makes me roll my eyes at his incessant flirting and over-the-top shenanigans, but he's part of our friend group. An integral part.

All my friends are dating hockey players. I live next to them, I party with them, I even work with them doing recruitment tours at the Hall of Fame.

It really is the end of an era.

"Is Heath leaving too?" Reagan asks Ginny, her gaze narrowed.

She shakes her head and fingers the end of her long, blonde braid. "No. He wants to finish school."

"And hang out with his awesome girlfriend," I point out. Heath and Ginny have been inseparable since they started dating last fall, and I can't imagine a world in which he goes anywhere without her.

"That too." She smiles, a little smitten and doe eyed.

The three of them talk about all the changes happening while I'm lost in my thoughts. There is this underlying excitement as they talk about it, even though their words are sad, and lunch includes no less than five group hugs. Sienna graduates next week with Rhett and Adam, and now that I know Maverick is leaving too, I feel an odd pang of sorrow.

Up until this moment, I've had a hard time feeling the same sadness as my friends that things were changing, maybe because I'm so ready for change myself that I couldn't wrap my brain around what they were feeling.

No matter where Sienna goes, we'll stay friends, and being friends with her, I'll also get tabs on Rhett. And since Adam is staying in Valley for medical school and dating my roommate, I know I'll see him too. Things were changing, but they didn't seem so permanent as Maverick leaving does.

Ginny leans forward and rests her palms on the table. "Heath is throwing him a party tonight at the apartment. Shirts are optional, but fun is not."

I feel my brows lift. "I'm sorry, what?"

She giggles, and her brown eyes light up with humor and excitement. "It's seriously the tagline for tonight. And you should see the amount of Mad Dog we bought."

A party where MD 20/20 is the drink of choice and shirts are discouraged? The knot in my stomach loosens at the ridiculousness that I've come to love about our group. "Only a party for Maverick would require a tagline."

Chapter Two

JOHNNY

A knock at the front door sends Charli running toward it, barking.

Heath's voice calls from the other side. "Mav? Are you home?"

I pull open the door and step back to let him in. My buddy sets a large box on the coffee table in the living room.

"I think I got everything, but I'm going to do another pass to make sure."

I move forward and open one of the flaps to see inside. "What is all this?"

"Your shit." He plops down on the leather couch. "Video games, headphones, books." He shakes his head. "I had no idea I was hoarding so much of your stuff. You should see how empty my room looks now."

I pull out a pair of Beats headphones. "I gave these to you."

"*Loaned*," he says definitively. He has a hard time accepting gifts, which is too bad for him because I like giving them.

"I thought you might say that." I walk over to the kitchen

counter and pull a new pair of headphones out of the box they shipped in yesterday. I toss them at him.

He sits up and cradles the box, turning them over and then sliding the headphones out. "No way!" He smiles, but his excitement is short lived. He sets them on the table next to the box. "Mav, no. I can't accept these. They're like three hundred dollars."

"So?"

"So?" He chuckles.

"Take your pick, but I'm leaving one of them behind. And whatever is in that box is yours too. The less I have to move, the better."

He sits back on the couch and glances around the apartment. It was never very lived in. I spent most of my time hanging out at his apartment with Rauthruss and Scott upstairs, but it's been home for the past year, the dorms the year before that. Two years I've been at Valley U, two of the best of my life, and now I'm leaving. It's surreal.

Classes are done Wednesday, and when everyone's done partying and heads off for the summer, I will too. I don't need to be in Minnesota for another two weeks, but I've already signed a lease on an apartment, and Coach Miller said I could start using the workout and practice facilities as soon as I want.

The Wildcats season is over, and camp isn't until July. No rest for the wicked, though. If I want to keep myself from being sent down to the minor league team, I need to start contributing immediately.

"It isn't going to be the same without you," my buddy says.

"It wouldn't be the same regardless." I take a seat in the recliner next to him. "Rauthruss and Scott are both done, and there'll be a new group of rookies…" My voice trails off, and I'm hit with the finality of my decision.

I've signed, and there's no going back now. I hope I made the right call. My dad, for all his faults, is a smart man, and he seems to think I made a good decision. And believe me, he doesn't approve of many of my actions.

"I know. I'll miss playing with you, though."

"It isn't too late. You can come with me. We can start our pro careers together." I smile and pretend that I think there's a real chance he might take me up on it. He won't.

He isn't going anywhere until he has a degree. I respect that. Heath hasn't had the easiest path getting to where he is. He doesn't take any of it for granted. He wants a fallback plan. Me? Well, I guess the money in my bank account gives me the freedom to not worry about what happens if hockey doesn't pan out. And they say money can't buy happiness.

He points at me and then waggles his finger. "Two years, and then I'm coming for you."

"Can't wait," I say, honestly. He's already been drafted by the Coyotes, and I'm looking forward to meeting him on the ice. Who knows, maybe someday we'll even be on the same team again.

"The guys want to have some time, just the four of us, before everyone comes over. You ready?" His gaze drops to my bare chest with amusement.

"You said it was a shirtless party." I run a hand across my pecs. "I even put on some of that shimmery lotion Ginny's always leaving around your apartment. It really does catch the light and accentuate my best assets."

He laughs, shaking his head, and smiling at me. "Fuck I'm

going to miss you."

Upstairs at their apartment, we find Adam and Rhett outside on the deck. It's hot today, but there's a nice breeze. They stand and show off their shirtless torsos. I laugh, and Heath pulls off his T-shirt as well.

"Aww, you're all going shirtless for me? That's the best going-away present ever. Maybe we should just make it a naked party. Let's get weird."

"Keep your pants on," Adam Scott comes forward and hugs me, slapping me on the back twice. "Congrats, man."

"Thank you."

Rhett Rauthruss is next. He embraces me quickly and then steps back and adjusts the Bruins hat on his head. "I might have to start cheering for my home state team now."

"Eh, I don't care if you cheer for the team; just coming to watch me play will be enough." He's from a town not far from the Wildcats arena and moving back there after graduation to work with his family.

He laughs quietly. "Definitely."

Heath brings out the Mad Dog, my favorite drink, and hands us each our own bottle.

"Oh fuck, I don't know if I can drink an entire one of these," Scott says as he gets a whiff of the sweet liquor.

"Party rules," Heath tells him and holds up his bottle. He's the only one staying. Technically, Adam will still be in Valley while he goes to medical school, but the team won't be the same. "It's been a wild ride playing with the three of you, living together, drinking, just hanging out. Congrats to all of you."

"Cheers." Rauthruss is the first to clink his bottle against

Heath's, and Adam and I follow.

"Cheers." I take a long swig, swallowing down the emotion swirling with it. "Let's get ridonkulous!"

Their girlfriends are the next to arrive. Ginny, Reagan, and Sienna file out together and go straight to their boys. Dakota is with them, and when I get a good look at her, I bark out a laugh.

"That for me, sweetheart?"

"I heard shirts were optional," she says, batting her lashes and doing a spin that sends her red hair whipping around her head. The shirt, or scrap of white material, barely covering her tits, is held up by two thin straps around her shoulders, leaving most of her back bare too. She's lean, and tone from running, and her skin looks soft and tempting. She's gorgeous on any given day, but when she's trying to impress, she could kill a man.

"I approve. Every day should be a no-shirt day."

"You can't handle all this every day, Johnny Maverick," she says with a teasing tone.

"Man, but I'd love to give it the ole college try." I scoop my arm around her back and pull her against my hip. Just like I thought, her skin is soft, and she molds perfectly to my side.

She swats at my chest. "I think I might miss you."

"I'm definitely going to miss you."

Someone starts the music, and more people join us outside. Dakota starts to move away, but I tighten my grip.

"Dance with me?"

"Now?" She looks around. No one else is dancing, but I give zero fucks. I'll take any excuse to keep her at my side.

"Yeah. Now. Later. All night." She has a slender but athletic build, and she's a great dancer. I can't think of a better way to spend my last party at Valley than dancing all night with the best chick I know.

"Maverick!" a freshman teammate calls out to me as he approaches, holding up a bottle of Mad Dog.

Kota opens her stance to acknowledge him, and I reluctantly let her go. I always let her go. She's too beautiful. Too smart. Too rad. Too everything for me. Yeah, I'm definitely going to miss her.

With one last look in my direction, she hits me with those sexy blue eyes. "Enjoy your party, Johnny."

Chapter Three

DAKOTA

The guys' apartment is packed tonight. People crowd out onto the deck and into the living room. It's a real possibility we're over capacity on this creaky deck. But at least we're only on the second floor.

"Okay, so I know we were mocking the optional shirt tagline for the night, but holy shit, why did we not think of this sooner?" Reagan looks around from where we sit on a couple of loungers on the right side of the deck, and I follow her gaze.

She's not wrong. Most of the guys took off their shirts in honor of Maverick and some girls too. When I pulled the smallest shirt I owned out of my closet, I had no idea I'd be one of the most dressed people at the party. I should have. Everyone loves Maverick. He's easy to love. He's fun and generous, and he has this way about him where he makes people feel included and important. When he's talking to you, he gives all of him.

He's a shameless flirt, and I'm not sure how much of what comes out of his mouth is actually serious, but he makes people feel good, and that's worth something.

"First order of business next semester, throwing a shirtless party in our new apartment," I say to Ginny and Reagan. The three of us are moving in together now that Ginny can move out of the dorms. We're staying in the same complex, just moving into a three-bedroom place.

They nod eagerly as if they don't have hot boyfriends they see shirtless on the regular. I don't call them on it. It's a rare moment that my friends are by my side at a party and not with their boyfriends, and I'm enjoying it.

Everyone is trying to soak up time with the people they won't see, and my friends will see their boyfriends. Each one of them is not only coupled up, they're deliriously in love. And I feel like I'm never going to get past the talking phase.

Reagan says I'm too picky, but I really don't think that's it. I just want more than "Hey girl, what's up?" texts that are followed by a string of get-to-know-you questions that tell me nothing about the guy I'm talking to. There has to be a better way.

"Is that the same girl Maverick left with last night?" Ginny asks.

I'm already aware of exactly where he is and who he's with, but I watch with the rest of my friends as Vanilla Fields places a hand on his forearm and leans forward.

She's beautiful. Curvy, big blonde hair that looks like she walked off the stage of a beauty pageant, and she skipped a shirt altogether and wears a black lacy bra that barely contains her boobs.

"One of them," I say and force myself to look away.

I feel the girls' questioning gazes on me, and I explain how I stumbled onto him walking two girls out of his apartment this morning.

"He was looking for you last night," Sienna says. "It could have been you in that Johnny sandwich."

My chest flutters. "No chance. I would have gladly taken Charli to my place, though. The things that poor dog has seen."

"Well…" Ginny stands. "My man is looking far too sexy to be left alone."

Reagan nods in agreement. "Yeah, I need to go intervene before that girl standing next to Adam touches him one more time. Does anyone have bail money just in case?"

I snort-laugh. "No. Behave yourself. He loves you."

"He does. Doesn't he?" Dimples dot her cheeks on either side. "You good?"

"I'm good. Have fun."

Reagan and Ginny make a beeline for their men, but Sienna stays sitting beside me.

"Go," I say, aware she's probably staying so I'm not alone. "I'm going to get another drink and then do a lap and scope out the ab situation. Did you see Liam? I did not expect all those muscles under his polo shirts."

"Are you okay?" she asks. Her brows pinch together, and she studies me closely.

"Yeah." I smile and shift uncomfortably. "Of course. Why?"

"You and Mav… I thought maybe the two of you…" She doesn't finish either sentence, and I hang on her words, wondering why she might possibly think the two of us would be a good fit.

"Me and Maverick?" I ask, disbelief in my tone, but that fluttering thing happens in my chest again. "Why?"

"Just a feeling when you two are together." She shrugs and looks from me to him. "There's more to him than he puts out for most people to see."

"There is?" I take in his muscles and tattoos.

Vanilla Fields is still talking to him, and he laughs at something she says. His whole body shakes with it.

Sienna angles her body and rests her knees against mine. "When I had my skating accident last year and was in the hospital for a month, Maverick sent me flowers every single day. *Every* day. It was always some bright, happy bouquet."

"Sounds like he was into you." That wouldn't surprise me. Sienna is sweet, beautiful, and a super talented figure skater.

"No, that's the thing. He never sent a note or said anything about it. He didn't want me to know they were from him."

"I don't understand."

"I got curious and called the florist. They wouldn't give his name, but their description was enough for me to put the pieces together."

I try to picture Maverick walking into a flower shop and ordering a dozen bouquets. Surprisingly, I can see it. The thought makes me smile.

"People don't give him enough credit. He loves big and wild."

"And often," I point out.

"Jealous?" She smirks.

"No. Definitely not. I could never be with someone like that. He doesn't take anything seriously."

"All right." She places both hands on her thighs. "If you're not going to stop Mav from having a repeat with blondie over there, then do you want to dance with me?"

"Dance? Where?" It's packed out on the deck and in the living room.

"Rhett's room. He pushed everything to one side for us." She grins. "One last dance party?" She holds out her hand, and I place mine in hers.

"Absolutely."

It's just the two of us at first, but the music calls to more people, and by the third song, Rhett's room is packed with girls dancing and singing along.

And where girls gather, boys are sure to follow. Smiling and feeling free and happy, I glance over and catch Maverick watching me from the doorway. His signature smirk is in place, but his eyes don't light up with humor in the same way they usually do. My breath catches in my lungs, and I blame Sienna for the seconds that I hold his stare, wondering just for a moment if there could have been something more than friendship between us.

He strides toward me, and I pause my dancing. "Having fun?"

It's rhetorical. Johnny always has fun. It's his only mode. I'm sticky and breathless from dancing, and my throat is thick, making it hard to breathe. All the talk of lasts and people leaving has made me emotional. The alcohol probably isn't helping.

Johnny moves to the beat in front of me. We've danced before, but I've never felt this awkward about it. I'm so aware of every breath and the strum of my pulse, growing faster with every second.

His chin dips, and he circles my waist with a strong arm, taking over and swaying us to the music. My body tingles everywhere his warm skin touches mine, which, thanks to the lack of shirts, is a lot of surface area.

I stare anywhere but at him—down at our feet, at Sienna, who flashes me a smile as Rhett pulls her from the dance floor, probably to a secluded corner somewhere to make out. I look anywhere but up at Johnny's face until I can't take it any longer.

The tips of my ears burn with that feeling of being watched, and I lift my head and lock my gaze on his. I wonder if he feels it too—this sadness that we won't have chances like this again. Sure, we might see each other again someday, but it'll never be like this. It's a now or never moment, and you can't be in that moment and not wonder what if. Right?

I can't read anything on his face. The smell of vanilla hits my nostrils, and I turn to see the blonde from last night dancing beside me. When I glance back, Mav's gaze slides from her to me again, squashing whatever moment we were having.

Vanilla falls in behind him, and he presses closer against me.

I lean in so he can hear me over the music. "I'm going to get some air."

"Want some company?"

A light laugh escapes my lips as Vanilla glides her fingers around his stomach. No Johnny sandwich for me tonight.

"I'm good," I say and step away, letting her have him. I blow out a shaky breath. It's probably time to switch to water.

When I reach the kitchen, Adam's pulling on a T-shirt, and Reagan has her purse on her shoulder.

"There you are," she says. "Are you in for one last late-night game of sardines?"

I nod. The fresh air should help the heat coursing through my veins.

"Have you seen Mav?" she asks, looking around.

"I don't think he's going anywhere except to his apartment for a repeat with the chick from last night, and I'm pretty sure Sienna and Rhett are off somewhere having sex."

"I'll grab everyone," Adam tells us and drops a kiss to Reagan's lips. "Meet you outside."

I run into my apartment to grab my phone. I left it earlier tonight when I headed to the party because I don't have any pockets and couldn't wear a bra either to stick it in.

I'm scrolling through notifications as I walk back outside. In the short time I was gone, Adam's managed to gather everyone. Even Maverick.

The eight of us walk toward campus in the dark. We've done it a hundred times before. It's sort of our thing. Late-night parties often led to some combination of us and whoever we were talking to at the time playing sardines on campus. But tonight, as the school year is coming to a close, everyone is paired up except Mav and me.

"I'm surprised you came," I say as I fall in beside him. It's a short walk, but we wander slowly. The happy couples in front of us spend as much time hugging and kissing as moving their legs forward.

"Are you kidding? This was my idea. One last time." He stares straight ahead, and his jaw flexes.

"What about Vanilla?"

He shrugs. "Maybe she'll still be around later."

Of course she will. The party won't stop without us, and when we get back, he'll have a selection of girls to pick from.

"Besides." He moves closer, and his arm brushes mine. "You're my favorite partner, and we get to hide tonight. I have the perfect spot. Been saving it up for this."

When we finally reach campus, Maverick leads me to his perfect hiding spot while the rest of the group gives us a head start.

Over the years, we've set some boundaries to where we can hide, but we've never lacked creative ways to play the game. Inside fountains, under tables, behind trees and columns. It's so much more than finding a good hiding spot. Staying quiet and still, things Maverick always struggles with, are what usually get people caught.

Tonight, staying quiet isn't a problem. I'm lost in my thoughts, wondering what next year will be like. Will those of us still at Valley come here? No, probably not. It won't be the same. I can't believe I've fallen into the same bout of melancholy my friends have. It isn't sadness that they're all leaving. I'm happy for them. They're all going to do incredible things. The problem is, I'm not.

"Everything okay?" Mav asks as we approach the library. They're doing construction on one side. Heavy, translucent plastic hangs down, covering the work area.

"Yeah." I force some pep into my tone. "Yeah, I'm good."

"Not sad we're all leaving?" He sticks out his bottom lip into a pout.

"I am, but I'll still talk to Sienna, and she'll fill me in on Rhett, and Adam isn't going anywhere."

"And me?"

"I'll miss Charli," I say with a cheeky grin. "Will you send me pictures of her occasionally?"

"Babe, if you want dick pics, then you just gotta ask."

I laugh despite myself, and he holds back the plastic to let me go ahead of him. A light hangs above me, casting a soft glow on the area, but otherwise, the space is open.

"What are they doing here?" I ask as we both step in, and Maverick lets the sheet fall back into place.

"I'm not sure. Maybe outdoor seating."

"Oooh, that'll be nice." I picture it—sitting outside studying or chatting with the girls. That makes me think of Sienna not being there, and my heart hurts again.

When I turn to face him, Maverick's gaze is pinned on me. Like earlier, he smirks, but his eyes are hard and swirl with emotion I can't decipher. I'm blaming the shirt. This shirt was designed with college boys' dirtiest fantasies in mind.

"Won't they be able to see us with the light?"

"I don't think so," he says, staring out. From our side, it's only darkness. "I couldn't see the guys working yesterday when they were in here."

"Go outside and tell me if you can see me."

The sheet makes a crinkling noise as he steps to the other side.

"Anything." I wave my hands at my side.

"Little bit of movement, but when you stand still, I can't see anything."

"What about now." I step closer to the plastic but keep my hands next to my body.

"No."

One step closer so that I'm almost standing directly against it. "Now?"

He chuckles. "No. Can I come back in before they spot me standing out here?"

I glance at my phone. "They shouldn't have left yet."

"Yeah, well, they're all going to be anxious to find us and go back and bang."

"And you're not? Vanilla might have found another set of abs to go home with by now."

"I'm coming back in."

"Wait," I order. His footsteps outside stop. Curling my fingers around the bottom of my shirt, I roll the fabric up. The breeze buds my nipples, and I smile at the daring move knowing he's clueless. "Anything?"

His response is delayed, and I panic for a second, thinking maybe he can see me.

"Nah, nothing, babe."

The light flickers above me, brightening and then dimming again. Quickly, I right my shirt and pull back the plastic separating us. "I think we're all good."

Mav and I sit side by side against the library wall. He pulls out a bottle of Mad Dog from his jeans pocket and offers me a drink. Humoring him, I take a small sip before handing it back.

"I'll never understand why that's your drink of choice."

"It's sweet and sticky." He winks and caps the bottle, then sets it between us. "Actually, I drink it because it pisses my dad off."

"Why does it piss him off?"

"It isn't exactly the kind of alcohol you serve at a black-tie function."

"Let me guess." I find myself smiling. "You would sneak it in just to get a rise out of him?"

He doesn't answer, but his expression says everything.

The wind blows my hair around my face, and I tuck it behind my ears and then hug my knees to my chest. Despite the warm weather during the day, the night air is chilly.

"When are you leaving?" I ask, keeping my voice low in case our friends are now looking for us.

"Not sure." He bends his legs and rests his elbows on his thighs. "You're staying all summer?"

"Looks like it," I say glumly. "I got another 'so sorry we've gone with another candidate' letter today from an internship I applied for." The last one. I'm officially out of options.

"There's gotta be something out there."

"I've tried. I applied all over Arizona, and anywhere I thought my car could make it without breaking down. Either it's unpaid, or it's so coveted that they have their pick of the best candidates."

"You're the best candidate," he says.

"Thanks," I mumble. My grades are good, but since I quit track, the only other selling points of my resume are intramural spikeball champion and working at the Hall of Fame. It's a great job, but at this point, I could do it in my sleep.

The phone in my hand lights up with a dating app notification.

Wyd, sexy?

"I literally cannot." I groan. It's the last straw. I swipe the screen angrily and delete the app off my phone.

Mav's upper body shakes, and he smiles, holding back laughter. "I take it online dating isn't going well?"

"Every single conversation I've had goes the exact same." I lower my voice. "Hey, girl. What are you doing? Wanna exchange pics?"

"I don't trust online dating."

"Afraid of being catfished?"

"Nah, it's just a vibe when you're with someone. You can't know that through a few texts."

He might be right about that. All I know, I feel nothing for these guys that I'm talking to. "Well, I'm done. Talking to guys is bullshit. Maybe you have the right idea. Hooking up, no feelings, and no chatting about hopes and dreams." I glance up at him. He's still staring at me, but he's not laughing.

"It isn't really like that."

"What's it like?" I humor him. "Tell me all your moves, Johnny Maverick."

He stares at me intently. A small smile on his lips. Playful. Cocky. Charming.

Reaching out, his fingers push back the hair that's blown into my face again. My breathing quickens as the calloused pads of his fingers scrape against the nape of my neck. He moves closer, and I swallow. The wind carries the sweet scent of liquor on his breath and something clean and masculine, his soap, I think.

For a split second, I think he's going to kiss me. He doesn't, of course. That would be crazy. Instead, he tilts his head to the side, eyes searching my face as his fingers are still on my collarbone spreading warmth across my skin and low into my belly.

The light flickers above us, and I quickly look up. I don't know why, reaction, I guess. When I drop my gaze, he pulls back, and then Rhett's voice slices through the night. "There they are. Behind the plastic."

"They found us." I'm thankful for something to say that breaks the awkwardness between us, but then Rhett's words register. Really register. *Oh my god.* I turn to Mav, and he bites his bottom lip, and his eyes dip to my chest.

He totally saw when I flashed him.

Chapter Four

DAKOTA

The following morning, I'm up making my morning smoothie an hour later than normal, thanks to the late-night party.

Life hack, a jug of protein powder, and a tub of peanut butter will feed you for weeks. Also, it's cheap when you factor in the number of meals for the price.

I'm not exactly destitute, but money is tight. I have student loans that pay for school and the apartment, but my Hall of Fame money has to cover everything else.

Reagan stayed at Adam's apartment, so ours is quiet. I take my drink to the couch and pick up my phone. Out of habit, I look for the dating app, then remember I deleted it. I toss my phone on the cushion. It is better this way. I was going to end up on one of those TV shows for women who snapped if one more guy asked me if I was DTF after the second text exchange.

A knock at the door gets me up, and I don't even question who it is. You never know around here. But Maverick is the last person I expected as I pull the door wide.

"Hey. What are you doing here?"

He does a quick scan of me. I'm still in a tank top, no bra, and running shorts, and he isn't bashful about soaking up every inch of bare skin.

"I have a proposition for you." His deep voice rumbles down my spine.

I step back to let him come in, then cross my arms over my chest to conceal how much my nipples seem to like his voice and the way he scopes me out.

"Propositioning a girl this soon after one left your apartment is a bold move," I say as I grab a sweatshirt draped over the back of the couch and pull it on. I sit, and he does too.

"Not that kind of proposition."

I note that he doesn't try to deny he took Vanilla home again last night. Whose name, I sadly learned, is Claudia, and now I feel bitchy calling her Vanilla. Shame. It was so catchy.

I angle my body to face him now that he can't see my nipples saluting him. "What's up?"

"How would you like to intern with the Wildcats this summer?"

"The Wildcats? As in the professional hockey team located in Minnesota?"

"That's the one." His mouth curves up.

"I tried the Coyotes and the minor league team in town, too. My adviser said those internships get hundreds of applicants and fill up early. The Wildcats have spots still open?"

He runs a hand over his messy, dark hair. "Yeah. They've already interviewed a bunch of people, but Blythe said if you sent over your resume this morning, she'd take a look."

"Blythe?"

"She's the VP of marketing. Seems cool."

My lips spread into a wide smile. It's dumb to get my hopes up, not to mention all the logistics of an internship in freaking Minnesota, but I can't help the butterflies in my stomach. "Really? You're not screwing with me?"

"Not screwing with you. She's waiting to hear from you. They're a couple of hours ahead of us, so I wouldn't wait too long."

"You did this?"

"I just asked. I had to call and get some information this morning, anyway."

I lunge forward and hug him. "Thank you, Johnny."

A few seconds pass with me squeezing him before he returns the gesture. I feel his laughter and the words as he speaks them. "You're welcome."

I pull back, stunned and giddy at the prospect of getting out of Valley for the summer. I need a change of scenery.

I glance at my laptop on the coffee table. I want to grab it and look up everything I possibly can about the Wildcats and Blythe, but he's still sitting here, and it feels rude after what he's done. He must be able to tell, though, because he juts his chin and says, "Go. I have to get to class anyway."

"Isn't it kind of pointless to go to class now?"

"Nah." He gives his head one quick shake. "I mean, yes, it's probably pointless, but I want to soak it all up before I leave." His hand falls to my thigh, and he squeezes. "Text me later and let me know how it goes?"

"Absolutely."

Within five minutes of emailing my resume to Blythe, I get a call from the woman herself.

Reagan's back home and she smiles at me from the kitchen while I talk to Blythe. I love her. She's already my hero: twenty-nine and the VP of marketing for an NHL team.

"The internship is eight weeks, working here in the main office. We try to give you opportunities in all areas, from selling tickets to creating content for our social media accounts." The longer she speaks, the more excited I become.

"It sounds amazing. Seriously, it's my dream job. I work at the university's Hall of Fame doing tours now."

"Johnny mentioned that. He also said we'd be crazy not to hire you."

My laugh is stilted, and I cringe a little at what all he might have said. "He's a good friend."

"It sounds like it, but I also think he might be right. You have all the qualifications and ambitions I was hoping for, and, honestly, I just have a good feeling about you."

"You do?" My smile widens, and I do a happy dance that she can't see. Reagan giggles from the kitchen.

"What do you say? Do you want to work for the Wildcats this summer?"

"Oh my gosh. Yes. Yes!"

She laughs. "Perfect. I will let our human resources manager know we've filled our last spot, and she'll send over some information on the dates, housing options, and probably a million other things I left out. She usually does these interviews, but she's out today, and I wanted to talk to you before someone else pushed through another applicant."

"Thank you. I am so excited. Truly. This is a dream come true." I have no idea how I'm going to get there or how I'll afford two apartments, but I'll take a bus and live in a crappy budget motel if I have to. Speaking of, she didn't mention the pay, and I'm embarrassed to ask, especially as she's congratulating me and telling me that she can't wait to meet me in person.

When we hang up, Reagan bounces over to me. "You got it?"

"I got it." I bounce back. "I really got it."

"I have to go to class, but I want to hear all of it again later." She starts for the door and pauses with one foot outside. "Don't forget, we're moving our stuff upstairs to the new apartment tomorrow." She hits me with a big grin again. "Ahh! I'm so excited for you. We are so celebrating later!"

The past few weeks have been one celebration after another, but I'm not complaining because this one is all about me.

My excitement lasts through my morning classes and into the afternoon as I lead a few tours at the Hall of Fame. That's what I do—convince top recruits from all over the country to come to Valley University. I take them around the workout facilities and training rooms, to the field, sandpit, arena, or wherever their sport is played, and then I bring them into the hype room for the pièce de résistance.

The hype room is where we show these epic videos showcasing the current and past players. It's different for each sport, but the vibe and the reaction are always the same. The setup alone is impressive. The circular space requires a code to get in and out and is completely soundproof. The screens take up every inch of the walls from top to bottom and three-quarters of the way around. The recruit and their family stand in the back, lights dim, and I just hit play. Okay, that isn't all I do. I am knowledgeable on all kinds of important facts for every sport on campus, but this room has proven to be the deciding factor on more than one occasion.

And, no matter the sport (golf can look badass in a hype video, fight me) and no matter how many times I see the videos when the music starts and it begins to play, even I get caught up rewatching. I'm always a little awestruck by the athleticism and sense of team that these videos capture. Sometimes it even makes me miss the time I was a college athlete. They didn't have the hype room four years ago when I came to tour Valley University and the track team, but I think I would have signed a lot sooner if they had.

I'm waiting for my last athlete, a tennis player named Natalie and her family, when the email from the Wildcats human resources department comes in.

I open it, barely registering most of the standard contract language, but the word *unpaid* jars me back to reality. Oh shit. I slow down and force myself to read it more carefully. Each word makes my smile fall and smacks me back to reality.

Eight weeks *unpaid*. I can't go that long without a paycheck. I have some savings, but not much. And definitely not enough to do that and cover the housing and basic living expenses.

I swallow down the lump in my throat and force a smile as Natalie and her family walk through the doors. I better get used to it. It looks like I'm going to be right here all summer long.

I know I'm lucky, and I'm genuinely grateful for this job, but the thought of spending the next two months watching my friends fall even deeper in love with their boyfriends while I tag along like a fifth wheel makes me ache for something new and exciting, and all mine.

Chapter Five

JOHNNY

Talking to my father is a little like playing hockey without pads. Everyone knows it's a bad idea, but occasionally you're fucking around, feeling lucky, and decide a quick no-hit game is fine. Everything is going great, and then all of a sudden, some asshole gets pissed and slams you into the boards, or you take a puck to the knee. You never see it coming, but after when you're hobbling off in pain, you feel like an idiot for ever considering the idea.

My dad isn't an asshole. At least he doesn't mean to be. I don't think. To be honest, I don't know him well enough to be the best character reference. Our conversations are few and far between. What I do know? I always hobble away feeling like an idiot.

"Did you get the samples?" I hear him puff on the cigar and then the ping of a driver hitting a golf ball in the distance.

"Yeah." I glance over at the unopened box with the Maverick logo on the side. "It just got here today."

"Great. Great. I sent some to the Wildcats office too."

"Cool." I lean back on the couch. The family business has never interested me. Probably because it was often the reason I was alone. Mom and Dad would be at the office working or at events networking, and I was left home with nannies.

By the time I was old enough to have any interest, I resented it too damn much. Now that I've got my own life and career, some of that baggage has lifted, and hey, free shampoo and deodorant.

"I'll have the company lawyer send the contract to your agent. We'll need to set up a professional photo shoot once you get to Minnesota."

It takes a minute for his words to sink in.

"Oh." I sit forward. "You want to endorse me?"

"Of course we do. Maverick Company has been endorsing you for twenty-one years. Who do you think paid for school and hockey gear? It's great timing with the new male line. We want to launch in early August, so there's a lot of work to do."

There it is. The sneak attack. Puck to the stomach. You're nothing without me and my money. My first endorsement deal and I can't even be excited about it. The company's just capitalizing on their investment.

"Right. Sure thing. I gotta go, Dad."

"Me too. I'm about to tee off. I'll set up the shoot with Hugh." Without a goodbye, he ends the call.

I slump into the leather cushion and let out a breath. Then, push to my feet and open the box to see what the hell I'm going to be endorsing.

I order pizza for the group and go upstairs, taking an armful of the free products with me. I drop them on the kitchen counter and wave my arms around. "You too can smell like me."

Heath quirks a brow.

"It's my first endorsement," I explain.

He smiles. "Congrats."

Rauthruss pushes forward and swipes a deodorant, uncaps it, and brings it to his nose to smell. "Maverick," he reads the label. "This is your family's brand, yeah?"

I nod. "New male hygiene line. It was unisex and female-geared before now."

He lifts his shirt and rolls it on his pits.

"Well?" I ask. "How is it?"

He angles his body, and Heath and I lean in and sniff his armpit

"Manly." Heath backs off with a smirk on his face.

"It kind of smells like coconuts," I muse.

I grab one of the body sprays and squirt it onto my shirt. It's not bad. Not great either.

"We're proud of you, my man," Heath says. "If I weren't so hungover from all the partying we've done the last couple of weeks, I'd suggest celebrating, but I don't think my body can take another night of drinking."

"Let's do something chill," I suggest. "Grab the girls, and we'll watch a movie."

The guys agree without any protest, and their girlfriends come over as the pizza arrives. Dakota too. She doesn't look as happy as when I saw her this morning.

When we settle in the living room, I take a seat next to her on the couch. "How was the interview?"

"It was great. Thank you again for connecting us."

Huh. She said great, but she doesn't seem very excited.

"So, are we Minnie-soda bound this summer?"

Her laugh is quiet. The movie is starting, and she leans closer and lowers her voice. "No. It didn't work out."

"Why not? Did you not like Blythe?"

"Not like her?" Dakota snorts. "I think I fell a little in love with her. Did you know she was on the Forbes thirty under thirty list? She's incredible. She turned down jobs at a ton of really high-profile places to work for the Wildcats."

"Okay, so you've got a lady boner. And I know she loved you. What's the problem?"

"Know she loved me?"

"Yep." There isn't a doubt in my mind. Dakota is a hard worker. Coach Meyers routinely requests that she does the tours for any hockey recruits. And I told Blythe as much.

She sniffs the air and tilts toward my shirt. "What is that smell? Did you trade Vanilla for… Coconut?"

"Body spray. You like?" I duck my head, bringing our faces close.

"It's… interesting. Why would you want to smell like suntan lotion?"

I shrug. "What's the problem with the job, Kota?"

She sighs and sinks back into the couch cushion. Her shoulder rests against mine, and I reposition us so my arm is around her. Our friends are lost in the movie and each other.

"It's an unpaid internship."

"Oh." Shit. I hadn't thought to ask about the salary. "Is that normal? Are they even allowed to do that?"

"Yeah, it's more common than you'd think. And I'd do the job for free in a heartbeat, but I can't afford living expenses here and there. Besides, logistically, it was a stretch. My car probably wouldn't make the trip to and from in one piece."

"You could ride with me. Shit, you could stay with me too."

"I am not living with you." Her icy blue eyes narrow at me, but her mouth twists into a playful grin.

"Why not? I'm a great roommate. Ask any of the guys." I jut my chin toward our friends.

"You don't even live here."

"I basically do." I squeeze her shoulder, which brings her farther into my chest. "Come on; it'd be great."

"I *could* start my dry cleaning and coffee service for all of your conquests."

"Conquests?" I arch a brow. I most definitely don't think of them like that. They're beautiful, smart women who want to have fun. And I am fun.

"Thank you, but it wasn't meant to be. I'll be fine. I have my job at the Hall of Fame, and I have Blythe as a contact now. Maybe next year they'll have an entry-level position."

I nod, holding her gaze. She looks away first to the TV. I'm bummed for her. She was so excited this morning. Charli's on the floor at my feet. I pat my lap, and she jumps up, makes a circle, and lays down. Dakota reaches over and scratches under her chin. Charli wiggles forward so her face is on Dakota's leg, and that's how we watch the rest of the movie.

The next morning, I'm packing up the kitchen in my apartment when my agent, Hugh, calls.

I accept the call and put it on speaker. "Talk to me, Hugh."

He chuckles. "Hey, Johnny. How are you?"

"Good," I say instinctively. "Packing up my apartment."

"When are you headed out?"

"This weekend, maybe."

"Glad to hear it. Listen, I have some paperwork for you on the endorsement deal. I emailed it to you, but I thought I should call. I'm concerned."

My brows pull together, and I stop packing, pick up my phone, and open the email he mentioned. "Why?"

I scan the contract from Maverick Enterprises. I don't know much about endorsement deals since this is my first, but nothing sticks out.

"I know this is your family's company, so I don't want to overstep…"

"I'm paying you to overstep, my friend."

"Frankly, Johnny, it's the lowest sum I've ever seen for a pro athlete."

My gaze drops to the number in question. Fifteen grand for doing nothing?

"I'm a rookie. You said yourself you didn't expect any big endorsements for me until next year."

"I did. You're right. But once you accept your first endorsement, others will look at that and your earnings from it to determine your worth. If you take a lowball offer out of the gate, you're telling others that this is all it takes to get you."

"Yeah, but it's my family's company."

"Of course. I understand, but I wouldn't feel good about you taking the deal if I didn't caution you first."

I mull over his words as I consider the number. I may not like how my dad phrased it, but he was right—Maverick Enterprises has been endorsing me for years.

"I don't care about the money."

He chuckles again. "Ah, I love rookies. In two years, I'm going to remind you of this conversation when we're renegotiating your contract."

"I don't even need it. Can't I just give it all to charity or something? Would that help?"

"Yeah. We could do something like that. Do you have a charity in mind?"

"No, but I'm sure my parents have one they like."

He's quiet for a beat.

"What is it?" I prompt him. We're still getting used to one another, but I gather that Hugh isn't someone who freely speaks his mind without a lot of thought and consideration.

"You're not Maverick Enterprises. You're Johnny Maverick."

"I know." Oh, how I know.

"All right. Then let's pick out a charity that means something to you. Give it some thought, and I'll check in later."

"Yeah… okay. I can do that."

"So we're accepting the offer?"

There's a knock at the door, and I call, "It's open." Before responding to Hugh. "Yeah, let's do it."

Dakota comes in with Charli. She stopped by to take her on a short run. She's sweaty, and her cheeks are red. Her tank top is rolled up to the line of her sports bra, and her shorts sit below her belly button. Charli's tongue hangs out as she trots to her water bowl. Mine too, girl.

Dakota waves and disappears back out the door without speaking.

"Great." Hugh's voice breaks the silence. "I'll get to work then."

"Actually, hold up. I have another idea."

Chapter Six

DAKOTA

I'm getting in my car after work when an unknown Minnesota number calls. I start the engine and blast the air conditioning while staring at the ringing phone in my hand. The vent blows warm air. It likely won't cool down until I get home. I switch it off and roll down the windows instead.

"Hello?" I answer when the breeze flows through my car.

"Hi, Dakota. This is Katherine Holland. I'm the human resources manager at the Wildcats."

Oh crap. I wonder if they didn't get my email declining the position.

"I am sorry I was out and didn't get a chance to talk with you. Blythe had great things to say."

"Thank you. I enjoyed talking with her very much." I pinch the bridge of my nose. Ugh. I had almost put that opportunity out of my mind, but now I'm back to feeling sorry for myself.

"I got your email declining the offer."

"Oh yeah?" This is beyond awkward. "The job sounds great. Perfect, actually, but I didn't realize it was unpaid."

I pull my hair away from my neck and let the breeze cool me off.

"I completely understand that but what if we could offer compensation for a similar position? Would you still be interested?"

"Yeah." I don't even need to hear what the job is. Having a foot in the door at the Wildcats would be huge.

"I was hoping you would say that." She laughs softly. "We have a unique situation with a sponsor-paid internship. They're endorsing one of our players and want someone to assist with the campaign: marketing materials and social media content. There is even a photo shoot with the player scheduled."

Ooooh. I would get to work directly with the players?

"Why wouldn't they just hire me directly instead of going through you?"

"Good question. Normally they wouldn't, but this is a unique situation, as I said, and Blythe pushed hard to make this happen. The sponsor-paid work likely won't take up all of your availability, and we're hoping to use you in our intern pool still when you're free. So, more work, but you will be compensated."

"What's the compensation?" I close my eyes. *Please be enough. Please be enough.*

"Twelve thousand for the summer paid in weekly increments, and it covers housing, too."

"I'm sorry." I chuckle as the number floats in my head, taunting me. "It sounded like you said twelve *thousand*." Fifteen hundred dollars a week? That can't be a thing.

Her laughter loosens the tension in my neck that I've been carrying since I had to decline the internship. "I did. It's a great opportunity and honestly not one that's passed my desk before.

I looked over the contract myself, and the deliverables don't feel out of line or beyond what I think you're capable of. Due to confidentiality, I'm not able to say the player or endorsement until after you've signed the contract." It sounds like she's shuffling papers as she continues. "I can tell you that you'll be required to assist with a photo shoot and marketing and advertising copy for each of their social media platforms. If there's anything you're worried about, we can talk about what that would look like."

"I can handle it. All of it. Whatever is needed."

"I love your confidence. And I'm sure you can. Blythe has agreed to supervise it, and there's nothing she hasn't seen before. The two of you will have no problem. If you'd like a day or two to think it over—"

"Yes! I mean, no, I don't need time. I'm a yes." I still have to figure out how to get there, but I will duct tape this car together and roll in on fumes if I have to!

After I tell Reagan and Ginny the news and we spend a good twenty minutes jumping up and down celebrating, I head downstairs to Maverick's apartment.

I knock, but the music inside is so loud, I doubt he can hear me. I open it a crack and poke my head in. Boxes are everywhere, stacked up on one another in the living room. I walk all the way in and shut the door. I can hear Charli whining but have to step through a cardboard maze to find her. She yips, and I bend over to pick her up before continuing through the apartment.

It's a one-bedroom, so there aren't a lot of places he could be hiding. I follow the music to his bedroom, but I still don't see him.

"Mav?" Charli wriggles out of my hold and runs toward the attached bathroom. I am so not going in there. I linger awkwardly. The song ends, and I hear his voice croon at his dog. "Hey, pretty girl. I know. I know. I'm going to miss this place too."

He walks out, shirtless, no surprise there, and pauses when he sees me. "Kota."

"I knocked."

He grabs his phone and turns off the music.

"Mi casa es su casa. What's up? I was just about to take a food break."

We walk out to the kitchen, and he opens the fridge to survey the empty shelves.

"Looks like I'm ordering. Want anything?"

"No. I just came to tell you the good news."

He puts his phone on the counter and leans back against it, giving me his undivided attention.

"I accepted an internship with the Wildcats!"

"No way?" His lips pull into a broad smile. "Congrats!"

"Thank you. I'm so excited. Technically it's an internship with a company called JM Holdings, but I'll be in the intern pool and just doing that on the side. They're endorsing one of the players. I wonder what they sell? It's probably hockey equipment or something equally boring."

He grunts.

"Boring to me," I clarify. "But I'm so excited!"

"I knew everything would work out."

"I am in shock still. It's too good to be true. The pay is…

incredible, and it covers housing."

"Where are you staying?" He bends down to get Charli's water bowl and refills it.

"It's across from the arena. The Legends, I think. It's a one-bedroom, looked pretty standard, but I won't have to worry about transportation which is a plus."

"That's where I'm staying. We'll still be neighbors."

"Oh, good. I'll have my side hustle as a fallback plan."

He chuckles. "Let's order some food and celebrate."

"The girls have already claimed all of my remaining hours until I leave. We're staying in tonight and then going out dancing tomorrow. No boys allowed."

"Boo. That's no fun."

"I do have a favor, though."

"Shoot."

"Could I still take you up on the offer to ride up together? I'll leave my car here and then rent something to drive back."

"Yeah, of course. When do you have to be there?"

"Monday," I say tentatively, hoping he hasn't made plans beyond that.

"Perfect. We can leave Saturday morning, be in Minnie-soda Sunday night."

"Great." I squeal. "I cannot believe this is all working out. It's too much."

"Nah, you deserve it."

"Oh, just one more tiny request."

He grins. "What happens on road trips, stays on road trips."

"What?"

"If you want to share a hotel room, maybe get naked and

wrestle, then by all means." He winks.

"Tempting," I say sarcastically. "But my favor does solve the shared bed situation. I need to stop by my dad's house and get a few items for the apartment. It's on the way, and that will save me from having to buy a bunch of stuff when I get there. We can stay there Saturday night."

"Ah, shit. The apartment isn't furnished?" He looks stunned.

"No, but I don't need much, and my dad said I could borrow a few things for the summer, so I don't have to take stuff from the apartment here. The couch is Reagan's anyway."

He nods thoughtfully. "Sure. I have room in the trailer for whatever you need, or you can borrow anything of mine. Maybe just crash with me." His eyes light up. "One bed… it was meant to be."

"There isn't enough room in your bed for me and the girls that hop in and out of it."

He chuckles softly.

"A bed, a chair or couch, and I'll be fine." I step forward and hug him. His body is warm and hard. "Thank you, Johnny."

A second passes with me squeezing his waist before his arms wrap around my back. When he speaks, the words vibrate against my cheek. "You're welcome."

REAGAN PLANS A WHOLE NIGHT OF DRINKS AND DANCING FOR THE four of us Friday night before I leave.

"It's the first summer we've been apart since we met." My

best friend holds my hand as we watch Ginny and Sienna on the dance floor. We're taking a breather and having our third shot. The bartender hates us. We keep making her split the shots into two glasses, so we don't get hammered too fast. Plus, it's cheaper because they almost always fill the glasses more than halfway. It's like a shot and a half combined. Score!

We toss back the half shots, and then Reagan takes my other hand. "I know that I've been preoccupied with Adam and all the drama with my mom, but I love you so much. I don't know what I would do without you."

"Rea." I squeeze her hands. My best friend is tough as nails. She had to be thanks to an absent mother who only shows up when she wants something from her beautiful and talented daughter. "It's only two months."

"I know." She pulls her honey-blonde hair over one shoulder and fingers a strand nervously. "It's just that with everyone graduating and leaving, it's starting to hit me that we won't be roommates forever. Promise we'll always be friends no matter where we live or how long we have to go without seeing one another?"

It's an easy promise to make. "I swear it."

I get to my feet and pull her into a hug. She had a shitty mother, and I lost mine at fifteen. We're so much more than roommates and friends. Neither of us has siblings, but I love her like I imagine sisters do, and there's no future I can imagine that doesn't involve us remaining close.

"Have you given any thought to the hockey hotties you're going to be working with?" She fans herself. "I saw the roster. Damn."

"I'm there for work, not to hook up." But she's right. I took a look at the roster, too, and *wow*.

"Yes, but you need the full *Wildcat* experience."

I shake my head. "Come on. Let's get one last dance party in and make it good because it's going to be six long weeks without seeing you shake it."

She smiles and shakes her boobs at me. "Nope. We're going to do virtual dance parties. I just decided. Once a week. Mandatory attendance."

"I'm in."

Chapter Seven

JOHNNY

Dakota's eyes are closed, brows pinched together as I drive. We just crossed into Oklahoma, and we're an hour from her dad's house in Kansas.

It's been a long ass day in this vehicle, and Dakota's so hungover from last night that she hasn't been much company.

"I need to stop and let Charli out. Do you feel like eating yet?"

She moans without opening her lids.

"A little grease to soak up the alcohol, and you'll be good as new."

"Fine." She sits up and stretches, sticking her boobs out in the process. "Where are we?"

"I don't know. All these small towns look the same." I pull into the parking lot of a fast-food restaurant and kill the engine.

As soon as I open the door, the air outside takes my breath away. "The humidity is killer. I always forget."

"Oh right, you grew up in Chicago. Arizona suits you so well." She gives her head a little shake. "Actually, scratch that. I think you could fit in anywhere."

"I'm choosing to take that as a compliment."

We walk Charli around in a grassy area between businesses. Dakota sits as if we haven't been doing that all day.

"What exactly did you girls get into last night? I can't remember ever seeing you this hungover."

"Shots. So many shots. We swore our loyalties to one another by dancing our hearts out and drinking Rumple Minze."

"Girls are weird."

She nods. "What'd you guys do?"

"Played Xbox and ate four large pizzas."

She snort-laughs and then stops and holds her stomach. "Did you hear that? My stomach just growled. I think it's finally awake."

"And wants pizza."

"That does sound good." She bites the corner of her lip. "There's this really great pizza place in my hometown."

"All right. Let's load back up then because I am ravenous."

When we get back on the highway, Kota is more alert and plays with the music while I drive.

"I'm going to let my dad know we're getting close."

"What are your parents like?"

She hesitates. "They're great. It's just my dad and me now. My mom died when I was fifteen."

"I had no idea. I'm sorry." A heavy feeling settles in the bottom of my stomach.

"It's okay. I mean. I don't know. I never know how to respond to that. Thank you?" She smiles.

It occurs to me that for as much time as I've spent with Dakota, hanging out, partying, joking around, I don't know that much about her. And I want to. "What does your dad do?"

"He's a firefighter."

"Badass."

"Technically, he's my stepdad, but he married my mom when I was five, so he's just Dad."

"And your real dad?"

"*Real* dad." She rolls her eyes. "He wasn't really into the family thing. He popped in occasionally when I was younger. I get a birthday card and a call on Christmas."

"I'm sorry."

"No, don't be. Be sorry that my awesome mother died if you want, but not that my sperm donor isn't part of my life. Some people just weren't meant to be parents. My real dad is one of those."

I wonder if my parents fit that criterion. They always made sure I had what I needed, but they were never very interested in doing the traditional parent activities like spending time together.

When we get close, Dakota navigates me through her hometown. I stop at the pizza place, and she runs in to get our order. Charli puts her paws up on the dash watching her.

Someone stops her at the doorway, and they embrace. Charli and I look on. My dog whines.

"I know. I know. She's coming back." I pat her head. Charli is a pretty friendly dog, but she's got a major crush on Kota. Who could blame her? Dakota watched her for me recently when I had to make a trip up to Minnesota, and she always gives her attention, pets her, takes her on runs. We're easy to please.

I check email on my phone. Hugh sent the final signed contract for my endorsement and my lease agreement. I lucked out being able to find a sublease for Dakota in the same building.

The Legends is usually booked up solid, but one of my new teammates was looking to offload his place while he moved back to his hometown to recuperate from surgery. I didn't even think about him taking his stuff with him. I just assumed it was furnished.

She's going to find out eventually that the endorsement is for the Maverick Corporation, but I couldn't risk her passing because of pride. I could see how much she wanted the job, and she shouldn't have to give that up because of something stupid like money.

She comes out a few minutes later with two large pizza boxes. I lean over to open the door for her, and the smell that takes over my truck is divine.

"Oh, man. My mouth just started watering."

"Right." She sits and flips open the lid revealing a sausage pizza. She frees a slice and takes a bite, then groans loudly. "You have to try it."

She holds out the pizza to feed me, and I take a huge bite that makes her laugh.

"You almost got my fingers."

"I'm so hungry. I hope one of those boxes is all mine." I reach for another slice, and she smacks my hand. "Only one bite. We have to save the rest to eat with my dad."

Dakota's dad lives in a quiet subdivision on the east side of town. I park the SUV along the road, grab our overnight bags and Charli, and follow her up the sidewalk to an entrance at the back side of the house.

The screen door creaks open, and a big, burly guy with a gray beard steps out. "DJ!"

"Dad!" She holds the pizzas with one hand to her side and hugs him with the other.

Her dad looks at me over her shoulder and gives me the appropriate dad once-over. Charli growls in my arms.

Dakota laughs and pulls back. "Dad, this is Maverick. Maverick, meet my dad."

"*Maverick*, huh?"

"Johnny Maverick, but everyone just calls me by my last name." I drop Charli to the ground and step forward to shake his hand.

He stares at the tattoos along my arm as he reaches to take my hand. "Jerry. Thanks for driving my DJ."

Kota rolls her eyes. "He always wanted a son. Hence the nickname."

Jerry smiles and holds the door open for us or, well, her. I get the feeling ole Jer might let it slam in my face if it weren't for Dakota holding it open with her foot while I shuffle through with Charli and the bags.

The house is small but has a homey feel. Everything is tidy and clean, but there are stacks of papers and clutter that my parents always kept out of view for guests.

We drop our stuff, and I feed Charli while Dakota and Jerry catch up. I try to hang back and give them some time, but Kota calls for me, and it's a good thing because one whole pizza is gone by the time I sit down.

"Can I get you something to drink?" Jerry asks. From the kitchen table, he reaches over and opens the fridge. "I've got Coke or beer."

"He wants beer, Dad," Dakota says at the same time I say, "Coke will be fine."

Jerry looks between us.

"Either one is great. Thanks." I wipe my palms on my thighs. I don't have a lot of experience with fathers. Especially girls' fathers.

I mumble my thanks as he sets a Bud Light bottle in front of me. I think I'm sweating. Must be the humidity. Charli jogs in circles around the living room, then the kitchen, checking everything out.

I whistle lightly and pat my thigh to get her attention. "Come lie down, girl."

"Ah, let her be," Jerry says. "She's been cooped up in the car all day. So, DJ, tell me about this job."

My friend lights up and goes into it, telling her dad every single detail.

"You don't know which player or what they're endorsing?" Her dad leans back in his chair and takes a long drink of beer.

"No, but I checked out all the guys on the team and their endorsements, and there wasn't anything crazy. My guess is that it's some diva who needs a handler to make sure he shows up to set and looks pretty. Maybe Jack Wyld." She looks at me. "He's got quite the reputation for partying."

"Jack's a nice guy. I doubt he'd do anything to jeopardize a lucrative relationship. The guys I've met have all been levelheaded and cool."

"Hockey players and levelheaded." Jerry grins. "That's funny, *Maverick*." The way he says my name is almost like he's mocking me.

Now I really am sweating.

I pull at the collar of my T-shirt to get some air.

"More ink, huh? What do all those mean?"

"Mean?" I drop my gaze to the tattoos on both arms.

"Back in my day, when a man got a tattoo, it meant something.

Now you're all covered in them, and it loses the sentimentality, don't you think?"

"*Daaad.*" Dakota pins him with an annoyed glare.

"No, it's fine. My dad said basically the same thing when I got my first sleeve done." I stretch out my left arm. "The truth is. Some of them have special meaning; others don't."

"Like decorating a house," Dakota pipes in. "Some items are sentimental, and others you buy because you thought they were pretty." She places her elbows on the table and looks at Jerry. "Do you still have the pink sofa?"

"In the basement." He nods.

"Oh, you have to see it." Dakota reaches out and touches my arm lightly. "The salesperson called it dusty rose, but it's the color of bubblegum."

Everything in my parents' house was white or gray. I think I might like a bubblegum pink couch. Jerry retires to an old recliner in the living room, and Dakota rinses the plates while I finish off the pizza.

"Going downstairs, Dad," she calls as we start down the creaky stairs.

"Leave the door open," he yells.

"Oh my gosh. So embarrassing," she mumbles and flips on a light in the stairway. "Welcome to my teenage hangout. I spent many hours down here watching TV and hanging out with friends."

"*Boy* friends?" I ask.

"Sometimes." She walks straight to the pink couch and sits down. She runs a hand along the fabric cushion as I take in the rest of the space.

My head grazes the ceiling fan in the middle of the living area.

The furniture is mismatched as if it's a collection of old furniture pieces Jerry couldn't bear to part with. A worn leather armchair, a plaid upholstered love seat, and the pink couch. A flat-screen TV is mounted on the wall, and a bookshelf sits underneath, holding dusty books and games.

"Did you have a *basement* where you took girls in high school?"

"Kind of." I take a seat next to her on the couch. It's hard, not a lot of give, and it sits low to the floor, making my ass sink down below my knees. "I had a pool house."

"Oh my gosh, of course you did." She rolls her eyes but smiles.

"This is a great color," I say and mean it. "Could be more comfortable, though. This thing is hard as a rock."

I try to bounce on it and then wiggle to get situated, but it's like sitting on a bleacher seat.

"My mom always wanted a pink couch. I have no idea why. It was a running joke every time we picked out new furniture." She plays with the hem of her shorts, staring down at the material between her fingers as she continues. "The day she found out her cancer had returned, she went straight from the doctor's office to the furniture store. I came home from school, and she was sitting on it and just smiling. She died two weeks later."

"I'm so sorry." I cover her hand with mine.

She lets out a breath and nods. "It is pretty uncomfortable."

"The worst," I admit. "But I dig it. My parents were all whites and grays. I like color."

She squeezes my fingers. "How come you don't have any colorful tattoos?"

I scan my arm. I'd never thought about it before. "I guess I'm whites and grays too."

"Oh no." She smiles. "You are a pink couch. Not quite right, but all about making people happy."

Chuckling, I move my hand. "Jerry seems nice."

"Nice? Really."

"Okay, he seems like a hard-ass, but he loves you, that much I got."

"He loved my mom so much. Even if I were a holy terror, because let's be honest, there were some rough high school years when I was awful, he'd still love me if only because I'm her daughter. She was going through chemo when they met. Can you imagine the kind of love that takes? He had no idea if she'd get better."

"But she did."

"Yeah." Dakota nods. "They had ten amazing years, and I guess that's more than most people get."

Dakota grabs two more beers, and we eventually move to sitting in front of the couch. It's a real bad sign for a piece of furniture when you'd rather sit on the floor than on it, but I'm having a great time.

She rests an elbow on the pink couch and angles toward me. "Tell me about your parents."

"We're not close. They were busy building the company when I was a kid. But they gave me a lot."

"I saw your dad at the Frozen Four celebration party. He seemed proud of you."

A laugh breaks free. "Sorry, I don't mean to laugh. He is proud in his own way, but I don't think he's ever said the word."

"He should. You've done some amazing things. Were they disappointed that you were quitting college to sign with the Wildcats?"

"Nah, they were all about it." I shrug. "I was never going to be anything but a hockey player."

"Don't sell yourself short, Johnny Maverick. I think you could be anything you want."

Chapter Eight

DAKOTA

He lines up the empty beer bottles between us. Upstairs is quiet. Dad must have gone to bed. It feels good to be home. Not a lot has changed in the three years since I moved away to college, but the basement feels smaller with Maverick in it.

He has that way about him, filling up space. Not just physically because he's a big guy, but his personality is even bigger.

The conversation has bounced from every topic imaginable—from my mom to all the horrifying things guys have said to me on dating apps.

"No way. He didn't say that." Mav throws his head back and laughs.

"He did. I would prove it to you, but I deleted the app. I asked him where his favorite place he'd visited was, and he said, the womb. Like, what do I do with that? How do you ever make a guy like that happy? I can't give that to him. Is he going to have some weird obsession with my *womb* when I get pregnant? So many questions."

"Again, this is why I don't do online dating."

"You do have a certain charm that might be misunderstood via text."

"Right?" He laughs and stretches out a long leg in front of him.

Charli is snoring at his side, and he absently runs a hand along her back.

"It's different now," I say. "Now that our friends are all coupled up. I see how happy they are. I want that."

"You know what you need?" he asks.

"Oh my god, I swear if you hit on me right now, I'm going to break one of these beer bottles and beat you over the head with it."

"First of all, ouch. That's some crazy bar brawl shit, Kota."

I laugh. I've seen Patrick Swayze in *Road House* one too many times, admittedly.

"Second, stop trying to force it. Enjoy the weirdos and the cringe stories. Have fun with it. Things will happen when they're supposed to. Life is a series of events that you can either let push you down or shrug them off and move on. I'm single and making the most of it."

"Oh, I know. I've seen you making the most of it. Two girls at a time. How does one girl compare after that, seriously?"

"You know the great thing about two girls instead of one?"

"Oh man, I feel like I should be taking notes. I cannot wait to hear this. No, Johnny, what's the great thing about two girls instead of one? Outside of the obvious two vaginas to stick it in thing."

He shakes his head. "It takes off the pressure. From everyone."

"The pressure? Seriously? You poor thing. Performance anxiety? I knew it."

"Think about it. You're hooking up with someone, and it's just the two of you. Every movement, every word is a back and forth trying to read one another and wondering how the other thinks or feels. Casual sex, especially when you get more than two people, is all about fun. No one calls the day after a threesome to see if you want to grab a coffee."

I give my head a shake, but I can't hide my smile. I understand what he means, though. It's about expectations.

You take people at their word, and sometimes they disappoint you. They make you feel special and wanted, they say all the right things, but you don't really know their heart. The upside? Eventually, people always show you their true colors.

And it isn't just in dating either. We have expectations in all kinds of relationships. I learned this lesson at eighteen when a man that I trusted, my high school track coach, made me believe that I was a talented runner who had a bright career ahead of her. Maybe I did, but he never really believed that. He was saying and doing whatever he thought would get him in my pants. It's kind of incredible the lengths some people will go to to keep you from knowing they only want sex. Expectations.

He grins back. "Besides, two chicks wanting me at once—*so* hot."

"And there it is. I'm going to be single forever. I appreciate your honesty, though."

We fall quiet. The only sound is Charli snoring.

"We should probably get some sleep." I struggle to get on my feet from the awkward position I'm sitting. Mav hops up and takes my hands, lifting me with ease.

He's so tall that he can't quite stand all the way up without knocking into the ceiling fan.

"Thanks."

He drops his hands but holds on to mine, lightly running his thumbs along the backs of my fingers. He smiles, the same friendly Maverick smile he always does, but my heart rate speeds up.

"Let me show you to the guest room." I change my tone to speak to Charli. "Come on, girl."

Why, yes, I am using the dog to get out of this situation. I've got images of Maverick with two girls stuck in my head, and I don't hate the view. What is wrong with me?

"My room is the last door on the right. Dad is last on the left, and he does own a gun. You've been warned."

He drops his bag on the bed, and Charli climbs right up, does a circle on the end of the mattress, and lies back down.

"Night, Mav."

"Hey, wait." He grabs my hand as I turn to leave.

"Oh right, the bathroom is across the hall. You can go first."

"Thanks, but that's not it." He looks uneasy as he shifts from one foot to another.

"You're making me nervous. What's wrong?"

"You told me not to hit on you, or you'd bust a bottle over my head, so I'm choosing my words carefully here."

I snort loudly then remember my dad is sleeping. I wiggle my hand free from his and then hold both up to show him. "No beer bottle. You're safe. As long as you don't invite me to a threesome."

"Don't knock it 'til you try it." He grins then his lips fall into a more serious line. "You're fire, Kota. You won't be single forever. You could have any guy you wanted."

I try to laugh it off, but he steps closer, and the bubble around us loses all the oxygen. "It's good to keep your standards high, but people can surprise you if you let them in. So they don't get it right over text, or they occasionally like to indulge in threesomes, it doesn't mean they aren't also capable of giving you the things you want."

He stops, but I can't find my voice to respond. I can't move either.

"That's it. That's all I wanted to say." He moves first and sits on the bed. Charli sticks a leg out in his direction, wanting to be closer to him but too lazy to get up. Johnny is kind of like that. People extend themselves to be near him.

I force my feet backward and hold on to the doorknob as I twist my lips into a friendly smile. "Thanks, Mav. I'll see you in the morning."

When I wake up the next morning, it's to Dad's and Johnny's voices. I check the time, then get up and change into my running clothes. I make a quick stop in the bathroom to brush my teeth and put my hair up into a ponytail.

The smell of bacon greets me as I walk into the kitchen. Johnny is at the stove, shirtless, and Dad sits at the kitchen table with a bottle of Icy Hot and Ibuprofen in front of him and his back brace on.

"Oh no, what happened?"

"Eh." Dad waves me off. "I tweaked it when we were loading the trailer."

"Why didn't you wait for me? Mav and I could have done it. It's barely seven o'clock. Are you that eager to get rid of me?"

His smile softens, and I slump into one of the chairs and steal a piece of bacon off the plate in the middle of the table.

"These came for you." Dad slides three identical envelopes in front of me.

I lift the top one, see the return address, and let it drop.

"Still bugging you to be in the school's Hall of Fame?"

I nod and fill my mouth with another piece of bacon. For six months, the high school has been sending me invites for the school's athletic Hall of Fame. I thought I'd successfully dodged them since the ceremony was last month, but apparently not.

Mav spins around. "That's awesome."

"It's unnecessary and unwarranted." I stand and drop them unopened in the trash. "I'm going for a run. Do you want me to take Charli?" I look around. "Where is she?"

Maverick's lips twitch, and he points with the spatula to the floor. I lean down and see Charli next to Dad's feet.

"You made a friend."

Dad grunts a response but bends down and scratches behind her ears.

Before I leave, I glare at Dad. "No more moving things while we're here."

He holds his tongue, but the unimpressed look on his face tells me he's going to do whatever he wants—stubborn old man.

I get only a few feet from the house when Mav falls into step beside me.

"Hey," I say, surprised. "Need to get away from my dad?"

"Nah, he pushed me out the door and told me no respectable man lets a woman run by herself. Something about the neighborhood not being what it used to be."

"Oh geez. I'm sorry. Also, I'm good. I can outrun most people."

"It's cool. I have to get back into the routine of it again anyway."

I start down my old path toward the high school. The neighborhood is older, lots of retired couples live here, and the streets are quiet this time of day. At the end of the block, we turn right.

I take us up and down each street scoping out the changes instead of taking the direct route to the school. The morning air is heavy with humidity. The sky is clear, and the sun is already hot on my skin.

By the time the track and football field comes into view, sweat drips down my back.

"Wow," Johnny says beside me. He's been quiet. "Nice field."

"The football team is like *everything* here," I mock in my best high school cheerleader voice.

"You don't sound bitter at all," he says sarcastically.

"Eh, I'm not really. They redid the field my sophomore year, and that included the track, so I benefited."

We come up short at the chain-link fence, staring in. A few morning walkers are moving along the rubber circle.

"How come you don't want to be inducted into your school's Hall of Fame?"

"I didn't say that."

"You tossed the invite in the trash." He quirks a dark brow.

"I don't even run anymore. Not for real, you know? I don't deserve to be in it, and even if I did, it's silly."

"So? Who cares if it's silly? And don't even get me started on the 'I don't deserve to be in it' nonsense. Who are you, the selection committee authority? Let them celebrate your general ballerness. I mean, you work at a Hall of Fame. You know how much it means."

I'm quiet. It's so much more complicated than that, but I appreciate him thinking I'm baller anyway.

"Come on. We should get back. It's another long day on the road."

We take a more direct path back to the house. A block before Dad's house, a guy has his back to us with the hood of his sports car up. Maybe the neighborhood has aged down since I lived here. Teenage me spent a lot of time running these streets hoping for a new, hot neighbor.

He turns as our feet hitting the pavement get closer, and my breath hitches. He takes me in, recognition dawning and his mouth curving up. "Dakota?"

My high school track coach leans down to grab a water bottle at his feet, his eyes never leaving me. I don't want to notice the sweat beading up on his chest and abs, but I do. Hans Hote. Coach McHottie is what we called him, and the name still fits. I manage to wave and keep my feet moving, one in front of the other. I push my legs harder as my pulse kicks up another notch.

"Morning," Johnny says, keeping my pace. My lungs burn as we round the corner to my dad's street.

"Want to tell me who the hell that was and why we sprinted away?"

"Nobody," I lie. "Come on. I'm starving."

Shortly after breakfast, Maverick and I walk outside, ready to make the last leg of our trip.

"Miss you, DJ. Knock 'em dead up there in Minnesota."

"I will." I wrap my arms around him and soak up the smell of his aftershave. "Thanks for letting me borrow the furniture."

I didn't see what they put in the trailer, but Johnny said they got a couch, chair, nightstand, and bed. The apartment will still be bare, but it's everything I need.

I pause before I get into the passenger seat. Maverick's already behind the wheel with his sunglasses on. Dad stands in the front yard. I miss him. I miss my mom. Years later, and I still sometimes forget that she's gone.

"Bye." I wave.

"Don't let him talk you into any tattoos," Dad warns. A small smile tips up the corner of his lips. "Drive safe with my DJ." His voice softens. "Bye, Charli!"

"I'm pretty sure your dad likes my dog more than me," Maverick says as he pulls away from my childhood home.

"Oh, he definitely likes Charli more than you," I confirm.

Chapter Nine

DAKOTA

It's dark when we get to the apartment. I'm too tired to scope out the surrounding area appropriately. We still have to get our stuff inside, and I have to unpack at least the essentials so that I can get ready for work tomorrow morning.

Work. *Squee!* I'm so excited about my first day.

Maverick pulls into a parking spot in the underground lot. Four guys lean against the wall, pushing off when Mav kills the engine and opens the door.

"Uhh…" I start uneasily. "Are we about to get shook down?"

Maverick shoots me a funny look then calls to them, "Hey, guys. Thanks for—" His voice cuts out as he closes the door and greets the guys. I stay in the truck, but I look them over more closely. They're in matching green shirts with the words, *Making Moves* on the front.

The guys listen to Maverick. He points to the trailer, and two of them head toward it while the others walk to a work truck and pull out a tarp and straps. Well, that makes more sense. He hired people to move him in.

Maverick returns to the truck and opens the door. "Ready to see your new place?"

"Yeah. Umm… I can grab my stuff first since it's at the back of the trailer. Can you help me with the big pieces? I think I can get the bed frame on my own, but not the mattress or the couch. Probably not the chair either."

He gives me a confused look. "You think they're going to move my stuff and not yours?"

"I—" Well, yeah.

"I called earlier. I figured as late as it was going to be, it'd be easier if we could bring in the small stuff and start to unpack while they get the furniture. You have a big day tomorrow."

"You didn't have to do that. Thank you."

He smiles big. "Come on. Let's check out your new digs."

We take the elevator to the second floor. Mav tells me that the first is a lobby, and the front doors open to the arena on the opposite side of the street. There is also mail, dry cleaning drop off and pick up, coffee (there goes my side gig), and a concierge desk.

The building locks down overnight, and I'll need the key card he flashes me to get in after nine. I'm giddy with excitement as he points to a door and says, "That one is yours."

He hands over the key, and I swipe it. A clicking sound and green light tell me it worked, and I push inside.

It's empty, as expected, but the space is huge. So much bigger than I expected.

I walk through a large entryway. The kitchen is on the left, and the living area stretches out in front of me. I move straight through to the windows on the far wall. The downtown lights up below, and my stomach flutters. Holy crap.

I want to twirl, and I'm so not a twirler.

"This is amazing."

"Setup is a lot like mine." He points to the right. "Bedroom and en suite." He stands next in an open doorway and flips on a light. It's a normal-sized bedroom with a decent walk-in closet and an attached bathroom. I can't stop grinning.

"Laundry closet is here." He opens a door where a washer and dryer should be, but it's empty. "Oh, shit."

"It's okay," I say quickly. "I'll figure out laundry. This place is incredible."

"You can use mine."

I definitely won't be schlepping my dirty panties up to Maverick's apartment, but I appreciate the offer.

We continue to explore. There's a small half bath on the other side of the kitchen and a dining area. It's perfect. I've never lived alone, and I'm suddenly really excited about it and a little nervous. This place is all mine for the next eight weeks.

Someone must knock because Johnny goes to the door and pulls it open for the movers, but I don't even hear it because I'm still too wrapped up in checking out every detail of the place.

I'm opening all the cabinets in the kitchen while they come in with the furniture.

"Where do you want it?" one of the guys asks.

I turn and see them holding the pink couch in my new living room. I can't help but laugh.

"Right there is fine."

Two more guys come in with the matching chair. My heart squeezes. *Dad, you sneak.* "By the window."

"He insisted," Johnny says. "You're going to have the most

uncomfortable furniture in all of Minnesota, but I figured you wouldn't have it any other way."

My eyes are teary, and I shake my head, unable to speak for a few seconds. "It's perfect." Like my mom is here watching me. "Let's go get the rest. I can't wait to sleep in my new apartment."

We get all the bags in one trip. Maverick wheels my oversized suitcase into my room.

"Thank you." I take it from him and try to lift it onto the bed. It is heavy. He moves in to help.

"I'd invite you up to see my place, but it looks like you're in a zone here."

He isn't wrong. I've got tunnel vision to get this place exactly how I want it before going to bed. "I have to find everything for tomorrow. What floor are you on?"

"Eleventh." He scoops Charli up in his arms. She's been busy checking out the place too. "What time do you have to be at the arena?"

"Nine. Just enough time to run and eat breakfast. Oh crap. Food. I didn't even think about groceries."

"We can go grab some stuff now if you want."

"No, it's fine. I have my protein powder and peanut butter somewhere, and my blender is in here." I pat the suitcase.

"No wonder it was so heavy." He smiles. "So you're good?"

"Yep! I'm going to unpack and then try to sleep."

"Text me if you need anything."

"Thank you." I walk him to the front door. He steps out into the hallway and then hits me with a grin. "Welcome, neighbor."

I skip my morning run and spend the time freaking out about my job and setting up the kitchen. I didn't bring a lot of kitchenware since it's just me, but I have a couple of plates, bowls, glasses, and a handful of silverware. I also grabbed one pan, one spatula, a whisk, and a potato peeler. Although the latter was an impulse grab, and I have no real plans to use it.

I set up my blender to make my smoothie. I can't find my jar of peanut butter anywhere, and I know I packed it. Reagan was making fun of me, tossing it into the air while I packed shoes. Oooh, I bet it's in the shoe bag.

The doorbell rings, and I freeze on my way to the bedroom like I'm caught in someone else's house. I wait for a second and then quietly pad over to the door and look out. No one is there, but there is something on the ground in front of the door.

Curious, I unlock and open the door. Several Trader Joe's bags filled with groceries sit outside and on the very top—a jar of peanut butter. Score! I could kiss Maverick.

When it's time for work, I make sure I have my purse, phone, and key card for the apartment and then take the elevator to the first floor. I smile at the white marble and the sunlight that streams into the open space.

A man stands at the door holding it open for people coming and going and there's a young woman behind the counter that I assume is the concierge Johnny mentioned.

I smile at her, and then the doorman greets me. "Good morning."

"Morning," I reply as I step outside. The street between the apartment and the arena is busy, and I walk up to the corner and cross with the others waiting. I take in the downtown area. Other tall buildings with company names surround us. Some I know, and others I don't.

I feel underdressed next to some of these people in their formal business attire: suits and no-nonsense pumps. I opted for a simple black dress and my red Chucks. Katherine in HR said it was business casual with an emphasis on casual, so I'm not too worried. Besides, who is going to see my shoes while I sit behind a desk?

I get a text from Reagan as I'm about to enter the front doors of the arena. I pause and move to the side to let people pass.

Have a great day with the hockey hotties. I expect roster details. EXPLICIT details. She added six eggplant emojis, a briefcase, and a kissy-face. I love her.

Inside the door, I stop at the front desk and give them my name as I was instructed to do. They make a call and tell me to wait in the lobby, and a few minutes later, Blythe herself appears.

She's stunning. Even more so in person. Power suit has nothing on the jumper she owns with every long stride of her legs. Her dark skin is beautiful against the cream color of her outfit, but the best part is the bright red heels on her feet. Oh, I think I've just found my new role model.

"Dakota." She smiles and extends her hand. Simple gold jewelry, a bracelet, and a ring—not on her ring finger. "I am so thrilled you're here."

"Thank you. I can't believe it. I keep waiting to wake up and be back in Valley."

Her dark brown eyes light up as she smiles. She hands me a

badge and leads me past the front desk. "This is the main entrance. You can also come in through the back near the training rooms, but this is probably easier coming from the apartment. Did you get settled okay?"

"Yeah. We got in late last night."

"We?"

"Oh, uh, I drove up with Johnny Maverick."

"Right. Of course."

We catch an elevator to the top floor. Everyone we pass smiles at Blythe or tips their head in greeting. I'm happy to see lots of people in more casual attire and lots of sneakers.

"This is me." She walks into a large corner office. The view from her window looks down to the same street as the apartment and a crossroads. "I'll run through all the details of your contract tomorrow after orientation, but this is where you can find me if I'm not in a meeting, and if I'm in here, then I'm always available if you have any questions."

Her office is tastefully and beautifully decorated. Very modern and chic and so her. The white desk has gold metal legs and is entirely clutter-free except for her laptop and a cup of tea. She motions to a large box behind me. "That's the product for the endorsement. I will bring it down to you this afternoon or tomorrow morning once you get your desk assignment."

My fingers itch to see what's in there. Protein bars? Athletic wear? The suspense is killing me.

We head back out of her office, and she leads me to a conference room. "Let me introduce you to the other two interns in our group."

Inside, people are moving around. Long tables are pushed together and face the front of the room where a projector displays a welcome PowerPoint slide. "Today is a general session for all interns. They'll go over everything and show you around the building. Lunch is catered and…" she trails off. "Am I talking too fast? Sorry, I tend to do that."

"No." I laugh softly. "I think I got it all. I'm really excited."

She smiles so genuinely at me before stopping next to a girl with shiny brown hair, dressed to kill like those people on the street that looked like they were off to bust through the glass ceiling. Only far more fashionable. She's career Barbie.

"Dakota, this is Quinn."

I greet Quinn and get a polite smile and once-over. Blythe takes a step next to a guy wearing a Wildcat tie that I don't think he's wearing ironically. "And this is Reese."

"Hello," he says and does a one-arm wave that's a little goofy, but I can tell already suits him.

I take a seat between them. This is so surreal. I cannot believe I'm here.

Blythe grins at her dutiful interns sitting together. "I'll check in with you all this afternoon. Welcome to the Wildcats."

Chapter Ten

DAKOTA

After several more welcome speeches from various members of the Wildcat front office, we're given a quick tour of the facilities. We start at the ticket office and then see all the main offices where most of us will be working. From there, we go down to the practice rink, which is sadly not in use, then we're guided to the game ice, which is also woefully empty, but wow, is it impressive.

Actually, the whole building is remarkable, from the green bleacher seats in the main arena to the fabulous paint job in the hallways with framed black and white photographs of the team over the years. It's like the Hall of Fame back at Valley decided to have a baby with a hockey arena, and that baby got all the functional qualities of the arena and all the extra fabulous genes of the Hall of Fame. There's even upbeat music playing softly over the speakers in the hallways.

I am in awe.

There's a buzz about the upcoming season. These people really love their hockey team, and I grin when Johnny's name is mentioned several times with other newly signed players they're excited about.

Admittedly, with every corner we turn that doesn't have a big, burly hockey player on the other side, I'm more disappointed. It's increasingly possible that my bestie got in my head with the whole hockey hottie nonsense. But come on, we haven't had one player sighting this morning.

Then when I can practically smell the sweat and pheromones, they just wave a hand toward a long hallway where the players work out, watch film, and dress, and instruct us to turn around. I was really hoping for a peek into the locker room. Not for a glimpse of a perfect ass, although that would have perked this tour right up, but because I want to see if it's as over the top as I imagine.

And now they're shuffling us back to the conference room. The slide on the projector reads Wildcat History and has a picture of a team from back in the eighties if the Burt Reynolds mustaches and mullets are any indication.

"Oooh, maybe now we'll get to meet some players," I say as I take my seat between Quinn and Reese. "I've got this whole image in my head where they parade them in front of us to show us what all our hard work is really about. Maybe Jack Wyld gives us a touching speech, and then we all get a fist bump and an autograph. Go, team!"

Quinn shoots me a weird look.

"Doubtful. Not after last summer." Reese's voice is quiet as he mutters the sentence out of one side of his mouth.

"What happened last summer?" I'm whispering, but I have no idea why.

"Last page of the handbook," he offers at my confused

expression and points the end of the green Minnesota Wildcats pencil in his hand.

I flip through the little paper booklet we were each given first thing this morning and skim the paragraph on workplace relationships.

"Seriously?" I whisper as I reread it, homing in on the *we strongly discourage dating between any Wildcat employees* clause. They provided helpful examples of Wildcat employees to further drive home the point. Manager and team member, coworkers, and intern and player. It doesn't explain what happened last summer, but the result is pretty straightforward.

It isn't like I was really going to date a player, but I am surprised to see it in black and white.

Jack does not come in to give us a rousing pep talk. Neither do any of the other players. After many more slides on the Wildcats and the internship program, we're finally shown to our workspaces, and all my hopes of a famous athlete sighting on my first day are dashed.

Exhausted from sitting too long, but still so giddy I can't stop smiling because *OMG, I work here*, I sit at my new cubicle in the intern pool. We're grouped with other interns in our department, so it looks like I'm going to be spending a lot of time with Quinn and Reese.

I spin in the chair, and Quinn gives me an amused smirk. I think I'm growing on her. She hasn't said much today except to let us know that her dad is friends with the owner, and she scores an invite to the season kickoff party every year. Am I jealous? Not at all. Am I going to befriend her in hopes she gets a plus-one? Maybe. Kidding... I think. I really need to get Reagan out of my head. I've worked around athletes for years. Still, this feels different.

Reese is also local, like Quinn. It's his second year interning at the Wildcats, but he's a lifelong fan, backed up by the many random stats and records he recites about the players any time one is mentioned. The first thing he sets on his new desk is a hockey puck.

It's after five, but we're waiting for Blythe to get out of a meeting and give us instructions for tomorrow. When she appears, the entire floor stops to watch her. She's got that something about her, and I swear she walks like every space is her personal catwalk.

"I'm so sorry. I got held up in a meeting. How was your first day?" She glances between us.

We mutter a chorus of tired "good".

"Go home and let your brains recover from information overload. We'll get started first thing tomorrow." She smiles, hands clasped around her cell phone. "See you in the morning."

Reese loosens his tie and pulls it off over his head. "Some of the other interns went to Wild's, the bar down the street. You guys want to grab a drink?"

"I'm in," I say, getting my purse. I'm too excited to go sit in my empty apartment.

Quinn stares down at her phone as she answers. "The players won't be there. They avoid this area during the summers. Even the ones that come into the arena."

Reese and I exchange a look, and Quinn stops messing with her phone long enough to look up and roll her eyes. "There are so many better bars in the area. The only appeal of Wild's is the hockey player sightings, but whatever, sure. I have a nail appointment downtown at seven, so I might as well stay."

"Great." Reese tucks his tie into his pocket. "Let's do it."

I text Reagan while we walk. She tells me that she and Adam are at the library but promises to call when she gets home to hear all about my day. I consider texting Maverick to see if he wants to join us, but I doubt he wants to be accosted by a bunch of eager interns. If they're anything like me, salivating for a first run-in, then he'd be sorry he showed. Or maybe he wouldn't. Johnny would probably eat it up.

Wild's has a cool vibe. It's your basic sports bar. TVs tuned to sporting events, Wildcats memorabilia on the walls, dartboards, and pool tables. It's bright inside instead of the usual dim lighting that gives off that *don't look too closely at the grime* mood of some bars. The table we sit at isn't sticky or rickety. I guess when you have pro hockey players hanging out, you have to step up the cleanliness.

"Are you a Wildcats fan?" Reese asks me. In a surprising move, Quinn offered to grab the first round and is at the bar getting our drinks.

"I guess so."

He chuckles, deep and throaty but friendly. Then points to Quinn standing on the quiet end of the bar next to two guys. The bartender brings the drinks, and she gives them a parting glance before heading back to us.

"Do you know Declan Sato or Leo Lohan?"

"No." I shake my head and then give the guys another up and down. "Oh, shit. Are they players?"

He nods as Quinn sets our drinks down with a triumphant smile.

"Guess they do come out in the off-season," Reese says to her.

"They aren't exactly the most social of players. They're no Jack

Wyld."

"Why? Because they don't chat up random puck bunnies at the bar?"

Oh snap, does he mean Quinn?

"I am *not* a puck bunny."

I'm with her in the horrified expression on her face. Slut-shaming is so nineties.

Reese's face pales. "Shit, I didn't mean you. I meant… never mind. I'm sorry."

She picks up her drink and fingers the straw. "Besides, if I were, my standards would be Jack Wyld high."

Oh, Quinn. I think I might like her.

"Anyway," Reese says. "Now you've had your first official sighting."

"Not like it matters since they're off-limits this summer." Quinn frowns.

I note she says *this summer* as if she fully intends to bag a hockey player someday—a top player by the sounds of it.

Reese drops his voice. "You can thank Jack for that rule."

"What do you mean?" I ask.

He shifts in his chair and leans in, resting one elbow on the table. "Last summer, there was an intern, Crissy, who was rumored to be hooking up with a player."

"Jack?" Quinn asks. "I doubt it. Probably some chick looking for attention."

"Maybe." He nods. "I didn't know her. I was in the media department last summer, but Crissy was doing a rotation in the social media department, like us, with Blythe at the same time she posted the picture." He sits tall and uses his hands like he's painting the scene for us. "Her, with a sheet pulled up to cover her, but obviously naked and then someone, allegedly Jack, lying in the bed behind her."

"Allegedly?" I ask.

"Just a back and part of a shoulder. Impossible to make out," Reese clarifies. "She posted it from the team's page, though with the caption, CHEATER. It blew over pretty fast since no one could be sure it was him. Besides, our captain can bang the entire state as long as he keeps playing like he's been. But, they put the no-dating-players rule in right after that incident.

"First of all, Jack doesn't do exclusive relationships, so the idea that he cheated is silly." Quinn purses her glossy lips.

"And second?" Reese prompts.

"It's dumb that they made a rule because one person couldn't keep their shit together."

"Wow," I say, stunned. I'm shocked at the gall it would take to do that. And to risk the job. I've seen pictures of Jack, and he's gorgeous, but to go to that extreme and publicly call him out?

We sit in silence for a few moments before Reese breaks the silence again. "Arizona, what led you to Minnesota?"

"The job, of course."

"I mean, lots of internships out there. Why one so far from Arizona?"

"Running from something?" Quinn asks. There's a sparkle in her eyes. I could have guessed she likes the drama, but it's confirmed when I see how ecstatic she is at the prospect.

"No. A friend from college recommended me for the job."

"Where do you go to college?" Reese asks.

A burst of pride sparks under my skin. "Valley University."

His smile spreads. "They won the Frozen Four this year."

I nod. "Yep."

"Man, they had a great season. I wanted to be in Kansas City for the final game, but I couldn't make it work."

"I was there, and it was awesome."

"Wait... a friend from college. You don't mean..."

"Yep." Another dose of pride. It was amazing to hear Maverick's name dropped so many times today. The people of Minnesota are really excited that the Wildcats signed him.

"What?" Quinn looks between us. "What am I missing? Who do you know?" She narrows her eyes at me.

"Johnny Maverick. We went to college together." It's weird to think of that in the past tense. He won't be there when I go back.

The corners of her mouth pull down into an unimpressed frown. "Never heard of him before today."

"You will," Reese says and lifts his beer bottle to the center of the table. "To the Wildcats."

Quinn and I touch our glasses to his. "To the Wildcats."

I stick with Reese, and he introduces me to a lot of people. Since he interned last summer and is local, he has all the inside knowledge, and I feel like I'm drinking from the end of a fire hose. I want to do such an amazing job this summer.

Quinn eventually ditches us for her nail appointment, but I'm glad she came out. She's unlike any of my other friends, but there's something about her brazenness that I kind of dig.

Speaking of friends, Reagan calls while we're playing darts. I excuse myself and find a spot at a quiet section of the bar.

My best friend's face fills the screen, and I smile back at her. "Rea!"

"Kota! I miss you." She sticks out her bottom lip. "Tell me about your first day. Was it amazing? Did you meet any hockey hotties? I miss you *so* much!"

"I miss you too." And I do. We've been inseparable for the past three years. There are few days since we met that I haven't seen or talked to her.

"And hockey hotties?" Her mouth pulls into a wide smile.

"A couple of sightings here at the bar, but just backs of heads. It's just as well. They made it clear at our orientation today that fraternizing with the hockey players is not cool."

"You can't date the players?" Her mouth forms a perfect O, and her eyes widen. You'd think I just told her I can't leave my desk to use the bathroom.

"Oh, come on, it isn't like I was in a real position to do that anyway." The only player I will be spending time with this summer is the one I'm working with on the endorsement. And Maverick, of course. Well, assuming he wants to hang out. He might be busy with team stuff.

"Please, you have WAG section written all over you," she teases. "The way you wore Maverick's number at the Frozen Four, and then he scored a hat trick. That's enough to convince any guy you meet there that you are the perfect accessory to a great season."

I snort-laugh. "Except I won't be here once the season starts."

"I believe in you. Make it happen."

Channeling my dramatic friend, I place a hand on my chest. "Hey there. Do you want to casually date for the next two months? I'm leaving at the end of the summer, but my vagina is so magical. I guarantee that you'll have a great season."

I giggle and look to Reagan, who I expect to be laughing along with me. Her brown eyes are even wider now. "Uhh, Kota."

"What?"

She points, and I swivel in my chair and come face-to-face with Johnny and Jack Wyld.

Maverick is chuckling under his breath, and Jack has an amused smirk. Holy hell, he's good-looking up close. The same height as Maverick, but broader and sporting just the right amount of scruff. His dark hair is slicked back. He's sex on legs. I retract my earlier words because I can see exactly how he might make a young girl go crazy and toss her sanity and job out the window.

"How much of that did you hear?"

"Enough to want to buy you a drink." Jack lifts his hand to signal the bartender.

"I'm going to hang up now." Reagan's voice draws me back to her smiling face on the phone. She singsongs, "Have fun."

She disconnects, and I have no choice but to face Johnny and Jack.

Maverick takes the seat next to me. "Jack, this is my friend Dakota. Kota, I'm guessing you know Jack."

"No," I say, then shake my head. "I mean, yes, I know who you are."

Jack extends a large hand. "Nice to meet you, Dakota."

Chapter Eleven

JOHNNY

"You should see your face?" I bite back a laugh as Dakota stares slack-jawed at Jack moving across the bar to Dec and Lohan. "I so didn't expect you to be starstruck."

"I..." Her mouth opens and closes a few times before she continues. "I was just caught off guard. Jesus, he's a lot." She shakes her head, making the long, red strands fall over one shoulder. She composes herself and hits me with a killer smile. "What are you doing here?"

"Jack called and said a couple of the guys were here." I lift a shoulder and let it fall. I spent the day unpacking and getting settled into the apartment. Hearing from the captain of my new team was a welcome interruption. "Do you think you can handle yourself meeting a couple more of my teammates?"

She rolls her eyes. "Of course I can."

We stand, and I lead her over to the guys.

"Johnny Maverick," Leo Lohan addresses me from his perch on a barstool. "Good to see you again, man."

"You too." The last time I was here, I met most of the team, but only a few are still in town during the off-season.

Declan tips his head in greeting. I'm not sure I've heard him speak yet, but he has a friendly mug.

"Guys, this is my friend Dakota. She's interning with the Wildcats this summer."

"Hey." Kota smiles and waves to the guys.

"How do you two know each other?" Jack asks her.

I toss an arm around her shoulders. "Oh, we go way back."

Jack's brows lift, and he nods slowly. "Magical vagina… I think I'm following now. She's the reason you got a hat trick in the championship game."

Dakota groans, and her body wilts under my arm.

"That's right," I say. "We didn't sleep together, but she did wear my number in the final period."

"So magical boobage." Jack grins and puts out a fist for Dakota.

She taps her knuckles with his, though not very enthusiastically. "Well, this has been mortifying. It was so nice to meet you guys. Let's forget this conversation ever happened, yeah?"

"Done," Leo says and adjusts the Wildcats hat on his head. "Ignore Jack. We do."

"She should be good at that if she's friends with Maverick," the quiet Declan pipes in. I'm rescinding that friendly mug comment.

"If they were handing out degrees for it, I'd have a doctorate," she confirms and knocks me with her elbow. "Can I steal you? I want to introduce you to someone."

"Gotta go, guys," I say. "She wants to show me off."

I dodge the elbow I know is coming and take a side step to safety. I've only been to Wild's one other time, but it's busier tonight than it had been then. Dakota weaves through tables and stops by the dartboards. A guy smiles at her in that way guys do with Dakota that she never seems to notice, and then his gaze slides to me, and his eyes bug out of his head.

"Johnny, this is my new friend and fellow intern, Reese. Reese, Jo—"

"Johnny Maverick," he interjects. "Man, I am so glad you're here. Could have used some of your points last season."

"Reese is a fan," Dakota says, eyes twinkling with amusement like she wasn't just fangirling over Jack a few minutes ago.

"This is the guy you're so pumped about?" A chick steps up beside him and gives me a once-over that makes me feel like I should shower. It isn't sexual so much as it's invasive.

"I thought you left," Dakota says, lips pulling into a big, mocking smile. "Johnny, meet Quinn."

"Nice to meet you." I shake both their hands.

"I came back after I heard Jack made an appearance," X-ray vision–Quinn says.

This Quinn chick smells like trouble. Hairspray, perfume, and a variety of other makeup and body products—lots of products. It has a smell, I swear. She's gorgeous and done up in a way that says she's down for wherever the night might lead her, but like she's hoping that's a six-course meal on a yacht.

When a chick looks like money, it either means she's rich, or she's looking to be. I'm polite as Dakota tells me how the three of them are working for Blythe this summer. Reese really is a fan, and he knows some of my stats from last season, which Dakota thinks is amusing and I think is awesome.

"We were about to start a new game." Reese holds up a dart. "You two want in?"

"Yeah, let's play doubles!" Quinn's eyes light up, and she reaches for my arm.

Dakota backs up, eyeing Quinn's fingers latched onto me. "We probably shouldn't be seen getting too friendly with you."

"Why not? Do I smell? I showered today and everything."

Dakota rolls her eyes. I love it when she does that. Don't tell her.

"We're not supposed to fraternize with the players," she says.

"What? Why not?"

"Long story," Dakota says at the same time Quinn insists it's fine.

"You guys go ahead. I was about to call it a night anyway." She looks at her new friends. "See you tomorrow."

Quinn takes a step closer to me, and her nails dig into my bicep. I'm starting to get the feeling she's hoping to fuck herself into some Louboutins. I don't like to judge, but she's a little too eager.

"I think I'll head back, too. I'm pretty beat."

"You don't need to do that," Dakota insists.

"Nah, I want to." I untangle myself from Quinn's grasp. "Ready, babe?"

When we step out onto the sidewalk, Dakota bursts into laughter. "Babe? Did you just babe me to stop a girl from following you home? Or did you get her number, and she's following in five?" She turns to look back at the bar entrance.

"That chick is dangerous."

"Quinn? I think she's all false bravados."

"Uh-huh." I don't buy it.

"Oh, come on. Like you've never hooked up with a puck bunny."

"These are professional puck bunnies, Kota. It's a whole new league." We shuffle down the sidewalk. The sun's setting, and the foot traffic has slowed from earlier.

"Did you eat dinner?"

"No, not yet. You?"

I step ahead of her to open the door, but Larry, one of the doormen, beats me to it and opens the lobby door wide as he greets us.

"Hey, Larry. Did you meet Dakota? She's interning at the Wildcats this summer."

"You're the new second-floor tenant?" he asks her.

"Yes."

"Pleasure to meet you."

Inside the elevator, she presses the numbers two and eleven.

"What do you feel like eating?" I ask.

"Are we really hanging out? I thought that was an act to get away from Quinn."

The elevator stops on the second floor, and she steps out. "I don't feel like going out."

"Let's order in." I place a hand on the door so that it won't close. "My place or yours?" I shake my head. "Never mind. Mine. I'm not sitting on that pink couch."

She laughs. "See you in fifteen."

I ORDER FROM THE FIRST PLACE I FIND THAT DELIVERS AND TAKE Charli out for a walk. Declan is coming back from the bar at the same time. A few of the guys, including him, live here, but the others are gone for the summer. It's still weird living somewhere without any friends nearby. Except for Kota, of course.

He kneels and holds out a big hand to my dog. She plods forward happily. Not a lot of people she doesn't like, but it's a few extra points for my new teammate.

"Are you getting settled okay?"

"Oh yeah. I dig Minnie-soda."

He smirks. "Good. Let me know if you need anything. I'm on twelve."

"Thanks, man."

I catch the delivery guy coming into the building, grab the food, and head back upstairs.

Dakota's waiting outside my door with one long leg crossed over the other. She changed out of the dress she was wearing earlier and has on shorts and a baggy T-shirt. Her hair is pulled back in a ponytail. Everything about her says comfort and casual, but she's a rocket no matter what she wears.

"I got food," I say, holding up the bag.

She takes it, and I let us into the apartment. Once Charli is off the leash, she jogs around the place, still scoping it out. Neither one of us has gotten used to this being our new place yet.

"Tell me all about your first day, honey," I say playfully as I grab plates and silverware from a box. I haven't unpacked much in here yet, but my TV is set up. Priorities.

Dakota's walking around the apartment, checking it out. She speaks without looking at me. "It was great. Most of the day we sat in a conference room going over the details of our intern rotation and boring human resources stuff, but then they took us around and showed us all the facilities. The arena…" She turns to face me. Her expression is adequately impressed. "It's the most beautiful thing I've ever seen."

"I know, right?" I bring the food and utensils out to the living room. I have a dining table, but Kota doesn't seem bothered by sitting in the living area. In fact, she sits on the floor, crosses her legs, and keeps on talking while I set a plate in front of her and then pull out all the food containers.

"It was my favorite thing we saw today, hands down. I didn't expect it to be so big."

"That's what she said." It's out of my mouth before I can stop it.

Dakota crumples up the receipt on the table from the food and tosses it at my face.

"It's the locker room for me. No matter how many I've seen, it's always something special when you walk into a new place. And the Wildcat's locker room is pretty epic."

"They didn't let us in there," she says with a frown. "They kept us very far away from anywhere players might be."

I scoop a big bite of noodles into my mouth and chew.

Dakota takes a much smaller bite, and her face twists up in disgust. "Uh-uh. What is this?"

"I thought you liked Thai," I say, mouth still mostly full. I'm so hungry. I can't even taste it. I skipped lunch while trying to get the living room setup.

"I do, but something is funky with that."

I offer her some off my plate, and she takes another bite and runs to the kitchen. She holds a hand over her mouth and mumbles something as she searches around.

"Trash can is under the sink." I think. I hope because I hear her spit it out, and then she pops back into view. "That is not edible."

"A spitter, huh? I am so disappointed."

Before she can roll her eyes—oh, well, almost before, I put my fork down. "Do you want me to order something else?"

"No, I'll find something." She opens a cabinet, then another before hitting me with one of her no-nonsense glares. "Johnny Maverick, did you buy me groceries and not yourself?"

"How do you…"

"Oh, please. You're the only person I know here."

I smile. "I was planning on doing it tonight."

"Okay. Let me come with you. I need to get a few more things anyway."

"Can I finish this first?"

"Do you really want to?"

My stomach rumbles. Yeah, maybe it's not the best plan. Something is definitely funky, or she's appropriately psyched me out anyway.

"Thank you, by the way." Dakota grabs a cart for us inside the grocery store.

"For what?"

"The groceries."

"Oh, that was nothing."

She drives the cart over to the produce section and stops at the bananas. "It wasn't nothing. It was really nice."

This is the part I hate about gifting things. I don't know what to do with the thanks. It was fifty dollars' worth of food, not a Rolls Royce.

"Welcome," I say and set a bunch of bananas in the cart. Oranges too.

"What do you need?"

"Everything," I say. "And healthy shit. I start working out with the guys tomorrow." My contract is a two-way, so if I want to stay in Minnie-soda and not be sent down to Iowa to the AHL team, then I have to step it up.

"Okay. Me too. Good, healthy food for a hot girl summer." She walks ahead of the cart, putting things in the front. "I'm going to put my stuff here so we can keep it separate."

That lasts all of ten minutes when I've forgotten and filled the cart with so much stuff I have to encroach her space. And I don't even know what's mine or hers.

We stare at the overflowing cart.

"Did you get everything?" she asks.

"Yeah, I think so." I look over the veggies and meat piled up and then glance toward the chip aisle that we purposely didn't go down because we both decided against it.

"You know," she starts. "We could get a couple of bags of chips and candy."

"Maybe some ice cream," I add.

She nods enthusiastically. "And start fresh tomorrow."

"Hell yes." I jog the cart down the aisle, stepping on the bottom rung and riding it until I get to the ones I want. Sour cream and onion potato chips. What was I thinking not indulging one last time?

The shelves are ransacked like before a winter storm or holiday weekend. I spot the ones I want on the top shelf, but even those have been picked over, and I can't reach them.

I step back on the cart, but even then, it's not happening.

"Fuck. I had my heart set on those."

Dakota clutches a bag of pretzels in one hand and Cheetos in the other. "Which one?"

I pluck them both from her hands and toss them into the cart. "Hop on my shoulders."

"What?" She laughs.

"I need that bag of chips, Kota. It's a matter of life and death."

"Can't we just ask someone for help?"

"Time is wasting. We still have to get to the ice cream aisle."

Laughing, she shakes her head but walks behind me.

I squat down, and she lifts one leg over my shoulder while holding on to my head for balance. "This feels like a terrible idea."

"I won't drop you. Promise."

She groans but links her other leg over, and slowly I stand with her sitting on my shoulders. I grasp her thighs. They're silky and smooth under my touch. I try not to concentrate on that because dropping her would really kill the moment. Also, I probably wouldn't get my chips.

I step up close to the shelving, and she leans forward, one hand in my hair and the other reaching for the chips. I glance up, and her T-shirt gaps giving me a view straight up. Oh fuck, I'm going to hell. All the sensations—her perky tits covered by some sort of lacy black bra, the feel of her sexy, silky legs, and the way she's fisting my goddamn hair. It's my new favorite porno situation. You know, the innocent encounters that you wish ended with the pizza delivery girl ripping off her shirt. Or, in this instance, Dakota climbing off my shoulders with my chips and feeding them to me naked.

"Got them!" she shouts.

I step back, and she tosses them in the cart.

"Now, put me down."

"I don't know. I got a pretty good view when you leaned forward. Maybe I want you to grab a few more things for me."

She smacks my forehead. "Oh my god. I was doing you a favor."

"I didn't mean to see. They were just there."

"They." She covers her face. "Oh my god."

I crouch down so she can get down. "Relax. Not the first time I've seen them."

Ah shit.

"I knew you saw them that night!"

"I didn't see *much*." I saw everything.

Her eyes narrow, but she's still smiling at me. I know she was flashing me behind that construction plastic back in Valley. When the light flickered, I could make out just enough to get a semi. To be fair, looking at Dakota fully clothed could do that to a guy. Okay, fine, it does it to me. I'm the guy.

She's a rocket. I dig her red hair and fair complexion and the way she rolls her eyes but smiles when I flirt with her, which is often. She thinks I'm joking. I'm not serious about much. But I've never said anything to her that I wasn't prepared to follow through on.

Chapter Twelve

JOHNNY

Tuesday late morning, I head over to the arena. Jack mentioned the guys still in town are working out, and truth be told, I need an excuse to get out. I don't like being alone. In Valley, it was the best of both worlds. I had my own apartment, but I was only a flight of stairs from Heath, Adam, and Rhett. Fuck, I miss those guys.

I pause in front of the arena doors and take a selfie, then send it to the group. Heath is the first to respond as I walk down the hall toward the weight room.

Payne: Sweet new digs, bro. Ice isn't the same without you.

He attached a picture of the Valley rink, and I have to admit, even being in this fancy-ass arena, I'm hit with a bittersweet feeling that I won't ever play there again.

Scott: You left a giant box of glow-in-the-dark condoms in the apartment. Want me to mail them?

Rauthruss: We're in the same state again! Let me know when

you're free, and me and Sienna will come down for dinner.

Maverick: That was a parting gift, Scott. Enjoy. Payne, love you, bro. FaceTime later? Rauthruss, yeah, man, let's make plans as soon as camp is over.

Damn, this is weird. I was only at Valley for two years, but it was more my home than any other place I've lived. I glance around. This isn't too bad, though. Not bad at all.

Jack, Declan, and Leo are lifting weights, music blasting. I stop in the doorway and take it all in. Goosebumps climb my arms as I glance around the weight room. It's fucking huge. So many machines, top-of-the-line shit. No expense was spared in here.

"Johnny Maverick." Jack checks the clock on the wall. "Nice of you to finally join us."

"Your text said you'd be here from nine to two."

The captain of the Wildcats drops the dumbbells in his hands and steps forward. "Just messing with you. You're in time for weights."

"Nice of you to conveniently miss the five-mile run." Leo smirks as he mops the sweat off his forehead with a towel.

Dec finishes guzzling from his water bottle and uses the back of his hand to wipe his mouth. "And the hour mobility session."

Five miles? Mobility? Already? Fuuuck. I ate a bowl of Lucky Charms and chased it with a dozen donuts while I watched *The Price is Right*. I know. I know. The healthy food was supposed to start today, but I couldn't let the junk food go to waste.

I step to the only guy I don't know in the room and offer him my hand. "Hey, I'm Johnny Maverick."

He's a big guy, several inches taller than me and like twice as wide. His grip on my hand is painful. "Hercules."

"No shit?"

Hercules drops my hand and walks over to the squat rack. He proceeds to put forty-five plates on either side until I'm not sure the bar can take any more.

"He doesn't talk much." Jack picks up his weights and goes back to curling the forties while chatting. "Ready to get to work?"

"Yeah." I nod and take a seat on an empty bench. We don't have to report for camp for another two weeks, but I am anxious to get started.

"Well, don't just sit there. Grab some weights, rookie." Declan smiles at me in the mirror. "Let Hercules have a little new blood."

The trainer in question grins.

"Don't worry." His voice is thick with an accent—Austrian, I think. He sounds like Arnold. Just about as big as him back in the Mr. Olympia days, too. He tips his head, indicating I should come closer. "Let's get some meat on those legs, huh?"

Oh fuck, this is going to hurt.

Jack huffs a laugh. "You made a friend. That's more than he's said to me all day."

Hercules doesn't respond, but one corner of his mouth tilts in amusement.

The giant trainer may not say a lot of words, but he doesn't need to. I finish one set, he adds more weight, and then waves a hand, basically telling me to get a move on.

Jack finally takes pity on me after an hour of sweating out the pound of sugar I inhaled this morning. I'm killing myself trying to keep up with everything Hercules throws at me.

He tosses me a towel. "All right, Herc. You've had enough

fun with the new guy. *For now.*" He looks at me. "Tomorrow, nine o'clock."

"I'll be here. I might not be able to leave. I'm not sure I can walk. My legs are dunzo." I lie on my back in the middle of the floor. Everything hurts, and I'm dying. I've got a lot of work to do. Less beer, less pizza, and way more weight training are in my future.

He crouches down and offers me his hand. "You need to meet Elsa."

"Elsa?"

"Trust me."

I take his hand, and he pulls me to my feet. Wowser, my thighs burn, but I follow him into another room to a waiting ice bath.

"Seven minutes with Elsa, and you'll be good as new." He slaps me on the back, and I stumble forward on wobbly legs. "See you tomorrow, Rookie."

While Elsa isn't the magic cure, I do feel better after a soak. I find Hercules still in the workout room and ask him to create a plan for me this summer. He grins, and I regret it immediately. Lastly, I have a meeting with Coach, and then somehow the day is over, and it's five o'clock. I head upstairs to the main offices, looking for Dakota. I have no idea where she sits, but I see lots of other people I assume are interns and wander until I spot her red hair. She stands outside of an office, shoulder leaning against the wall.

"What are you doing here?" She looks around.

"Picking you up from work. Let's go to dinner." Now that I'm not in so much pain or in threat of puking up breakfast, I'm starving. I'm going to need to get my nutrition on lock to survive training with Hercules.

"I'm waiting for Blythe. What are you doing here?"

"I work here." I wink.

"Right. I meant—"

"I know what you meant." I lean against the wall next to her. "I worked out with the guys and then spent seven minutes in heaven with Elsa."

Dakota's brows lift, and she pops a hip. "Do I even want to know?"

"Ice bath." I shift and hold out my arm. Standing still makes me realize how weak my legs are. I should have spent more time with Elsa. Or less with Hercules. "Ready to rock?"

She wakes the screen of her phone and checks the time. "Blythe is running late. She has the boxes and all the details for the endorsement. I still don't know which hockey player I'm working with. The suspense is killing me!" Her beautiful eyes light up.

My gut twists. I should have told her, I know, but then she might not have come to Minnesota.

"Can't you get it tomorrow?" One more day of ignorant bliss.

"Yes." Her shoulders slump forward. "I guess so."

"Great." I move my legs as fast as possible, which isn't all that fast right now, to get us out of dodge before Blythe returns.

When we're outside, I breathe a sigh of relief. "Where do you want to go?"

"I was planning on cooking. We did just buy a ton of groceries."

"Yeah, but I already ate all the good stuff." Man, I'd love another donut right now.

"I think I'm going to bake some tilapia and make a nice salad."

My stomach growls audibly, and I give her big, pleading eyes.

The kind that says, please feed me and keep me company.

Dakota rolls her eyes. "Fine, you can come, but only if you bring Charli and no complaining about how uncomfortable my couch is."

"Ooooo." I inhale with a hiss. "I'm not sure I can promise that. It's the most uncomfortable—"

I slam my lips shut when her eyes narrow, and my dreams of a home-cooked meal start to disappear. I make a motion like I'm locking the key on my closed mouth and follow her home.

Chapter Thirteen

DAKOTA

After dinner, I go with Johnny and Charli on a walk, and then they come back to my apartment. I get the feeling my place has become his new home away from home. I don't mind. I've had a roommate for so long. I've gotten used to always having someone around.

He collapses on my couch, groans, and mutters under his breath about how hard it is. I fill a bowl with water for Charli and then grab the nearly empty tub of ice cream from my freezer. We put a major dent in this last night.

I wave a spoon in front of his face. "Want some rocky road?"

"Oooooh." His hazel eyes widen with excitement, and then he shakes his head. "Can't. Hot girl summer." He lifts the hem of his T-shirt. "Time to start treating this body like the temple that it is."

His flat stomach taunts me. Maybe I could lick his abs and save myself the calories.

What... no. Ewww, no. Okay, not eww. Johnny is hot, but I need to get out and meet more people. If I spend every night holed up with him for the next eight weeks, I might do something stupid.

I laugh and sit in the chair with the tub, eating straight from the container.

He watches me lick the spoon, and I just know he's thinking something dirty. It's probably true ninety-nine percent of the time. I roll my eyes.

"I didn't even say anything." His deep laughter fills my living room.

"I could tell what you were thinking."

He smirks and sits up. "Doubtful."

He snatches me around the wrist before I realize what he's doing and pulls me on top of him, ice cream, spoon, and all.

"Johnny," I squeal as he sets me in his lap, arms around me.

"I changed my mind. Feed me, Kota." He leans his head over my shoulder and opens his mouth.

"No, this last bite is all mine." I bring the spoon toward my lips, and he whines.

"Kooooota."

I take a small bite and then feel bad and hold the rest out for him.

"Sweet. Your mouth touched it too. Bonus."

"My saliva on your ice cream is a bonus?"

He nods with a cocky glint in his eyes as he swallows. "Absolutely."

THE NEXT MORNING, I GET TO WORK FIFTEEN MINUTES EARLY, hoping to catch Blythe before rotations start. Again, I find her office empty. The lights are on, so I know she's here somewhere, but it looks like another day without finding out which player I'm working with this summer.

Thanks to Maverick, I know most of the guys aren't around for another week or two anyway, but, ugh, I want to know!

I head to my desk since I have time to kill. We don't start our rotations until next week, which means this week, we're with Blythe learning all things marketing department.

While I wait for everyone else to arrive, I scroll through the Wildcats social media pages. They're well done with a good mix of content: news announcements around game schedules and contracts, then there's game footage—photos and videos a lot like what we compiled for the hype videos back at Valley in the Hall of Fame, and finally, more personal touches like birthdays and casual photos of the team and staff.

Blythe and her team have created an engaging and visually stunning space on all the platforms. There are a lot of cool jobs at the Wildcats, and I'm excited to do all of it, but none of it more than working with Blythe.

I click on the team page to find some of the guys' personal pages. Jack's is the most obviously curated. He doesn't have any private photos or really anything that looks like he posted it himself. Still, he has almost a million followers.

Reese is the next to show. He drops into a chair with his sunglasses still on.

"Morning."

He slides the shades up and rests them on top of his head. "Morning, Arizona."

"I'm actually from Kansas."

"It's too late. You're Arizona in my brain now."

Quinn walks in just before Blythe. My new boss looks as stylish and gorgeous as ever. I'd kill to see her closet. She carries a box on her hip.

"This is for you," she says, dropping it on my desk. "Sorry, I didn't get a chance to bring it by yesterday afternoon."

"No problem." Ahhh, finally!

"Is everyone ready to get started today?"

I nod and bite my lip, anxious to dig into the goodies.

The three of us gather around while Blythe gives us a basic rundown of the day. Reese and Quinn are assigned the task of brainstorming content ideas for social media posts between now and when the development camp starts in two weeks, and thank the hockey hotties, she tells me to spend the day familiarizing myself with the endorsement campaign.

Quinn and Reese huddle together at his desk next to mine, and Blythe stands by while I open the box for my big hockey guy's endorsement.

"We'll need to work around the camp schedule to get a photo shoot," she says. "The sooner, the better because as the guys all return from break, things will get busier around here."

As she speaks, I dive in with enthusiasm to finally figure out what the heck is inside. My hand slides past the packing peanuts, and I wrap my fingers around the first item. I pull it out and smile. Body wash?

I keep going, pulling out more products—deodorant, body mist, aftershave lotion, and ... sack spray. There are a few different scents, all with names like Starry Night, Wild Fields, and Hailstone. Each fragrance is available in all the products so that you could have an entire collection of Starry Night, for example. Of all the things I imagined, this wasn't anywhere on my radar. I'm relieved, though. This is going to be fun.

I hold up the deodorant spray for balls for Blythe to see. She laughs. "Charming."

"What is it?" Quinn asks.

I toss it to her, and she reads the label, mouth twisting into disgust.

"Eww." She tosses it to Reese like she's playing a game of hot potato.

Reese catches it easily and chuckles. "Awesome."

"Which player is endorsing ball deodorant?" Quinn lifts a brow. She stands and comes over to get a better look at all the products scattered on my desk.

"I don't know, actually," I admit as I empty the box and set it on the floor. I glance at Blythe. She tilts her head to the side, a confused expression on her stunning face.

"Do you know?" I ask her.

"Yeah. I…" She smiles hesitantly. "Johnny Maverick. This is the Maverick Company's new product line for male hygiene. He didn't tell you?"

Heat rushes to my face. I shake my head side to side. An unsettling feeling takes hold of my chest. I look back at the products. The Maverick name and logo sit proudly on each one. *Oh my god.*

Quinn huffs, shoots me a suspicious glare, and goes back to her desk.

"Well, I'll leave you three to get started. Dakota, let me know if you need anything." She waves, indicating the Maverick campaign and the tiny little bottles on my desk.

As soon as she's gone, I pull out my laptop and bring up the contract for my internship. JM Holdings. Oh my god, how could I be so stupid? John Maverick. Did Johnny do this? Of course he did. But why? And what else did he do?

I grab my phone.

Me: Are you at the arena?

Maverick: Yep. I'm in the weight room. What's up?

Me: Have a minute?

Maverick: Of course. Come on down. I'll see if I can sneak you into the locker room for a tour while you're down here.

I stand and grab the Wild Fields sack spray. My cheeks burn with humiliation and rage.

"Everything okay?" Reese asks, looking up from his notepad. Quinn doesn't spare me a glance. I can't blame her. I know exactly how this looks.

"Perfect. I am going to take a walk while I brainstorm."

And I might maim a hockey player while I'm at it.

Chapter Fourteen

JOHNNY

Jack and I have music pumping in the weight room. Hercules is working with Declan and Leo on the other side of the massive room. I asked Hercules to come up with a training plan for me, and he did not disappoint. I'm not going to be able to feel my arms when I leave here, but the man came through.

When Dakota appears in the doorway, I smile and drop my weights. She scans the room for me, and while she does, I appreciate today's outfit—a light pink dress paired with those red Chucks again. She is smoking.

"Kota!" I call.

Her expression morphs into anger. Those sexy blue eyes narrow, and her chin drops as she glares at me across the room. *Ah shit.*

"You." She marches over to me and pokes my bare chest with a pointy finger.

"What? What?" I rub my chest and take a step back.

She holds up one of the products for the male hygiene line I'm now endorsing.

"Oh." It's a dumb thing to say. I knew she'd find out, and I knew she'd be pissed, but I hoped when the time came, I'd know what to say. I don't.

"*Oh?* Oh?" She comes at me again. She uncaps the spray and starts spritzing me with it.

I back up and put my hands up. Does that stop her? Hell to the no. I trip over a dumbbell and catch myself on a nearby bench, sitting and saying, "Stop. Okay. You're pissed. I get it."

"Pissed? You think this is pissed?"

"Uhhh…"

"Why am I working for your family's company?"

Jack, who was doing squats, stops and rests his elbows on the bar, watching our interaction in the mirror with a grin.

"They needed someone to—"

She spritzes me again. "Wrong. Try again."

"Blythe—"

Another goddamn spritz.

"Fuck, Kota. Cut that out. It got in my mouth that time."

"Serves you right." She holds it up like a weapon. "I'm going to ask you one more time. Why am I working for your family's company?"

"Because I didn't want you to miss out on an internship with the Wildcats."

"So you talked to your dad and got him to sponsor my internship?"

Ah, fuck. This is going to be bad. Her eyes are tiny slits of ice.

"It wasn't my dad. I sponsored your internship. I used the money they paid me for the endorsement."

She goes on a spritzing rampage, growling and cursing me.

Standing, I grab her wrist. We wrestle with the bottle, but I get it and hold it up high where she can't reach it. She looks like she might hit me, so I hold her against my chest with the other arm. "You deserved the internship. It's a great opportunity for you, and it isn't like I'm not getting anything out of this. My endorsement campaign is going to be baller. You're the best, and I wanted the best."

She wiggles in my hold. "Let me go, Maverick."

I comply, and she steps back, still glaring at me, but it doesn't look like I'm in immediate danger.

"I'm sorry, okay?"

"Sorry? My entire internship is a big, fat lie."

"It isn't. Blythe wanted to hire you."

"I don't want your money. Find someone else to do the endorsement."

"Kota." This is precisely why I didn't want to tell her. "Wait."

"No. I would have been perfectly happy working at the Hall of Fame this summer. Maybe they can still get me on the schedule."

She starts toward the door, and I jog in front of her, blocking the doorway. "You can't go back to Valley."

"Why not?"

"Because this internship is a great opportunity. Blythe is the best. You said so yourself. A summer working for her will look great on your resume."

"Let me tell you how much I care about my resume right now. I assume the apartment was also you?"

I don't speak, but she nods once and sighs.

"I might need a couple of days to arrange everything, but I will be out by the weekend."

"Come on. Don't do this."

"I have to get back upstairs." She pushes past me.

Fuck!

"I like her," Jack says as Dakota disappears down the hallway. "Ah, rook." He claps me on the shoulder. "You really screwed this one up, huh?"

"Yeah."

"I suggest groveling. A lot of it."

"You grovel?"

"For a chick like that… I think I just might."

"What is that smell?" Hercules says as he waves a hand in front of his face. "It's growing on me. Lavender? Sandalwood?"

I toss him the sack spray. "Wild Fields."

"I'm gonna…" I jab a thumb to the door.

"Go. I'll catch you later, rook." Jack smiles as I head to catch Dakota.

I get upstairs before I realize I don't have on a shirt. A couple of corporate guys give me a once-over, and I slow my roll. Dakota isn't answering her phone, and I don't know where she sits up here in the maze of offices.

I head back downstairs and finish my workout, but my head isn't in it. When I don't hear back from her by the end of the day, I go back to the apartment and text the guys for help.

Maverick: Pissed off Kota. Help!

Scott: WHAT THE FUCK DID YOU DO?

Payne: Ouch. Bet that had painful consequences.

Scott: Sorry, that was Reagan. She's looking over my shoulder now, FYI. (Don't say anything that's going to get me in

trouble for your stupidity).

Rauthruss: Ah shit. I hope you were wearing a cup.

Scott: Oh fuck. You paid for her internship?

Maverick: How do you already know?

Scott: Reagan's texting Dakota. You're right. She's pissed.

Payne: You paid for her internship?

Rauthruss: Oh shit, you paid for her internship?

Maverick: Yes, great. Glad we're all on the same page now. What do I do?

Payne: I got nothing.

Rauthruss: *shrug emoji*

Maverick: Scott?

Maverick: Heeeeeeeelp me!

Scott: Dude, I don't know. When Reagan gets mad at me, I kiss her. I don't think that's going to work in your case.

Payne: Ooooh yeah. Kiss her. That always works.

Rauthruss: I take off my shirt, but I'm guessing you've already done that.

Maverick: *shirtless selfie, flipping them off* You guys are useless.

Maverick: I still love you. Xbox later?

Payne: Meet you online at eight. *kissy face emoji*

Rauthruss: I'll be there. I might even let you win (Probably not).

Scott: Brainstorm session before? I'll see what I can get out of Rea.

I SHOWER AND WAIT OUTSIDE OF DAKOTA'S APARTMENT FOR HER to get off work. I bring Charli as a backup. She can't say no to Charli.

When she steps out of the elevator, I push off the wall and wait for her to come at me, fists flying.

"What are you doing here?" Her tone has lost all the anger, but she isn't happy to see me either.

She opens the apartment, and I follow her inside.

"I'm sorry. I should have told you."

"Yes, you should have."

She crosses her arms over her chest and leans against the kitchen counter.

"I knew you wouldn't take the job if you had any idea that I'd arranged it. And I wanted you to take the job."

"I get that you think you were doing me a favor, but now all I can think about is how I didn't earn this job."

"You did, though. Blythe offered you the job, remember?"

"No one will believe that. You should have seen the way Quinn looked at me today. I want my talent to stand on its own."

"And it will. I am just providing the opportunity."

"I can't stay, but since I have already cost you money with the move and apartment, I spent the day working on concepts for your endorsement photo shoot. I emailed them to you. I have no idea if any of the ideas are feasible, but it should be a start for whoever you get to take my place."

She starts toward her bedroom. I follow her. So does Charli. She's a loyal little creature, and she knows something is up.

"Let me buy you dinner to make it up to you."

"You think buying me something else is going to fix this?" The scowl on her face tells me no. "I'm going for a run. I need to clear my head."

She shuts herself in the walk-in closet.

I don't know how to make this right. Think, Johnny, think.

I haven't come up with anything when she steps out dressed in her running clothes.

"I'm so sorry I didn't tell you before. I wanted to, but I also really wanted you to take the job."

Her glare softens only slightly.

"I was trying to do you a favor. That's true, but it's because I really believe you're the best person for the job."

She grabs her phone and ear pods.

I shadow her back out of her room and through the apartment. She says nothing as she leaves for her run.

"Stay," I tell Charli. I'm not dressed for a run, but I'll keep up with her step for step, for as long as it takes to make her understand.

She's halfway down the stairs to the lobby. Damn, she's fast. I can't lose her. I have to fix this. I take the stairs three at a time. They're an odd size and curve around. I'm almost to the bottom when I lose my footing. I jump the rest of the way and catch myself by ramming the left side of my body into the wall.

She glances back at the commotion. "Are you okay?"

"Fine."

Her gaze flicks to my leg as I put weight on it and limp forward, still trying to get to her. I rub at the outside of my knee. Fuck, that hurt.

"You're not fine. Sit down." She points to the bench in the lobby.

"I just need a second." I hobble over to it and sit.

"Does it hurt to touch?" Her eyes search my face as she places her fingertips on the side of my knee.

"I'll be fine in a minute. I hit it against the wall. It hit back harder." I lower my voice. "Please don't go."

I wince as I get to my feet.

"I think you should have that looked at."

"If I do, will you stay?"

She laughs, and I breathe a tiny sigh of relief that she's no longer trying to run away. "Who do we call? Your coach? Your agent?"

"I'll check in with the trainer first thing tomorr—"

She silences me with a sexy little growl. "I've seen you get slammed to the ice and look like you're in less pain than you do right now. You need to have it looked at now."

"I'll call Hugh. He'll know what to do." I'm still holding her hand hostage while I dial.

She points for me to sit again, and then she takes the seat beside me and brings my hurt leg up on her lap. I like her when she's all bossy and takes charge. And when she's not glaring at me.

Scratch that. I like her all of the time.

Chapter Fifteen

DAKOTA

Hugh sends Maverick to see the team doctor. I help him out to his SUV. It takes us more time to drive around and park than it would have to walk, but since I'm taking as much weight as I can handle off his leg, it seemed the safer choice.

I pull up to the back entrance of the arena, where the team doctor is waiting for us.

After only a few minutes, Dr. Anderson tells Maverick that he thinks he has a sprained MCL and sends us to the hospital for an MRI to determine the severity and ensure he didn't tear the ligament.

Mav is quiet in the passenger seat as I drive. I don't think he really expected the doctor to find anything, and I can't imagine the thoughts going through his head. When we get to the emergency room, I force him into a chair while I sign him in.

"Dr. Anderson said you could be back as quick as a week or two," I tell him.

"Great," he says in the most mundane tone I've ever heard from him.

"It's going to be okay." I rest a hand lightly on his thigh. It has to be. I feel awful. I know it wasn't my fault, but it would never have happened if I hadn't been running away from him.

He looks down at my hand, and then his stare locks on mine. "Don't leave."

"I'm not going anywhere. I'll be right here." I scan the magazine selection and pick up a copy of *People*.

"That isn't what I meant. Stay here in Minnesota. Don't go back to Valley."

I set the magazine back on the table and sigh.

He angles his body, holding an ice pack to his knee. "I did it for you, but I did it for me too."

"There are lots of people that can do the job." Even better than I can, but I leave that out. I would have worked my ass off for that job.

"Maybe, but they're not you. I wanted the best, but I also wanted you."

I try to read his serious expression. "Why?"

"Because… leaving Valley was hard. The guys, you, Reagan, Ginny, Sienna, you were more than just my friends."

I nod. I get that. I love my dad, but outside of him, my family is made up of my crazy friends.

"I shouldn't have lied to you, but I want you here. You're like a little piece of home."

"Mav." My voice cracks.

"Don't go. Not now. I need you." He drops his head into my lap.

My heart splits open, and he nudges a little farther in. He's vulnerable and unsure and so unlike my friend. "Okay. I'm here. I'm not going anywhere."

"Thank you." He doesn't move his head, and I slide my fingers through his thick, dark hair.

"I'm not taking your money, though."

"We'll figure it out," he says. "Just don't go."

It's late when we get back to the apartment. No tear, thankfully, but he did sprain his MCL and needs to rest for at least a week, maybe longer. He crutches to the elevator, and we start toward the second floor so he can get Charli.

We left her at my place when we went to see the doctor, and she is very excited to see her owner return. I pick her up and let Maverick give her a few pets.

"I'll take her out and then bring her up to you."

"Cool. Thanks." He sits on the couch and blows out a long, tired breath. "I'm just going to rest here for a second."

It's hard to see him like this when I'm so used to the happy-go-lucky guy I've been friends with for two years. I take Charli outside and then up to the eleventh floor. I knock on Maverick's door and wait.

When he doesn't respond, I try the doorknob in case he left it open for me, but it doesn't budge. I didn't bring my phone, so I can't call him. I knock and try again a little louder. "Mav, are you in there?"

He must have been exhausted if he passed out without his dog. Charli curls up in my arms.

"Guess you're staying with me tonight," I tell her. She snuggles in tighter against my chest.

Back on the second floor, I push into my apartment and come up short. Maverick lays on the pink couch. His mouth gapes open, and one tattooed arm is over his eyes.

"Correction," I say quietly, putting Charli on the ground. She jogs over and jumps up next to him. He doesn't open his eyes, but wraps an arm around her in his sleep. "I guess you're both staying with me tonight."

I WAKE UP TO THE WHIRRING SOUND OF MY BLENDER IN THE kitchen. I left my bedroom door open in case Maverick needed something, but I slept through the night.

I glance at my phone for the time. I have an hour before I need to get to work. I swing my legs off the bed and move toward the kitchen.

"Morning," he says when he sees me. He's leaning on one crutch. "Did I wake you?"

"My alarm was going off in fifteen minutes anyway." I hop onto the counter. "A couple of barstools would have gone great in here."

I scope out his concoction. "What are you making?"

Instead of answering, he grabs two glasses and pours half into each. "Try it."

"You should be sitting down and icing your knee."

"I will. All day," he grumbles. "I'm sorry I fell asleep here. Boy, am I sorry." He raises one arm and rotates it. He lost his shirt at some point, and the button of his jeans is open. I can see just the band of his black boxers.

My body tingles. Maverick has a great body. I've seen him shirtless more times than I can count, but after last night watching him be so vulnerable and mixing that with the ripped guy standing in my apartment making me a smoothie, that tastes… well, delicious, I'm a little too aware of how hot my friend is.

"I'm going to get ready." I start back toward my room, taking my smoothie with me.

"Yeah, I should head upstairs and get comfortable, I guess."

"Do you need any help?"

"Nah, Charli will follow." He finishes off his smoothie and places the empty glass in the dishwasher.

"How are you going to take Charli outside during the day?"

"I'll manage," he clips, and I slam my lips together to keep from smiling or calling him broody. A broody Maverick. I never thought I'd see the day.

"Okay. Well, if you need anything, just text me. And we should talk later. We still need to figure out everything with the endorsement and the apartment." I wave a hand around my fabulous new place. I really do love it. After only a few days, I'm going to be sad to leave it. "I did some searching last night, and I found some apartment listings I'll check out this week."

"This place is already paid for," he says. His tone and insinuation make it clear he thinks I'm being silly.

"You can sublease it."

He chuckles. "God, you're stubborn. And the internship?"

I lift my heel and curl my toes into the hardwood floor. "I will continue on one condition."

"Name it."

"I want to be unpaid like all the other interns."

"You're doing more than the other interns."

"Do we have a deal?"

"No." He leans on his crutches. "Look, the job you're doing for me is worth every penny I'm paying. If you want to reimburse me for the other bullshit, fine, but I'm not letting you go unpaid all summer for a job I'd hire out regardless."

"The Maverick Company could have done all of it for you. My being here is pointless."

"Not to me." He hobbles over, so he's standing in front of me. "I was always going to hire someone else to oversee the endorsement. I don't want them calling any more shots than is absolutely necessary."

"Why?"

"Because..." There's bite in his tone that makes me hold my tongue. He roughs a hand through his hair. "My dad looks out for the Maverick Company first and foremost. I don't have anyone. I guess I wanted a third party to look out for me, and I knew you'd do that."

"Johnny." I reach out and rest my hand on his chest. I'm angry at his dad and sad for him all at once. Also, I think he severely overestimates how much power I have. The Maverick Company has the final sign-off on everything I create. "You have lots of people. Me included. Although, I'm a little nervous about how much faith you're putting in me. I don't have any idea what I'm doing."

"I trust you." One side of his mouth hitches up.

I hope that trust isn't seriously misguided. "I should get ready for work. We can figure out all the details tonight. Are you going to be okay on your own today?"

"I'll be fine." He heads toward the door. "Have a good day at work, honey."

I shake my head as I watch him leave and then wander back into my room.

He's back a minute later. He doesn't knock, and I scream as he walks into my bedroom while I'm taking off my T-shirt.

"Oh, shit, sorry." He hops around on one foot and faces the other direction.

"What are you doing back?" I ask, fumbling for my shirt and pulling it over my head inside out.

"I had an idea."

My heart still races as I kick my bra toward the closet. "You can turn around now."

He smirks. "Three times now you've flashed me. I think you're doing it on purpose."

"You wish."

"Hell yeah, I do. You've got great tits. Are they fake?"

I'd like to toss a pillow at him, but don't because he's injured. "What's the idea, and why are you back in my apartment?"

"I was thinking… maybe you could move in with me?"

My brows lift, and he continues. "Hear me out. I have a two-bedroom, and we're obviously going to be hanging out most nights anyway."

"Obviously," I parrot.

"Would you rather live with me or some stranger?"

I laugh, and his smile gets bigger.

"It'll be fun. Come on, just give it a chance. We can do a trial run today." He hops to the couch and sits.

"I thought you wanted me to move in with you? My place is a one-bedroom."

"I do, but if I hang here today, it'll be easier to take Charli out. That elevator is slow as fuck, and the stairs are not my friend right now. Plus, I can rummage through your panty drawer."

"Oh my god, perv. Stay out of my room."

"Kidding." His smile falls. "But in all seriousness, my knee is screaming this morning."

"You can stay as long as you want." I point toward the couch. "In the living room only. And I will think about the rest."

"Thanks. This is going to be great, roomie."

I SPEND THE MORNING WORKING WITH REESE, LOOKING THROUGH approved photos to go with the content he and Quinn created yesterday. Then we mockup all the posts for Blythe to approve.

"So, Arizona, I heard Maverick got injured."

"You did?"

"It was in the sports section this morning. MCL sprain."

"That's right."

"Sucks. Right before camp is not a good time to be getting injured." He lifts his brows.

"He should be fine in a week or two. He's tough."

Reese leans back in his chair, pen lifted in his hand. He clicks it as he says, "Yeah, but by then they may have already decided to send him to Iowa."

"Really? Just like that?" Three days ago, everyone was talking about how he was the future of the Wildcats, and now they're ready to cast him aside? I knew it was important that he get treated and back on his feet quickly, but I had no idea they'd write him off so fast. Brutal.

After lunch, I review the endorsement contract more closely. The deliverables are outlined, but otherwise, it's vague. They want photographs of Johnny with some of the products for the launch, and they even provided examples from some of their print and online ads. There are a lot of smiling women putting lotion on their hands, others with shiny, just styled hair. It's a little stiff and boring, if I'm honest.

But whoever designed the new line for men did so with a new, younger vibe. The names of the products themselves are fun, and the colors and bottles are more modern. Johnny is the perfect person to endorse it, despite his reservations, which I totally understand. I can't imagine what it's like to feel as if your parents care more about their company than you.

For the rest of the day, I think of nothing else. I take everything I know about my friend and build a campaign that puts him and his personality front and center. Maybe the endorsement has no merit on whether the Wildcats keep him or send him down to the AHL team, but I work like it might be the difference.

Before I leave, I email Blythe my rough concept and then stop by her office on my way out.

"Come in," she says. Her feet are kicked up on her desk, and instrumental music plays quietly. She brings her feet to the floor and sits upright. "I was just looking over your ideas. They're good. Really good."

"They are?"

She nods enthusiastically. "I especially like your idea for the photo shoot. It's perfect for Johnny. Your knowledge of him really comes through. I could practically hear him in your summary."

"I'm not sure if that's a compliment, channeling my inner Maverick, but I had fun coming up with it."

"It shows."

"It's a little different than their other campaigns. Do you think it's too far?"

One of her shoulders lifts slightly. "No, I think it's exactly what they need to sell this new line, but we should run it by them before you do the photo shoot."

"Okay. Yeah, I was planning on doing that after I had it all detailed out."

"The tricky part will be scheduling and finding locations for the shoot. The Wildcats have agreed to let us do it here, but it can't look like it was shot here. Nothing that seems like the Wildcats themselves are endorsing the products. That sort of endorsement costs a lot more than what they're paying."

"While we're on the topic, I want you to know that I appreciate what you and Johnny did to get me here."

"You didn't know," she says, and I shake my head. "I pieced that together yesterday."

"I wouldn't have taken the job if I had," I admit. "But I am going to do my best to prove I'm the right person to be here regardless."

"I'm glad you're here, Dakota. I suspect Johnny had ulterior motives, but I think his career is going to benefit." She points to her laptop. "You've already proven it, at least to me."

"Thank you so much."

"I can talk to Coach Miller about letting us use the locker

room for the photo shoot. It's probably going to be a hard no the week of camp."

"What about next week?"

Her brows lift. "You think you can get it ready that quickly?"

"Absolutely. I'm so excited to work on this."

"Okay, then. I think he'll be okay with that, but I'll double-check." She cocks her head to the side and studies me. "You and Johnny Maverick…"

Heat floods my face. "We're just friends."

"I don't like telling people what to do with their personal time, but unfortunately, relationships between players and interns have caused issues in the past."

My heart flutters in my chest. "I understand. You don't have anything to worry about with me."

"Good. See you tomorrow, Dakota."

Chapter Sixteen

DAKOTA

When I get back to my apartment, Maverick and Charli are still here. Maverick's hurt leg is stretched out along the couch, and his laptop is in front of him. He's wearing a headset and playing some video game.

"Hey," I call, dropping my purse and laptop bag on the counter.

"Die, Rauthruss," he says and tips his head up to me. "Ah fuck, fuck. Dammit." The screen goes red. "You win again, fucker. I'm going to get you. I gotta go. Dakota just got home. I'll catch you guys later."

"Hey," he says with a sheepish grin. "How was work?"

"It was good. How's the knee?" I pick up a warm ice pack from the floor in front of him.

"Fine." He runs a hand over his messy hair. "I didn't realize it got so late while I was fucking around with the guys. I hope you don't mind Charli and I stayed here all day."

"I don't. I told you it was fine, but it looks like you went up to the eleventh floor." I point to his laptop.

"Yeah, I got really bored. You need a TV."

I don't point out the obvious that he could have stayed in his apartment instead of schlepping his laptop back down here. I'm glad to see him.

"Let me help. I can grab whatever you need."

"You've done enough. It was easier taking Charli in and out only going up and down the one flight of stairs." He stands and grabs his crutches. "We'll get out of your hair. Hand me that."

He juts his chin to the laptop.

"How are you going to carry it?"

"Stick it in the back of my jeans."

"Mav, this is stupid. Just hang out here." I resist reminding him that it's technically his place since he paid for it.

"Really? You don't mind?"

"No. I think I'd like the company. I'm not used to living alone. I'm starving, though."

I go to the kitchen and look for something to eat. We bought so much food the other night, but I don't feel like cooking. I grab mini rice cakes and take the bag to the living room.

"You really need a TV," he says.

"I could show you my plan for your endorsement?"

"I read over your email. It looked good."

"Well, today, I expanded all of it to give it more Maverick personality." I pull it up on my laptop, and I talk him through it while we devour the bag of rice cakes.

"I was thinking it would be cool if they named one of the scents after you."

"I don't think they're looking to redo anything."

"Then one of the scents they've already named. You could be Starry Night."

He chuckles. I go to my purse and bring out a few of the samples. I hold the one in question under his nose.

"Uh-uh," he says. "That one burns my nose."

"Okay, what about this one?" I uncap another deodorant and let him sniff.

"I like that one." He inhales a second time.

"It's my favorite too."

"Yeah. What's it called?"

"Hailstone."

"That one, but I can't ask them to rename it. That'd cost money, and they've already given me enough."

"No problem. It was just an idea, but let's use this scent in all the pictures. It will create a believable and cohesive campaign. Johnny Maverick wears Hailstone."

"Done. Now can we talk about the TV situation? Specifically, the lack of one in your apartment. I found a steal online. It can be here in an hour."

"I can't afford a TV. Besides, this is nice."

"Be nicer with the glow of a seventy-inch flat screen. I'll never beat Rauthruss playing him on this tiny screen." He lifts the laptop and lets it drop back to the couch cushion.

"How is he? How's Sienna?"

"They're good. Really good. Sienna's teaching figure skating and yoga, and he's running hockey camps. I'm hoping they'll come down sometime next month if they get a break."

"It would be good to see them before I go back to Valley. Who knows how long it will be before we're all back together."

"I'm not worried. You girls can't go very long without seeing one another, and the guys won't want to leave their girlfriends."

"True."

"I think if you carry the laptop and Charli, I can stand to crutch up the stairs one last time tonight. Then we'll have TV. Charli likes TV."

"Oh my god, you're hopeless. Surely we can find something to do."

We sit silently for a few seconds.

"Do you want something to drink?"

"Definitely." He follows me into the kitchen.

"All I have is wine or vodka, but I didn't get a mixer."

"We'll chase the vodka with the wine."

"That sounds like a terrible idea."

"Or a really great, fun idea. Come on, what else do you have going on?"

The answer to that is nothing, and two hours later, I'm drunk and back in the kitchen dancing and looking for food that doesn't require microwave or oven usage. Somewhere in my inebriated brain, I'm aware that I can't be trusted with either.

I grab the Cheetos and take them to the living room. Maverick is kicked back, shirt off, staring at me with hazy eyes.

"It's almost gone." He hands me the wine.

I tip it back and finish it off straight from the bottle. A little drips on my shirt, and I wipe at it, then say fuck it and pull my shirt over my head.

"I spilled," I say as if that's a good reason to be in my bra around my friend.

"It's cool. Nothing I haven't seen before."

"We match now." I point between us.

"You look better shirtless than I do."

I look down at my cleavage and then at him. His chest is defined, abs chiseled, plus all that ink. "I don't know. Tie?"

He smirks. "You think I look good shirtless?"

"Of course you do. You're hot, Johnny Maverick." And he is, but I don't think I've ever said that out loud before.

"You too. Like, fuck hot."

"What does that even mean?" I ask through laughter.

"It's pretty self-explanatory. *Fuck* hot."

"Yes, but you say it like it's an exclusive list, not half the population."

He snorts. "Learn to take a compliment, woman."

"Thank you." I set down the bottle and squeeze my boobs together. "They're not fake."

"No? Let me feel."

I drop my hands, not really expecting he'll do it. Although this is Johnny Maverick we're talking about so of course, he does. His big palms cover the lacy material of my bra, and he squeezes lightly.

"Damn, Kota. These are good."

"Thank you. I grew them myself."

He keeps squeezing, and the longer his big hands manhandle me, the tighter my nipples become.

He notices and glides a thumb over the peak through my bra.

"Okay, that's enough show and tell," I say through a shaky breath. I find my shirt on the floor and cover myself.

"Sorry. Been thinking about your boobs for so long, I wanted to make sure I copped a real good feel to last me the rest of my life."

I snort-laugh. "You've been thinking about my boobs?"

"I think about lots of people's boobs," he says with a grin.

"Right. Of course." I'm suddenly really aware of how drunk I am. "I should sleep, or I'm going to be a wreck for work in the morning."

He's quiet, and now I'm all flustered. I don't know how he's always so cool and casual.

"You can crash here if that's easier, or I can help you upstairs."

"This is fine. Awful couch is growing on me."

I grab him a pillow and blanket. He's taken off his jeans and is just in his boxer briefs. He's hard, and I don't want to notice, but I do, and my body warms everywhere.

"Here you go."

He takes one end of the pillow and uses it to tug me onto the couch next to him. "Running away?"

"Being the sane one," I say.

His gaze drops to my lips, and I wet them with my tongue instinctively.

"Sane is boring. Let's be wild. Take off your shirt again."

Chuckling, I shake my head slowly from side to side. "I'm going to bed."

"Fine," he calls, lying back and crooking an arm behind his neck.

I walk across the apartment to my bedroom, pause, and look back at him. "And locking my door."

"No worries there, Kota. You're safe. I'm waiting for the day you beg me to kiss you."

He's out of his mind. "You're going to be waiting a very long time."

"Maybe. Maybe not. Night, Dakota. You know where to find me."

The next night, I come home to an empty apartment. Reagan calls as I'm sitting down in the living room.

"Hey." I hold my phone out and smile at my bestie. "What are you doing?"

"We're going to The Hideout tonight. You?"

"No plans." I run a hand along the pink fabric of the couch. I swear I can smell Maverick and Hailstone.

"Everything okay?"

"Yeah. I'm tired. Maverick and I drank wine and vodka last night. Two out of ten stars. Do not recommend."

She laughs, and something shifts in my chest. I miss her something fierce.

"I wish you were here."

"Ditto. It isn't the same not waking up to the roaring noise of a blender every morning." She plays music in the background and sets her phone down. "Ready?"

"For?"

"Dance party. Come on." She motions for me to get up.

Reluctantly, I do. I place my phone on the arm of the couch and dance.

"Any more hockey hottie run-ins I should know about?"

"No," I say. "Well, unless you count Maverick. I, uh, may have let him feel me up."

Her brows raise, but she continues dancing. "I need more information."

"We were drinking. I spilled on my shirt and thought it was a good idea to take it off. Then I told him to feel my boobs to prove they weren't fake."

"You do have great boobs," she says. "Then what happened?"

"I went to bed. I cannot hook up with Maverick. He's… Maverick."

"Do you want to hook up with him?"

"My boobs were certainly into the idea." My body tingles, just like it did last night. "There is no way. Not happening."

"Okay. Well, then you need to go out with someone else and let them feel you up before your boobs start calling the shots. You've deprived them for too long."

I snort. She might not be wrong. "Who would I possibly go out with? I work all day. The hockey guys are off-limits and I'm not hooking up with another intern—that'd be a weird work environment."

"Dating app?"

"I deleted it. The options weren't great."

"So reinstall it." She smiles at me. "You are in a new zip code. New options. Better options, maybe."

"Yeah. Maybe."

Talking to Reagan loosens me up. We sing and dance through two more songs, smiling and laughing at each other as we show off our moves.

"Kota?" Mav calls. The door is open a crack, and Charli pushes through.

"I'm here. Come in."

Maverick walks in on his crutches. Reagan turns down the music.

"I gotta go," she says, out of breath. "Love you."

"Love you too."

I end the call as Maverick takes a seat on the couch. "Were you at the arena?"

He nods. "Yeah, I had to talk to Coach."

"How'd that go?"

"He's pissed I hurt myself."

"Will you be ready for camp?"

"Hope so." He rests an arm along the back of the couch. "What are you doing tonight? Do you want to go out? Dinner? Drinks?" He grins. "Dancing?"

"You can't dance right now."

"I can sit in a chair and let you dance for me like you were just doing. In fact, maybe we should just do that here so you can take off your shirt again."

I roll my eyes. "About last night. I shouldn't have let that happen. We're friends."

"Could also be friends that bang."

"Even if that weren't explicitly against the rules of my internship, it isn't a good idea."

"Why not? You said you think I'm hot. I think you're hot. There's no TV." He waves to the empty wall in front of us. "What the fuck else are we going to do?"

I chuckle lightly. "I love how it's just that simple for you."

"It's as simple as we make it." He shrugs. "I'm not going to suddenly stop being your friend just because we have hot, freaky sex."

"Hot, freaky..." I give my head a shake to stop the images flashing in my head. "Not happening."

"All right. Well, next best thing... dinner?"

Chapter Seventeen

JOHNNY

Dakota insists we order in so I can rest my knee. She's probably right. Coach Miller was not happy that I'd managed to injure myself so close to camp. But I'm already tired of sitting around all day long.

Kota is sitting in the chair with her laptop while I scroll through my phone.

"The food should be here by now," she says and narrows her gaze at the door as if she thinks that's going to help speed up the delivery person.

"Maybe they left it at the door."

"Without knocking?"

I stand and hop toward the door without my crutches.

"Mav!" she yells after me, but she laughs. There's a knock at the door when I'm one hop away.

"Perfect timing," I say, pulling open the door.

"Uhh… hi." A woman stands in the hallway holding a brown take-out bag. "I think this is yours. I ordered from there too, and they dropped both at my place. I didn't realize until after I ate one of your egg rolls. Sorry."

I smile. "Seems like a fair trade. Thank you."

She hands over the bag and then lingers. "You're Johnny Maverick, aren't you?"

"Yeah. Have we met?" I'm giving her a discreet once-over to decide if she's one of the hundreds of people I've met this week at the arena.

"No." She places a hand on her forehead and laughs lightly. She's pretty, late twenties, maybe, and has thick black-framed glasses that make her look a little like a librarian. "This is embarrassing, but I'm a fan. I was so glad when the Wildcats signed you."

"Thank you. Sorry, I didn't catch your name."

"Right. Oh my gosh. I'm Anika. I live in the apartment next door."

"Nice to meet you." I open the door wider. "This is my friend Dakota's place. She lets me hang out and annoy her. I'm on the eleventh."

Dakota walks toward us and waves. "Hi."

"I'm sorry to have interrupted," Anika says as she returns the wave and takes a step back. "Have a good night."

"You too."

After I shut the door, Dakota giggles and takes the food from me. "You have fans."

"Don't worry. You'll always be my favorite."

I hop back to the living room and sit down. Dakota gets everything else, bossing me around and insisting I sit still while she plates our food and brings it to me.

She eats with one hand, messing around with her phone with the other.

"Are you going to work all night?"

"I'm not working." She sets her phone down. "I'm signing up for a new dating app."

"I thought we agreed those were trash."

"This one is for people serious about dating and not just looking for hookups."

"So, it's for old people?"

She glares.

"Let me see." I beckon with one hand. "I can help."

"You said you don't do dating apps."

"I don't, but I still know what dudes like."

With a sigh, she hands over her phone and then comes to sit next to me. She hovers, crowding my space as I tap out answers and write a bio.

I had good intentions when I offered to help, but when she's this close, I remember how much I want her and decide to fuck with her instead.

"Granny panties? You said I wear granny panties?" She tries to get her phone, but I turn and hold it out of reach.

"People in serious relationships want this. Trust me. Thongs scream hookup."

"I trust you to know jack about serious relationships." She climbs over me. Her hair falls over my shoulder, and her face is so close to mine. I stop messing with her and turn to hand it back, but her lips are shiny and right fucking there.

I wanted to kiss her long before last night but since then it's all I can think about. And the way she hesitates, gaze dropping to my mouth before she snatches her phone... I'm pretty sure she's thinking about it too.

We settle back in our spots—me on the couch and her in the chair.

I'm lost in fantasies where she tosses the phone down and begs me to kiss her. I guarantee I'm a better option than whoever she's going to find online. Fuck that noise.

"You should ask out Anika," she says without looking up. It takes me a few seconds to remember who she's talking about.

"Your neighbor?"

"Yeah, why not? She was pretty and seemed nice."

"I know you think I pursue every chick that meets that criteria, but I do have some restraint."

She raises both brows and smirks at me before going back to her phone.

"I should head up to my place."

"Why?"

"Umm, because that's where I live. Unless you've decided you want to be roomies?"

"You're welcome to sleep on the couch as long as you want, Mav."

"I knew you didn't want to get rid of me. So… roomies?"

She bites on her bottom lip. "Are you planning on hanging out at my place every night, regardless?"

"Pretty much," I say with a nod.

"What about…" She stops herself and blushes.

"What about what?"

"Girls, Maverick. Are you going to be bringing random girls home?" The color in her cheeks creeps down her neck.

The thought hadn't even occurred to me. Not when I can spend the evenings with Dakota all to myself. I hold up my hand like I'm taking an oath. "I will not bring random girls back to the apartment."

"Then, yeah, might as well. I'll feel less guilty if you can find someone to sublease this place." With that, she stands and heads toward her room. "Does the spare room at your place have a locking door?" She grins playfully.

"What'd I tell you, Kota." I lie down and tuck an arm behind my head. "Not until you beg me."

THE NEXT MORNING WHEN DAKOTA WAKES UP, I HAVE JACK, Declan, and Leo over to help move her stuff upstairs.

She comes out of her room wearing a big T-shirt, red hair all mussed, and sexy as hell. "Oh, no."

"Oh, yes," Jack says, and his gaze drops to her long, toned legs.

"I see you all continue to travel in a herd even after college." She runs a hand over her bed head. "I'm going to need coffee. A lot of it."

"Already on it." I pick up the tray and offer her a cup. Part of the deal for getting the guys to help was coffee. The other was agreeing to go to a party at Jack's house next weekend—like a party is a real imposition. I think Jack just wanted to make sure I'd come and get to know some of the guys outside of workouts. That and he was probably hoping for another run-in with my hot new roommate.

"What are you all doing here so early?" She looks at me. "We're going to need some ground rules on acceptable times for your friends to come over."

"Don't worry, babe. It's a one-time occurrence and for a good cause. They're moving you in with me." I dangle a key card in front of her face and then put it on the counter.

Jack picks up the chair in the living room, and Dec and Leo each grab an end of the couch. She watches them carry her mom's furniture out of the apartment with a sleepy, dazed look.

"What is up with you this morning?" I ask. "You're usually all bright-eyed and bushy-tailed first thing."

"I didn't sleep well."

"No? That sucks." I lean against one crutch. "Everything okay?"

Her blue eyes lift to mine, then drop to take in my bare chest. I fight off a smile. Ah, shit. No way. Is that guilt? Embarrassment? This is awesome.

"You dreamed about me, didn't you?"

Her face flushes. "No, of course not. No. Absolutely not."

"You're a shit liar, Kota." I let the smile break free.

She rolls her eyes. "And if I had, it would just be further proof that I need to get out and meet some new guys."

"I think the lady doth protest too much."

AFTER WE GET KOTA MOVED IN, THE GUYS TAKE OFF, AND THEN so does she to meet up with some of the other interns for brunch. I'm on the third day of sitting on my ass, and I am booooored. I don't like being alone. It doesn't take a genius to make the connection between how much time I spent by myself as a kid and my need for people and attention as an adult.

I flip through the channels, take Charli for a short walk, text the guys to see if anyone's up for some video games. Everyone's busy except ol' Mav.

Scrolling through my contacts, I decide to call my mom. She probably won't answer, but at least I can leave a message. It's been a while since I've checked in. I move to Kota's pink couch and lie down, staring up at the ceiling as it rings.

"Hello?" my mother's voice answers from the other end. I love how she always answers like she doesn't know it's me calling.

"Hi, Mom."

"Johnny. Oh, I've been meaning to call you."

"You have? I thought you were in Italy. I was expecting to get your voice mail."

"I am. Doris and I are outside of the restaurant waiting for a table for dinner, but I talked to your father yesterday, and he said you had some sort of injury. I assume you're calling to get the name of some doctors to get a second opinion?"

"No. I just wanted to catch up and see how you're enjoying Italy."

"Nonsense. We have some great contacts in the city."

"I've got it under control, really. Dr. Anderson is great, and we did get a second opinion just in case." I shift on the couch and extend my leg out to elevate it like I was instructed. "How's Italy? How much longer are you there?"

She doesn't answer right away, and I can hear her talking to someone else in the background in Italian.

"Sorry, Johnny," she says when she's turned her attention back to me. "Our table is ready. I'll have my assistant send you a list of top doctors. Tell them who you are and that if necessary, your dad and I will fly them to you."

There's zero chance I'm doing any of that, but I understand that it's just her way of showing she cares. Time and attention aren't on the table, but money and resources they're happy to share.

"Thanks, Mom."

"Love you, honey. I'll call when I get back to Chicago."

She hangs up before I can say it back.

I toss the phone to the end of the couch and then reach down to the floor to pick up Charli and place her on my chest.

"Love you too," I say quietly.

Charli licks my face.

"What are we gonna do, girl?"

She licks again in response, eliciting a chuckle from me.

The TV is on as background noise. My stomach growls, but I don't feel like moving. I must fall asleep because the next thing I know, Dakota is standing in front of me with an amused smile.

"If you think the couch is so uncomfortable, then why do you keep sleeping on it?" She dangles a bag in front of my face.

I sit up, and the smell of something greasy and fried hits my nose. My mouth waters. "What is this?"

"It's lunch." She drops it in my hands and then goes to the kitchen and gets a cold ice pack, and swaps it out with the warm one on my knee. "Is that okay? Do you need anything else?"

She takes a seat on the chair, kicks off her shoes, and pulls her feet up under her. Her brows pinch together. "Maverick?"

The concern in her tone snaps me out of it. "Sorry. What?"

"Are you okay? You look a little pale?"

"Yeah." I clear my throat. "Perfect."

She keeps staring at me. My chest tightens, and I'm struggling to come up with something funny or teasing to reassure her I'm fine. I am fine, but I'm caught off guard that she thought of me while she was gone, that it occurred to her that I might want something to eat. It's dumb, really.

"You brought me food."

"Yeaaah," she says, slowly drawing out the word. "I thought you might be hungry. No biggie, if you're not. It's grilled chicken and sweet potato fries. I know sweet potato fries aren't healthy, but—"

"Thank you," I interrupt her, and my voice cracks, so I clear it again.

She hits me with a smile that chases away the loneliness. "Welcome."

Chapter Eighteen

DAKOTA

I throw myself into my new job and ease into living with Johnny. He made room in the living room for my furniture, which we never use, but I love seeing it every day.

Another thing I love seeing every day? Johnny, shirtless. I know, I know. I hate myself a little for admitting it even to myself.

But I'm going on a date tonight with a guy I met online. Marco is twenty-three and a grad student at UMN. He seems nice, and he's cute-ish. I'm not sure he's my soul mate, our conversations so far have been stilted and a little awkward, but I'm holding out hope that we're better in person. And even if it's a total waste, hopefully, it'll clear my mind so I stop having dirty fantasies about my new hot roommate.

Dressed and ready for work, I walk out of my room to find Johnny three feet away doing pull-ups in the doorway of his room. He put up some adjustable bar, and, wow, his back is impressive.

"Morning," he chirps as he continues to lower and lift his body.

I force my gaze down and mutter the greeting back.

"Smoothie is on the counter."

"You're too good to me." I pick it up and take a drink. He has really improved on my morning drink, and it tastes even better when I don't have to make it.

He joins me in the kitchen, hopping around on one foot.

"Where are your crutches?"

"My bedroom, I think. I don't know. I'm good."

I shake my head and move closer to him so he can lean on me. "When do you go back to the doctor?"

"Today, actually."

"You didn't say anything. Do you need me to drive you?"

He grins. "Nah, I'm good. Though I do like when you go all mama bear on me."

I roll my eyes. "You really make a girl regret being nice."

He chuckles.

Before I leave, I find his crutches in the living room and hand them over. "Later, loser."

At work, I spend the day running errands for Blythe with Quinn and Reese. There are a million things to do in preparation for camp, which starts next week. There are goody bags to put together, signage to hang, setting up rooms, and finalizing schedules. So many schedules.

By the time we're finished, I am so ready for a chill night in, but I go home and get ready for my date with Marco. I text the girls to calm my nerves while I wait.

Ginny: What's he look like? What's he do?

Reagan: What are you wearing?

Sienna: Where's he taking you?

Their rapid-fire questions make me even more nervous. Marco said he'd text after he got out of class and was on his way. We're meeting at a bar not far from the apartment. I wanted to be close enough that I could walk or Uber home if it's late but far enough away that I wouldn't have to worry about Johnny and his teammates stopping in and embarrassing me with their ridiculousness.

Two nights ago, Marco and I were having our first phone conversation after exchanging a few texts. Jack and Declan stopped by the apartment to see Maverick—they've been checking in on him almost every day. Anyway, they must have read it on my face that I was talking to a boy because they proceeded to yell out things like, "Honey, come back to bed." until I locked myself in my bedroom. I'm not sure what their plan was. They probably don't know either. Ridiculousness.

Right now, I could use a dose of Maverick's ridiculousness, though. He isn't home, and, holy crap, I am so nervous I can't stop the butterflies in my stomach. He always knows what to say to take my mind off things. I respond to the girls and then text Johnny to see how his appointment with the doctor went.

Maverick: Good. I'm at Wild's. Come hang out?

I hold off another five minutes waiting for Marco, then say screw it, grab my purse and say goodbye to Charli. I can leave from Wild's when Marco is close.

I find them on the far side of the bar, Jack and Johnny. Johnny swivels on the stool when he spots me and hops down. His big grin makes my insides mushy. He wraps me up in his arms and pulls me to his chest. "You made it! What are you having? I'm buying."

I'm temporarily too distracted by him to speak. Listen, Johnny

Maverick is a good-looking guy. My not wanting to hook up with him has absolutely nothing to do with how he looks. From his dark hair to his smile to the tattoos… oh the tattoos. He's chef's kiss perfection if we're going just by the hot scale. I couldn't build a better guy.

He's fuck hot to steal his phrase, but he doesn't take anything seriously. To him, sex is just an activity like watching TV or dancing—who he does it with doesn't matter as much as the activity itself. I want more than that. I want the sex, but the who matters to me.

Tonight, though, sigh, tonight he is in dress pants and a black collared shirt. The sleeves squeeze his biceps and show off some of the ink, and his hair has gel in it. He's dressed up and not in his usual jeans and a plain T-shirt, or honestly, more often than not, no shirt at all.

"I can't stay," I say when I find my voice.

"Woman, if you go back to that apartment, I will follow you and drag you out. We need a night out."

It suddenly dawns on me. "Where are your crutches?"

He raises his arms to his side. "I'm good to go." He rocks his head side to side. "Dr. Anderson says I'll be ready for camp."

"Mav, that's great news."

"I know. Now, what are you having? Champagne? I want to celebrate."

"I really can't."

"What, do you have a hot date or something?" Jack asks.

"Actually, yes. I'm going out with Marco."

"The guy you met on Hinge?"

"Yes."

"I don't like it," Mav says.

"Well, too damn bad." I laugh, nerves breaking.

"You don't know anything about the guy. What if he's a creep?"

"I can handle myself."

He tips his chin up and looks down at me. "Where are you going?"

"I'm not telling you that."

"Share your location with me."

"What?"

"I promise I won't use it unless you don't come home or answer later."

I'm quiet as I consider it.

"What would Reagan say? Should I text her and see?"

"Ugh. Fine. But I swear if you show up—"

He holds up his hands. "I won't."

I look to Jack.

"No promises here," he says.

Johnny leans against the bar. "Is this what you're wearing?"

"Yeah. Why?" Maverick has me second-guessing the navy skirt and white tank top I'm wearing. "I want him to know I tried, but not too hard."

"You look perfect."

I can tell he's holding something back. "What is it? Just tell me. I still have time to change if needed."

"Nothing, honest. You look gorgeous. I'm just glad it isn't the black dress is all."

"What black dress?"

"The one you wore to the Frozen Four party. Short, straps cross in the back." The idea that he knows my wardrobe shoots a zap of excitement through me.

"I don't even want to know how you remember that."

"Babe, that dress." He places his hands together, fingertips touching his lips. "That fucking dress." He groans.

"I'm not sleeping with him."

"Good." He barks out a laugh. "Then maybe you should wear it. The poor guy will be miserable sitting across from you all night." He pushes off and stands tall.

I get a glass of wine, and in the time it takes me to drink it, several more of Maverick's teammates show up. And as more of them arrive, girls make their way around us.

I check my phone—still nothing from Marco.

"Are you sure you can't blow off this guy and hang?" Johnny asks. "We're going to dinner and then… who knows."

"I really can't."

"Why not? I'm a way better date."

Behind Maverick, I spot Anika, my neighbor from the second floor, among the girls that have corralled around the players. I raise my hand to wave to her, and Maverick turns, tipping his head. "Hey, neighbor."

"Johnny Maverick," she says and smiles. "I didn't recognize you."

"Same. You look great," he tells her. One thing I love about Johnny, he never shies away from giving people compliments. And he means them, always.

"Thanks." She smooths a hand along the spandex of her black dress. She is dressed to impress tonight. "What are you two up to? I haven't seen you around."

"I'm trying to convince Dakota to come out to Beverlee's with me."

"Oh." Her eyes light up. "I've heard that place is great. Some friends and I tried to go last week, but they're booked up for months." The girls she's with start to walk off and she steps after them. "It was good to see you guys."

"Wait," I call to her before she leaves. "You should go with Maverick."

"Me?" Her smile broadens, but she ducks her head a little shyly.

"Yeah. It's perfect. I can't go. I have a date." I look at Johnny. "But you two should go out and celebrate getting rid of the crutches. It's a big deal."

I've put him in a position where he can't say no, but Annika is beautiful, seems nice, and I don't get any puck bunny stalker vibes from her. She's a fan, sure, but that's probably half the nearby population.

"Uh, yeah, if you're up for it," he says.

"Really?"

He nods and places both hands in his pockets.

"Okay. Yeah. I just need to tell my friends."

"Sure," Mav says.

When she walks off, he closes the space between us and lowers his voice. "What was that?"

"I'm sorry, but she seems really nice, and she's beautiful. Those glasses with that dress." I give him a thumbs-up.

He chuckles softly.

"This is good. You need to go celebrate, and this way, we're both out meeting new people." I slide from my chair. "I'll see you later."

Outside, I let out a long breath and start back toward the apartment. As I enter the building, my phone pings, and somehow

I just know. I know he's blowing me off at the last minute.

Confirmed when I pick up my phone and read the apologetic text claiming something last minute came up at work, and he's so sorry, let's reschedule, blah blah blah.

I kick off my shoes inside the apartment, scoop up Charli, and call Reagan.

"Are you calling me from the bathroom to tell me how great he is?" I can hear her smiling on the other end. "Or do I need to text you in five and claim there's an emergency?"

"He canceled."

"Oh, honey. I'm so sorry."

"I'm not." I hit the video button, needing to see her face.

She accepts and appears on my screen, brows scrunched together as she studies me. "You're not?"

"No. Ask me why not." I lie down on the pink couch. Johnny's scent still lingers from the night he slept on it, or maybe it's from being in his apartment. I wonder if it'll always smell like him now. I kind of hope so.

"Why not?"

"Freaking Johnny Maverick. That's why."

I CONSIDER GOING OUT SO THAT I'M NOT SITTING AT HOME thinking about how I forced the guy I like to go out with someone else because I don't want to like him. Maverick and I don't make any sense. We want different things.

Instead, I go to bed early. I'm lying awake listening for him to come home when it occurs to me he might bring her back here, and I'll have to listen to them having sex. He said he wouldn't bring random girls home, but it would really serve me right. Maybe if he sleeps with Anika, I'll be able to get the thought of kissing him out of my head.

I doze off at some point and wake to Mav's deep voice saying hello to Charli. I sit up and listen closer, trying to tell if there's someone with him. It's quiet, and I tiptoe to the door and press my ear to it.

"Kota." His deep voice makes my heart race, and I jump back. He raps lightly on the other side. I don't answer, and he says, "I know you're in there. Or your date dumped the body back at your apartment. Smart move, actually."

Stepping back, I open the door. He smirks, one arm resting against the doorframe. "You're alive."

"Yes. I'm alive and home safely."

He walks in, pushing past me.

"Please, come right in," I say sarcastically.

He sits on the end of my bed and unbuttons his shirt so it hangs open. "How was your date?"

"Great. Yeah. How was yours?"

"Don't bullshit me, Kota. I checked in a few times. You either invited him here or left your phone behind."

"You weren't supposed to check on my location unless I didn't come home."

"I had a feeling something was off, so I checked."

"Okay, so he canceled. Whatever."

"His loss."

"Maybe," I say, then change the focus to him. "How was your

date with Anika?"

"She's nice. Cool chick. Works as a nurse. Said if I hurt my knee chasing after you again, she'd take a look for me."

"I sincerely hope that doesn't happen again."

"Depends."

"On?"

"What it's going to take to get you to admit that there's something between us. I feel it, and I know you do too. Otherwise, you wouldn't have pawned me off on someone else like I'd invited you for a weekend orgy instead of dinner."

"I set you up to avoid confronting my feelings?" I roll my eyes. Dammit. Am I that transparent?

"Yeah. I think that's exactly what you did. And she's nice and beautiful, but I'm not going to see her again. Or anyone else. Not until you tell me this isn't happening."

"What isn't happening? Us hooking up once and ruining our friendship? No thanks, Maverick."

He stands and walks toward where I'm frozen to the spot near the door. "Why is it so hard for you to separate sex from everything else?"

"Because it is."

"That's a bullshit answer. If you're not into me and I misread you, then fine, but don't play it off like I'm not offering more than some quick fuck. Give me a little credit. I dig you. You dig me. What's the problem?"

"You're exasperating." I throw up my hands. "I'm not interested in casual sex. Not with you. Not with anyone."

"Fine then, it won't be casual. Nothing about the way I want to fuck you is casual." His hand reaches up and caresses the curve of my neck. My skin tingles and warms at his touch. Is he serious right now? Does he even know what he's saying?

"We can't. It isn't a good idea. We're friends. I have my internship to think about." I step away from him, cross my arms, and avoid his gaze. "Drop it, okay?"

My pulse thrums loudly in the seconds before he speaks.

"Sure thing." He stops in the hallway. "See you in the morning. Night, Kota."

Chapter Nineteen

JOHNNY

Dakota avoids me something fierce for the next two days. She comes home from work later than before and goes out with Quinn and Reese in the evenings. We're in deep avoidance. And I'm the ridiculous one?

I've been keeping busy, though. After feeling sorry for myself and my bum knee for a few days, I decided to suck it up and get to work. I'm working out my upper body and core and doing therapy on my knee. I can start working out for real next week, and it couldn't come any sooner. Camp starts Tuesday. Damn, that was a close call. One more fuckup like that, and I'll be spending this winter in Iowa.

Today is going to be a good day, though. We're shooting the endorsement photos, so Dakota can no longer avoid me.

I don't understand her. No, actually, I think I do, which is why it baffles me that she won't admit she wants to have sex with me as much as I want her.

I get to the shoot a few minutes early because I'm dying to see her in a place she can't run away. Outside of the locker room,

Quinn clutches a clipboard to her chest. "Hi, Johnny Maverick."

"Hey." I tip my chin to the door behind her. "Is Dakota in there?"

"Yeah, they're all waiting for you." She holds the door open for me and follows me inside.

The Wildcats locker room has been quiet the past couple of weeks, but today it is chaos inside. Her instructions were simple—be in the Wildcat locker room wearing swim trunks. I'm intrigued.

Dakota spots me immediately and hurries forward, weaving through the people standing around doing who knows what.

"What is all this?" I ask when she steps in front of me.

"It takes a lot of people to make you look good," she teases.

I rake a hand through my hair. "This isn't what I was expecting."

"Would you prefer I take some photos on my cell phone?"

"Uhh…"

"I was kidding." She wraps a hand around my forearm and pulls me with her. "This is going to be a big promotion for Maverick Enterprises. They pulled out all the stops."

I keep my mouth shut, but I highly doubt dear old Dad is responsible for any of this. This is all Kota.

"I don't know what I'm doing," I admit. It's a little intimidating as more people turn to look at me and start yelling for everyone to get into position.

"It'll be easy. Just do what you do best." She smiles, her blue eyes dancing with mischief. She's sexy as hell, and this is not a great time to be noticing, but seeing her in action at work all lit up like she is now is a major turn-on.

"What I do best?"

Her smile gets impossibly bigger as she walks backward, and

I follow because there's just about nothing I wouldn't do for her.

She comes up short next to the showers. "Take off your shirt."

When Dakota moves to the side, I get the full effect. Big standing lights and other photography equipment are angled toward the middle shower. Dividers block off the rest of the open space, and in the cubby underneath the showerhead, the entire new product line is displayed.

"Kota, this looks killer."

Blythe steps up beside her, fingers clutched around her cell phone as she speaks quietly, "We only have the room for an hour. Let's make sure we get what we need before Coach Miller kicks us out."

"Right." Dakota straightens. "Let's get a few of you standing in the shower first, and then we're going to do some with the water on. It'll be like you're taking a shower with no one watching. Except we'll be watching and filming, so don't embarrass me."

I chuckle, and she continues. "There is bottled water, that cherry energy drink you like, and some fruit and other food over there if you need anything." She points. "Reese and Quinn will be helping me by taking some behind-the-scenes footage." The two other interns wave awkwardly behind her. "I think that's it. Just be you."

"Just me, huh?" I'm not sure anyone has ever encouraged me to *be myself*.

People start moving into position, music starts playing, and a bright flash goes off.

"Whoa." I lift a hand and blink away the stars that are now flickering behind my eyelids.

"Sorry. Just checking the lighting," someone says before

another couple of flashes pop.

Dakota's hand takes mine. I know it's hers even before I open my eyes again.

"Are you okay?" she asks.

"This is weird, and what is this music?"

Her brows lift, and she smirks. "Johnny Maverick doesn't want to be the center of attention?"

"I know. Crazy, right? No one is more surprised than me."

"You're going to be great. I promise. Trust me?"

I glance around at all the people waiting for me to get my shit together and nod. "Yeah. Okay. Let's do it."

"Good. Now take off that shirt, Johnny Maverick."

Chapter Twenty

DAKOTA

Maverick removes his T-shirt, a shy grin tugging at his lips. I can't believe I'm having such a hard time getting him to take off his clothes. Who would have thought?

He balls up the fabric and tosses it at me. I hand it to Reese, who stands by shaking his head. All morning he's been giving me the same look like he can't believe I'm putting a great hockey player through this. I don't care. This is going to be gold. I've seen Maverick without his shirt on, and it's hot enough to sell just about anything.

"A roomful of women would kill to be you right now," Reese says, passing me a clear bottle.

"I'm the only one that can do it without swooning at his feet." I roll my eyes, but my stomach flips as I open the baby oil and step into the shower with Maverick.

"Whatcha got there?" he asks, eyeing me warily.

"Oil. It'll give us that wet look without water."

I squirt some of the cool liquid into one palm. "Sorry, it's a little cold."

I start on his chest and rub the oil into his skin in small circles. "On a scale of one to ten, how badly do you want to make a joke about me finally having my hands on you right now?"

"Shhh. You'll ruin this moment for me if you speak." He meets my gaze and grins.

My face warms as my hands slide down his abs. Okay, so maybe a little swooning. His muscles are hard, and his skin is warm. The oil makes every single part of him pop—each muscle and line and every tattoo. His body is covered with ink. I've seen them all numerous times in his shirtless debacles, but I've never inspected them this closely.

I run a finger along the outside of one on his side, tracing the hockey stick. It isn't new, but the ink inside of it is. Four numbers: 13, 44, 19, and 23. His Valley jersey number, as well as Heath, Adam, and Rhett's.

"When did you add these?"

"Right after the Frozen Four."

"It's really nice. Turn around and let me get your back."

"You scratch mine, and I'll scratch yours," he mumbles as he complies. "Sorry. Only so many things I can hold back at one time. I deserve a freaking medal."

"You can have a cookie when we're done."

"Will you feed it to me with your shirt off?"

I rub harder, digging my fingernails into his skin.

"Sorry. Sorry. Out of line. But actually, I kinda like that. Mark me up, baby."

"Oh my god." I smack a hand down on his lower back. "I'm working here."

"I know. I'm sorry. If I don't say them out loud, my dick will take action, and I cannot get hard right now," he whispers. Although his whisper is loud enough, I turn around to make sure no one heard him.

"Oh my god, Maverick. Shhh. I will send Reese in here to finish oiling you up if you hit on me one more time. Hooking up with players is not allowed. Remember?"

"We're not hooking up," he says and then mutters, "You made that abundantly clear."

"Yes, I know that, and you know that, but I don't want it to look like... you know."

He turns his head to look over his shoulder. "Like we're super attracted to each other and might break the rules at any moment?"

"Yes," I admit. I've thought of nothing else for the past two days. I know it's a terrible idea, but it doesn't stop the fantasies from playing in my head on a loop.

He holds my gaze for a beat, nods, and faces the other direction again. "Got it. You want me, but no one else can know. Sexy, secret romance. I can dig."

I growl under my breath and drop my hands. That'll have to do because if I keep touching him, it's going to end with me wringing his neck or shoving him up against the shower wall to shut him up with my mouth. And why am I starting to like the sound of the last one a lot more than I do the first?

The photographer, Lindsey, introduces herself to Maverick, and then it all begins. He stands awkwardly, hands at his sides with this sort of half grimace and half smile on his lips. I can't imagine how I'd feel with a roomful of people standing around staring at me with my shirt off, but I really thought Maverick would feed off the energy.

I give it a few more minutes. He finds me in the crowd gathered around watching him, and I can't read the expression on his face, but I know he's uncomfortable.

"Hey, Lindsey," I say, approaching the photographer. "Can I have one second?"

"Sure." She stands tall and drops the camera to her waist.

"More oil?" he asks and shoots me a sheepish grin before looking at the ground.

"Do you have your phone on you?"

"Yeah." His dark brows pinch together. "Why?"

"You were right. This music sucks."

He pulls out his phone, unlocks it, and hands it over. I scan the playlists. There are so many. He used to put together music for the morning skate on game days back at Valley, and I've heard they're pretty entertaining. He'd let each of the guys pick one song, and he'd compile it. Just another of the many charms of Maverick.

"Any favorites?"

He crowds my space, and I hold out the phone so that he can see it better. His silky-smooth arm covered in oil brushes against mine. Heat radiates from him. Shit, this is not good. Do I really want to hook up with Maverick?

He smiles and, fuck my life, I know the answer. I do. I really, really do.

"That one." He points.

"Okay, I'll get it going. Loosen up. Have fun with it."

"I'll try," he says. "I don't want to mess this up for you."

I pop a hip and rest my free hand on it, then give him a quick but blatant once-over. "Not possible."

"Switch the music playing over the speakers to this," I say to

Quinn, handing her Maverick's phone. "And do not snoop in his phone."

She chews her gum, jaw working while she stares at me with an annoyed and disbelieving glare as I boss her. Things have been friendly between us, and I don't want to ruin it, but I have to fix this, and I don't have time to worry about how much she might hate me when this is over.

Ignoring her, I look to Reese. "Can you grab a hockey stick from... wherever they keep hockey sticks. Bonus if it's Maverick's. We need to get him comfortable and fast."

"On it." Reese claps his hands and jogs off.

Blythe holds back a smile. "Do you have what you need?"

"I think so. I want this to work. It has to work."

"It will." Her ever-present phone rings in her hand. "I have to step out to take this. You have it under control here."

"I hope so," I whisper as she leaves me scrambling.

The bass of the music changes the mood almost immediately. Everyone, including Johnny, relaxes a little with an old, catchy Pitbull song, but when Reese places the hockey stick in his hands, I want to cry with relief. His shoulders relax, and his smile is genuine.

He wraps a big hand around the end and holds it up, aiming the other end at me and winking. Swoon. Damn it all to hell. Swoon. I roll my eyes and cross my arms over my chest. "Okay, everyone, let's do this."

The rest of the shoot goes well. Really well. Lindsey takes a bunch of shots with Maverick and his hockey stick, and then Quinn and I start handing him products. He poses with them in all sorts of ways. Some are silly and ridiculous, others serious. How does one spritz ball spray and make it look sexy?

But by far, the best material is when we turn on the shower and have Maverick wash himself. Okay, it sounds seedy. It isn't. I mean, he looks... *so good*, but he has fun with it, smiling and keeping the vibe really cool and casual. His dark hair slicked back, his hands working over his chest. Maverick meets my eye and smiles. I try to smile back, but I don't seem to have control over any part of my body. If I did, I'd surely be able to ignore the ache between my thighs. I can't imagine what he sees in my expression. I don't even know myself what I'm feeling.

But whatever it is, that smile on his face falls and is replaced with heat that has a direct line to the butterflies swarming in my stomach.

I want him. And he wants me too.

Chapter Twenty-One

JOHNNY

I'm shocked when Dakota comes home early from work. I'm doing sit-ups in the living room, and instead of heading straight to her room, she plops down on the couch with a tired groan.

"Long day?" I ask, stopping at the top of a rep.

"Being in charge is exhausting." She grins. "But totally awesome."

"You killed it."

"I actually believe you." She kicks off her shoes and goes into the kitchen.

I follow her, and she pulls out two wineglasses and then uncorks a bottle of wine, pouring two and handing me one of them. She hops up on the counter. Energy and excitement vibrate off her. "Even Quinn told me good job before we left."

"Look at you making friends."

"Yeah, she invited me to hang out tomorrow."

I make a sound like a buzzer going off. "Wrong answer. You're booked tomorrow."

She cocks a brow and takes a sip of her wine. "I am?"

"Yep, Jack is having a pool party. Starts early, will definitely go late."

"I don't think that's a great idea," she says, pulling that wall back up between us.

"I promise not to let you strip off your clothes and sleep with anyone," I say with a playful roll of my eyes as if I'm doing some noble deed instead of keeping her from hooking up with any of my teammates. It has the desired effect, and she smiles.

"Ha ha."

"I'm serious. It'll be fun. We cannot stay in this apartment another day. My couch is going to have a permanent indent of my ass."

Her gaze drops to my butt, and then she catches herself.

"Spending time at a pool does sound fun."

I clap my hands. "All right. It's settled."

"Is it okay if I bring a friend?"

"You're bringing me. Aren't I enough?" I pretend to be seriously injured, and she rolls her eyes.

"I want to invite Quinn. She's the only sort-of friend I've made here."

"What about Reese?"

"He has plans."

"Fine, but if you need any help with sunscreen or—"

She holds up a hand. "I've got it."

The tension between us seems to have eased, and I'm glad she isn't avoiding me anymore. "What do you want to do tonight?"

"I'm not sure. I'm tired. I don't think I want to go out."

"Let's order in." I grab my phone. When I look up at her to ask what she wants, she has a weird expression on her face. "What?"

"Thanks, Mav."

"For?"

"It would have been a lonely first couple of weeks here without you."

"Right back at ya."

The next afternoon Dakota comes out of her room with a beach bag under one arm and a hesitant smile.

"Are you sure this is a good idea? Should you even be swimming?"

"Yeah. I'm good. It isn't like I'm going to be diving off the side and getting crazy."

She doesn't look convinced until I add, "I'm not drinking, so that should help me behave… mostly."

"I feel like I'm going to regret saying this, but let's do it!"

Jack lives about twenty minutes away in a ritzy neighborhood where the homes are big and the yards are bigger. A few other teammates live nearby, and I can see why—it's a cool spot with a private lake.

"This is a house for a single person? A bachelor no less?" Dakota shuts the passenger door and comes around to the front of the SUV, all while gawking at the mansion in front of us.

"A single person with lots of friends."

Cars are already lined up in the circle drive, and I recognize a few of them as teammates. Jack himself answers the door, pulling it open before we have a chance to knock.

"Hey, come in. Glad you two could make it."

"Thanks for having me," Dakota says, slipping into her professional voice.

"Phones in the basket. James has the paperwork, and booze and food are in the kitchen. Enjoy."

"Paperwork?" Dakota asks.

James, Jack's agent, steps forward with a tablet. "Standard NDA."

"You're kidding?" Her blue eyes widen. "I'm not signing that."

I don't think James knows what to say or do at her refusal. On second thought, I have a feeling James has seen it all.

"I'll vouch for her," I say. "Plus, she works for the team."

I take her phone and mine and drop them in the basket, then grab her hand. "Come on, before they toss your delinquent ass out."

We stop in the kitchen for drinks. I don't miss the way Dakota runs her hand along the marble countertop, taking it all in. I know it's an impressive kitchen, but seeing her response makes me appreciate it a little more.

"What do you want?" I ask and grab myself an energy drink.

"What are my options?" she asks, still walking around touching appliances and cabinet handles.

"Anything your tiny, black heart could want."

"Let's go with vodka and tonic. Any limes?"

"Yep."

"Of course, there are limes."

I make her drink and then take it to her. "Are you going to mock everything?"

"Sorry. I'm still spinning on the whole NDA thing. Do you make chicks sign those?"

"Me? No, but I didn't just sign a sixteen-million-dollar contract."

She mouths the words sixteen million.

"Yeah, and that doesn't even include his endorsements." I hold out my arm for her. "You ready to do this?"

She takes my arm, and the smell of her fruity shampoo floats under my nostrils. "Ready."

Outside, the party is already going strong. A lot of guys from the team are here, some of their friends and girls. So many girls. If you want to inspire young kids to grow up and be hockey stars, just drive by one of Jack Wyld's pool parties—ass and titties galore.

The music pumps, and people shout hello from the pool. Dakota sticks with me as we make the rounds. I chat with everyone, introducing her when needed. She already knows most of the team, but I make sure to talk her up to the guys she hasn't met yet. Easy to do, if I'm honest.

It's late afternoon, and the sun sits high in the sky. Dakota pulls her long hair over one shoulder and squints.

"I forgot my sunglasses," she says.

"Do you want my hat?" I ask. "It'll keep the sun off your face."

"What about you?"

I shrug. "I don't burn, and I have my shades."

I place my Wildcats hat on her head. It's too big and falls down low on her eyes. "Adorable."

I'm pretty sure there's an eye roll, but I can't quite make it out under the brim of the hat.

"Should we brave the pool?"

"You don't have to babysit me," she says. "I can mingle and make new friends."

"Trying to get rid of me, so you don't have to admit how attracted you are to me right now?" I tug on the collar of my T-shirt. "I kept it on just for you. I don't want you to embarrass yourself drooling over my hot bod."

"Yeah, that's it," she says sarcastically. "You figured me out."

Just for that, I take off my shirt, and man is my grin big when her gaze sweeps over my bare chest. I don't know who she thinks she's fooling. Not me.

"Okay. Go away now. My friend is here." She points to Quinn coming out the back door.

I hold a hand over my heart like she's wounded me. "Ouch."

"I'm sorry, but you know the rules. I can't have them wondering if something is going on between us."

"Knew you couldn't handle all this temptation. I'll be in the pool. Come find me when you're ready to admit defeat."

Declan is sitting on the edge of the pool with his feet dangling in the water. I take a seat next to him. From this position, the whole party is in view.

"It's kinda like you're the lifeguard sitting up here watching over everyone."

He chuckles quietly. "Might need to be. How's the knee?"

"Good." I stretch out my leg. "I did a light workout this morning, and I should be able to participate in camp this week."

"I'm getting excited. Vacation always feels too long." Declan is a quiet guy, so usually, when he talks, I listen. He's going on about hockey and the upcoming season, but it's background noise because, across the yard, Dakota's stripped off her dress and is standing talking to Quinn.

The black material of her bikini top pushes up her tits, and the tiny bottoms are just a step above a thong. And my hat. Damn, her wearing my hat in that outfit shouldn't be so fucking sexy. Why is everything she does such a turn-on? It's really inconvenient in this battle of her not admitting the attraction between us.

As if she can feel my eyes on her, she angles her body and meets my gaze. I don't know if she can see my eyes pinned on her ass from behind my shades, but just in case she can't read the lust pumping through my veins, I dip my chin and push my sunglasses down, so she knows I see her. I always see her.

I swear she shakes her ass at me as she flips her head and turns back to Quinn. It's going to be a long fucking day.

Chapter Twenty-Two

DAKOTA

This party is nuts. It's a lot like the huge parties back at Valley but with better alcohol and more girls that look like they model on the side. Who am I kidding? They probably *do* model on the side.

The sheer number of girls is pretty incredible. There are easily two girls to every guy. I doubt that's an accident. Threesomes for everyone!

As afternoon turns into evening, the music gets louder and more people strip down to their suits. Quinn and I sit in lounge chairs next to the pool. Every once in a while, we get sprayed with water, but we have a great view without being in the middle of the team and puck bunnies.

"Come with me to pee," Quinn says. Despite how she rubbed me the wrong way when we first met, she's growing on me. She wears her insecurities like armor, and it makes her a tough nut to crack, but underneath all the name-dropping and obvious hero-worship of the players is a cool girl.

"All right." I swing my legs to the side and stand. My skin is warm from the sun, and the ends of my hair are still wet from a dip in the pool earlier.

Maverick stands between us and the pool house at the back of the property.

He's with Jack and Leo and a group of girls that just arrived. I swear every group of girls that walks outside is somehow more gorgeous than the last. These girls aren't playing. They strut out, already stripped down to their suits, hair done, high heels, and a waft of perfume floats around them. I'll give it to them. They know how to make an entrance.

A tall brunette with legs that never end and boobs that even I'd like to cop a feel of smiles at Maverick and leans in closer, resting a hand on his forearm. Listen, I've got nothing against puck bunnies. You do you, girl, but can you just not look at Maverick like he's the next conquest on your list of players. I will cut a bitch that does him dirty.

I waggle my fingers as we pass by. His head turns to watch me, and I have to admit it feels good to have him check me out when there is an endless supply of drop-dead gorgeous girls here.

At the pool house, sliding doors open to a large open-concept space. There's a bed on one side and a living area on the other. There's even a small kitchen. It doesn't look like it's used often. It has a whole just-staged vibe with lots of whites and blues.

Quinn goes into the bathroom, and I sit on the edge of the bed to wait for her. I wish I had my phone. I'd love to talk to Reagan right now. I miss her.

Two of the girls that were talking with Maverick come in while I'm still waiting for Quinn. Including the boobalicious brunette.

They don't see me initially or just don't acknowledge my

presence.

"His contract is less than a mil," the brunette's friend says as they walk back toward the bathroom. When they realize it's occupied, they linger.

"I don't care. I want to make my own money." She pushes up her boobs and adjusts her bikini top. She's working it. I would too. They really are something. "And Johnny Maverick would be a great career boost. His family already has money anyway. I bet he'd invest in my fashion line."

"Yeah, you just have to make him fall in love with you first."

They both laugh.

Quinn reappears as I'm imagining all the different ways I could make this girl disappear without going to jail. "Ready?"

"Yeah." I stand and glare at the backs of the two girls as they walk into the bathroom together.

"Did they say something to you? You look murderous. Even more so than usual."

"I feel it," I mutter as we walk outside. My gaze goes right to Johnny. He's smiling and laughing, totally oblivious to the chick inside who's ready to con him. "I have to pee."

"What? We were just in there."

"I'll be quick. Go ahead and make sure no one steals our seats."

"Okay."

I catch Johnny's eye, and he shoots me a confused look as I turn on my heel and head back inside the pool house. Tapping my foot impatiently, arms crossed over my chest, I stand outside of the bathroom door.

When it opens, the brunette's smile falls, and she lifts two perfectly arched brows. "Can I help you?"

"Actually, yes, you can," I say so sweetly that she buys it for a second. Her lips are coated in a super shiny nude gloss that reflects on the light as she smiles. I take a step toward her, and she backs up even though she's got a good foot on me in those heels she's wearing. "Stay away from Johnny Maverick."

"O-kay." She laughs. "I can stay away from him, but I can't guarantee he'll stay away from me."

"I'm sure you are a lovely person, and truth be told, your boobs are the best I've ever seen." I pause to collect my thoughts. I'm getting off topic. I swear I understand why guys end up sleeping with girls like her. Even I feel a little dumb with them sitting up staring at me. I can't focus, and I have my own amazing boobs I could stare at all day if I wanted. "Back off."

"Why? What's he to you?"

What? Like he's a thing instead of a person. "He's my... friend."

"Awww, I'm sorry you got friend-zoned, and now you want to ruin every other girls' chance with him."

I want to smack the smug look off her face.

"How about we let him choose?" She gives me an unimpressed once-over and then looks over my head. I whip around to see Johnny watching our interaction with a shocked expression.

I flatten myself against the wall, wishing I could disappear into it. Boobalicious and friend saunter past me in a victory walk toward Maverick.

"Come on, Johnny. Let's take a swim."

"Yeah, uh, I'll be out in a minute. I just need to talk to Dakota." He tips his head toward me and waits for them to leave. He shuts the sliding doors. I don't move. Crap, I know I overstepped going all psycho chick on them, but I'm so angry about how blatantly they want to use him like nothing else matters but his money.

"I'm sorry," I blurt out when he starts stalking toward me with a dark expression on his face. "She was talking about getting you to fall in love with her so you'd invest in her dumb fashion line. I lost my shit. Temporary insanity. I've been in the sun too long."

He doesn't say anything as he crowds into my space.

"I'm sorry," I say again in case he missed that part.

"Don't be. You're fuck hot when you're jealous." His lips finally twist into a cocky smirk, and he steps within an inch of our bodies being flush.

"It wasn't jealousy. I was being a good friend. I don't want to see you get played."

"I've been rich my entire life, Kota. I know how to spot a chick that's only into me because of money."

"Oh."

He rests a hand against the wall and leans in. The brim of his hat that I'm still wearing on my head keeps him from getting closer. "Admit it."

"Admit what?" My breaths come in quick gulps as his hazel eyes lock on me.

"Admit you were jealous." He fingers a strand of my hair with the hand on the wall, and the other comes up to caress my cheek. "Admit it, and then I can finally kiss you."

"I'm not kissing you. Hockey players are off-limits, remember?" I bring my palms to his chest to push him away, but in a swift movement I don't see coming, he picks me up and carries me into the bathroom. After he shuts us in and locks the door, he deposits me on the ground and backs me against the wall.

"What are you doing?" I ask, pressing my shoulder blades into the cool wall. I need to hold on to any anger I can because my body feels anything but angry.

"The door is locked, and no one can see or hear us," he whispers, resting a palm on the wall above me and leaning down, so his mouth hovers near my neck. "I know your internship is important to you, and I don't want to fuck that up, so I need to hear you say the words."

"Your ego will be fine." I roll my eyes.

"This has nothing to do with my ego. I know you want me. The same way I want you. So are you only holding back because of the internship, or is it something else?"

"Johnny." My voice breaks. I can't give him what he wants. Internship rules aside, we're not a good match. He lives for the moment and doesn't take anything seriously. I want more than that. Plus, we're friends and roommates. It's a lot to risk.

"Dakota." The hand not on the wall skims across my cheek, and he drags a thumb across my bottom lip.

They part, and the tip of my tongue touches his skin. He brings his thumb farther into my mouth like he wants me to suck on it. I do, heat pooling in my stomach, and then bite it. He pulls back, chuckling, and smears his wet thumb down my neck to my collarbone and dipping into the valley of my breasts.

"You're stubborn and very sexy." He slides that hand back up and cups my neck, holding my face in place as he brings his lips so close to mine, I can almost feel them. "Admit it, Kota. I wanna taste you."

I shake my head and issue my own challenge. One I'm most definitely going to regret. "Make me."

Maverick doesn't respond right away, and the faint sound of

the music outside is the only noise interrupting the quiet pulsing between us. He takes the hat off my head and places it on his backward. Then he resumes his position crowding into me. One of his legs goes between mine and forces my feet farther apart. He tucks my hair behind my ear and toys with a strand near the nape of my neck.

I keep my hands at my sides, refusing to break. This feels so much bigger than a kiss. Giving in now and admitting I want him, it'll be disastrous.

He lifts my left arm over my head and pins it against the wall while his nose grazes along the side of my neck. Then he brings my other hand to meet it and works the elastic hairband on the left over the right, effectively tying them together. My breaths come in quick, shallow gulps. The barest hint of a smile tugs at his lips. One of his large palms continues to hold mine against the wall while the other caresses my face and then my neck. Somehow that hand seems to be everywhere and not in the right place either.

I lift my chin to show him I'm not backing down. I will not be the first to break. He tilts his head like he's going in for a kiss and then pulls back. His lips move, and I realize he's mouthing the words of the music outside. Something about not wanting to be my friend.

My heart is pounding in my chest.

I wanna kiss you until I lose my breath.

He's full on smiling now as he whispers the words against my lips. And despite how much I want to resist him, I smile too. I still don't give in, though. I push against his hand and bring my hands around his neck, caging him in now and bringing my face closer. Just like he did, I zone in on his mouth and tilt my head, only redirecting when my lips are millimeters from his.

My hands still tied together with the elastic are around his neck, and I finger the thick locks, pulling a groan from him. I don't think I've ever been so turned on in my life, but I'll die before admitting how much I'm enjoying this.

He growls and uses his chest to push me back until my shoulders bite into the wall. If he gets any closer, he'll be flattening me into the drywall.

"Admit it." He holds his mouth over mine. "Please."

My heart hammers in my chest. "I was jealous."

He rubs his nose against mine and hums lightly. He drops the quickest, softest kiss onto my lips and pulls back. I melt into it, but it isn't enough. I need the ravenous, desperate kiss that was leading up to.

He's going to make me beg. And I will. He was right. Damn him.

Chapter Twenty-Three

JOHNNY

A noise outside of the bathroom catches my attention.

"Fuck," I mutter. "I didn't lock the outside door."

She stills in front of me. Motherfucker. She was seconds from begging me. I know it.

"I'll go out first," I tell her and nip at her bottom lip. "Meet me at the truck."

"I don't think that's a good idea."

"Fuck good ideas. This is happening." I step into her one last time and run a single finger from her neck to the middle of her suit top and slip my finger under the string. "Get in the goddamn truck, Kota."

She ducks under my arm and goes out the door. I blow out a breath and count to thirty before I follow. Jack is in the kitchen mixing a drink.

He looks toward the now open sliding glass doors and then back to me. "Seems one of us is having a good time."

"I'm going to take off, man," I say. "Thanks for having us."

"Already? Things are just about to get wild."

Yeah, they are, but not here.

"We'll do it up another night when I'm not nursing an injury."

"I'm holding you to that." He tosses back the drink and then holds out a hand.

I take it, and he pulls me closer. "Do I even want to know what's going on with you and the intern?"

"Probably not," I say honestly.

"Not my pussy. Not my problem. Thanks for coming, rook. See you Monday."

Dakota is nowhere in sight, so I take that to assume she took my instruction. I wave to the guys. Most of them are too busy drinking or hooking up to care anyway.

Kota sits in the passenger seat with her phone. I can feel the distance she's put between us as I slide into the driver's seat.

I play music, knee bouncing. It's a short drive, but every second I worry she's changed her mind. Not about us. I know she feels it, but about acting on it. She has a lot better impulse control than I do. And also more to lose. I get the need for discretion.

At the apartment, I whip into a spot and cut the engine. She still doesn't speak as we take the elevator to the eleventh floor. I unlock the door and scoop up an excited Charli.

She steps inside and looks to her feet. "Maybe we should get some distance and talk about this in the morning."

"Running away?"

"Being responsible."

"Being responsible or hiding behind it?"

She glares. Setting Charli on the floor, I step to Dakota.

"Tell me what you're afraid of?" I cup her neck. When I touch her, the blue in her eyes darkens like two giant mood rings.

"This job is important to me."

"I know. I won't say a word. It stays between us."

"What if they figure it out?"

"How? We're friends. They know we're friends. No one is trying to catch us, baby." I rub my thumb along her cheek. "That rule was meant to keep crazy interns from lashing out at players who fucked them over. You're not crazy, and I'm not going to fuck you over." I smile at her. "Well, you're not *that* crazy."

"I want more than one night."

"Good. I'm going to need more than one."

Her expression still doesn't give. "We'll still be friends?"

"Always. I just plan to know you a little more intimately." My hand slips under the hem of her dress, and I slide a palm up her thigh to her hip and then untie the side of her bikini, so it falls open. Then do the same to the other. It drops to the ground at our feet.

"Say you'll be mine for the summer." I bite her shoulder and walk two fingers across her hip bone and down to the apex of her thighs.

When she doesn't answer, I glide one digit over her sensitive clit. A hand shoots out and grasps my forearm, steadying herself on me.

While teasing her, I drop kisses along her neck and collarbone. "Hop on, baby, let's go for a ride."

I curl one finger inside of her and then add another. Slowly, I pump in and out of her. She drenches my fingers as her pussy squeezes them tight.

She wraps her arms around my neck and rolls her hips.

Pinching her clit, I ask again, "Be mine."

"Johnny." She gasps. She's close, and I want nothing more than to feel her come on my fingers.

"I take care of what's mine."

"I don't need you to take care of me," she says even as she rides my fingers harder.

"Need and want, baby. Look up the difference." I push a third finger into her tight pussy.

Her body shakes, and she lets her head fall against my chest. "I *need* to come."

"And I *want* to be the one that gives it to you. Be mine, Dakota."

She nods. It isn't the enthusiastic screaming answer I was hoping for, but I put her out of her misery anyway. Rubbing my thumb along her clit, I continue to pump her until she cries out and goes limp against me.

With the hand that was inside of her, I lift her chin so I can finally kiss her the way I've been dying to. Her eyes are still a darker blue and hooded as I lower my mouth to hers. She opens immediately, and I tangle my tongue with hers.

Fuck, this is going to be a good summer.

"I gotta take Charli for a walk and feed her. Stay mostly naked."

I can read the hesitation on her even before she says, "I need to take this slow."

"Slower than riding my hand like a joystick?"

She narrows her gaze.

Chuckling, I kiss her softly. "We've got all summer. We can take it as slow as you want." I take her hand. "You can *slowly* fuck my hand again in my big comfy bed."

Chapter Twenty-Four

DAKOTA

I shower and then hide out in my room while Maverick takes care of Charli. I'm stalling, giving myself time to talk myself out of it, but thirty minutes pass, and I still want to do this. Whatever it is. Friends with benefits? Fuck buddies? I don't like any of the labels, but I want a lot more of his hands on me. And inside of me. My face warms. A summer of sex and fun. Maybe it's exactly what I need.

When I finally emerge from my bedroom, I wonder if it's going to be weird between us, but my question is answered as I spot a shirtless Johnny in the living room holding up two bottles of lube. "Do you like a tingling sensation, or are you more au naturel?"

"What happened to slow?"

"I just want to be prepared like a good Boy Scout."

"You were never a Boy Scout."

"No, but I'm just as good with my hands."

I laugh, and the worries I had disappear. We can do this. We can be friends and also have a little fun exploring the chemistry between us. But I meant what I said about needing to take it slow. Insane chemistry or not, jumping straight from kissing to letting him put his dick inside of me in one day isn't something I'm comfortable with. "Maybe we can just watch a movie or something?"

He tosses the lube on the coffee table. "Yeah. Movie. We can do that."

While he flips through options, I sit on the couch with Charli. "Which one? You pick."

"*Crazy, Stupid, Love.*" The other is a Tarantino film, and gore is not my thing.

"You just want to stare at Ryan Gosling for two hours." He sits next to me, and Charli crawls over me to get to him before settling on the other side of him.

"Duh."

He tickles my sides and pulls me so my back rests against his chest. His arm circles around me, and his palm splays over the top of my thigh. I keep waiting for the weirdness, but it never comes.

For the next two hours, he doesn't make any attempt to make out with me, and somehow that makes me want him even more. Did I say I wanted to take things slow? Because what I really think I meant is I'm not ready for sex. I want everything else, though. The bottles of lube are taunting me.

"I love Steve Carell," he says. "We should do a binge of *The Office*."

"Yeah," I agree, not really thinking about it. He sits forward and grabs the remote so he can navigate to it, and he plays season one, episode one.

When he sits back, I place my hands on his shoulders and sling a leg over him, so I'm straddling his lap. An amused smile tips up the corners of his mouth. "Need something?"

"Sex is off the table. For now," I clarify. "But I want to take care of you."

"I took care of myself while you were stalling in your room." He winks. "I'm good, Kota."

His arms circle my waist. I can feel him hard underneath me despite his saying he's good.

I lean back and grab the lube. "Which do you prefer?"

"That one." He nods toward the one that tingles with a giant smirk on his handsome face.

I toss the other one back on the coffee table and scoot off his lap, then drop between his legs.

"Oh fuck," he says as if he can't believe this is actually happening.

He stands and pulls me to my feet. "Bedroom. I've been fantasizing about having you touch my dick in there for so long."

He pulls me along behind him. It smells like Johnny in here. I don't get a good look around because the lights are off, and he kisses me while bringing us down to the mattress. His kisses are possessive and hungry. Nipping, licking, biting, groaning. Just like he does everything else, it's all out with nothing left to the imagination. When I do something he likes, he makes sure I know it either by verbally responding in grunts and groans or pumping his hips against me.

We lie on our sides, kissing until I hook a finger under the band of his sweats, letting his dick spring free. He helps me get them off and continues to kiss me. I turn my head, and he lavishes my neck while I uncap the lube and squirt some in my hand.

He's thick and long, and it twitches when I wrap my fingers along the base. I work my hand up and down, coating him in the liquid.

I'm wearing another baggy T-shirt, and he ducks his head under it, eliciting a laugh from me. It's cut short when he bites my nipple through the lace of my bra. He does the same to the other and then sucks hard until my nipple peaks.

While I pump my hand around his length, he kisses everywhere he can access.

"Does it tingle?" I ask.

He pops out from under my shirt and pulls my bottom lip between his teeth. "Touch yourself and find out."

I hesitate, and he guides my hand down my shorts, encouraging me. My fingers are wet from the lube and warm from his skin, and I don't know which is hotter, that or the way he watches me while gripping himself and pumping in slow, steady jerks.

"Does it feel good?"

"I liked your fingers on me better," I admit. "But yeah."

"Tradesies?"

Smiling, we switch, and he dives his fingers eagerly into my shorts, taking over as I try to mimic the way he was jerking himself.

For the second time tonight, my orgasm builds as he rubs my clit.

"Are you close?" I ask. "Want my mouth?"

"I want your tits," he says.

"You want to fuck my tits?"

"Oh fuck." He groans. "That isn't what I meant, but damn right I do. I won't last that long, though. Show them to me. You have the best tits."

I lift my shirt and bra for him. He rubs harder and pumps into my hand. "Oh goddamn, Kota. This is beyond anything I imagined. So far beyond."

He waits for my orgasm and then leans forward and suctions his mouth around my nipple, sucking hard while I explode around his fingers. He follows a few pumps later, still holding my nipple hostage as he shoots on his stomach.

"So fucking beyond," he repeats.

I wake up Sunday morning with Maverick's lips on my neck. I don't know how many times he made me orgasm last night (That's a lie; I was totally counting, and it was four), but my body doesn't care. The light touch of his mouth on my skin already has my insides on fire.

"Wanna go out for breakfast?" he asks.

"What if someone sees us?"

"Then all they'll see is two friends out sharing a meal."

"Okay," I agree readily. I'm starving, and I need some fresh air to decide how I feel about everything that went down last night.

He hops up and tugs my hand to pull me to a standing position. We slept shirtless, and he appreciates the view for a few seconds before sliding his gaze back up to my face.

"See something you like?"

"Yeah, sorry. You mentioned fucking your tits, and now it's all I can think about. Did you mean it?"

My nipples harden. I guess I did. "Maybe not before breakfast, but yes."

"Something to live for." He winks and steps back. "I'm gonna shower. Joining me?"

"I think I'll go back to my room. I need clothes anyway."

"K." He pauses, then grips my hip and yanks me forward until I'm flush against him. His mouth covers mine, and he kisses me hard before pulling back again. It feels so easy and simple and *good*. "Pick you up from the living room in thirty."

We shower and get dressed separately, then head off in search of a restaurant with an outdoor patio since we brought Charli along.

"Are you nervous about camp?" I ask when our food comes. Development camp starts this week, and everything I've learned about it from working with Blythe and Reese is that it's a grueling week for rookies.

"Yeah, but excited too." He takes a bite of eggs and then breaks off a piece of bacon for Charli.

"No wonder she likes you so much," I say.

"Girls like to be fed. Duh." He breaks off another piece and holds it across the table for me.

"No thanks."

He pops it into his mouth and leans back with a huge grin on his face. "I've got something else you can put in your mouth after breakfast."

"Eww. I'm eating here."

He busts up laughing. "I'm sorry. I can't hold them in when they're that easy."

I roll my eyes. Yeah, I think Mav and I are going to be just fine going back to being just friends after this summer.

Tuesday morning Blythe gathers all the interns to work the first day of camp. She splits us up into different areas: check-in, lunchroom, floaters to walk the floor in case anyone has questions, and Reese even gets assigned to Coach Miller as a backup equipment runner. The camp is open to the public, so there are people at the ticket office and even working the concession stand.

"I'm starting to understand now why Blythe was running around frantic for the past two weeks," I say to Quinn.

We're placed on player check-in. They're set to arrive by bus from the hotel any minute. Two long tables are pushed together, and we stand behind it, ready to cross off names and show them where to go for breakfast.

It's quiet, and we're standing around waiting, and then suddenly it's chaos. A huddle of men stands in front of us, and Quinn and I check them off as fast as we can.

When Johnny shows up, my pulse jumps higher. He smiles and gets in the line next to mine. I feel his eyes on me as I check in Tyler Sharp and point him in the direction of the breakfast area with a goody bag.

"Johnny Maverick," Quinn says as he steps up to the front of the line. "The party was boring after you two left Saturday. I never thought you'd be one to leave a party before it ended."

He smiles, and I can feel how much he wants to look at me, but doesn't. "Called it an early night."

"Too bad. It was fun." She holds out the goody bag.

"I had a good time too," he says and finally slides his gaze to me. "Thanks." He pauses. "Hey, Kota."

I woke up next to him this morning, his big beefy arms trapping me in place and not letting me get up for the day until he did, and somehow he's able to play it off like we haven't seen each other all weekend.

I waggle my fingers. "Hey, Johnny. Good luck at camp this week."

"Thanks. I had my Lucky Charms this morning." His lips twitch with amusement. I'm pretty sure he's referring to the multiple orgasms he gave me with his mouth, and heat pools in my stomach at the memory. He lifts the bag. "Later."

Chapter Twenty-Five

DAKOTA

Wednesday morning is the same. Camp runs all day long, but after check-in, Quinn and I are able to go back to our desks.

I check my email and see that Lindsey, the Wildcats photographer who shot Maverick's endorsement, has sent me proofs. I squeal as I open them. Hundreds of photo thumbnails fill the screen, and even before I click on one, I know they're good.

I start at the beginning, laughing when I see the deer in headlights expression on Johnny's face for the first twenty or so photos. Even stiff and unsmiling, he's handsome. As the photos progress, I watch him relax and grow more comfortable.

Lindsey captured so many good ones, but the scenes where he's in the shower are by far my favorite. His dark hair slicked back, smirk in place, holding the Maverick Hailstone body wash in one hand, the other sudsing himself up. I find the photo where his dark eyes cut through the camera, and I know it's the one where he's making eye contact with me. My whole body tingles. This should have been a freaking commercial. I'm buying it. All of it.

After I go through it twice on my own, I call Quinn over.

"Damn. The camera loves him."

"I know. They're so good. Even better than I hoped."

"Nice job," she says.

I'm a little thrown every time she gives me a compliment. "Thanks. Oh, hey, can you send me the behind-the-scenes footage you and Reese captured?"

Technically, all the endorsement contract asked for are photographs with the products and ad copy concepts. Still, I want to put together an entire social media campaign for them with the footage, if any of it's usable.

They signed off on my photo-shoot concept, but they instructed me to focus on the products. Whatever that means.

"Yes. I went through all the photos and put my favorites in a folder. I'll send everything, though, in case you have a different eye. Design isn't really my thing."

"Really?" I give her outfit a once-over. She looks like she's wearing something straight out of a magazine.

"This was put together by the sales lady," she admits. She lifts a foot to show off her strappy sandals. "Right down to the shoes."

"Cute," I say.

"There. Sent," she says after clicking a few buttons on her laptop. "I'm going to do a coffee run. Want anything?"

"I'll go." I stand and wave her off. I promised Maverick I'd stop by and let Charli out, since he will be at camp all day.

I do that first, spending a few extra minutes petting Charli. She's a great midday boost. Then I stop at the coffee shop next door to the arena. I look through the photos Quinn sent while I wait for my order. I open the favorites folder first. She might think she doesn't have a good eye for design, but so far, all the ones she selected are great options. They show off another side of Johnny that the professional photos don't.

In one, he's smiling while talking to the photographer as they both stare down at the display on the camera. In another, he's high-fiving Reese. He's good with people, and these photos show that. It humanizes him in a way the posed images don't.

Next, I look through the folder with images that didn't make the cut into the favorites. My body warms, and I don't need a mirror to know I'm blushing as I click on a photo of Johnny and me. My hands work over his stomach, spreading the oil. He looks up at the ceiling with a pained look. My face isn't visible, but I bet it matches his.

"Dakota?" the barista calls, and I can tell by her expression it isn't the first time she's tried to get my attention.

"Sorry." I put away my phone and thank her for the coffees.

I spend all afternoon selecting images for the endorsement. I'll be sending them everything we took, but I still take extra care to highlight my favorites and even recommend some behind-the-scenes ideas for their social media, which is not very exciting from what I've seen. Johnny has more followers on nearly all platforms than they do.

I take everything to Blythe's office late after camp is over, and most everyone else is gone.

"Do you have a minute?"

"Yes." She waves me in. "I was just looking over the photos from the Maverick campaign. You got some great content."

"I know. I'm really excited about how it turned out. I put together a whole plan. Can I show you?"

She laughs lightly and indicates I should sit.

I walk her through all my ideas, talking a mile a minute. She listens, nodding along.

At the end, I take a breath. "What do you think?"

"I think it's great, honestly. You made the most out of the limited time and resources available. The behind-the-scenes photos and videos alone should capture a lot of buzz. Send it over as is."

"Really? It isn't too much?" It's way more than they asked for, but I couldn't help myself. I want Johnny's first endorsement to be amazing.

"Yeah, Dakota. Really. The worst they can do is not use some of it. More is better than not enough. Do you have the contact in their marketing department?"

"Yes." I've already composed a dozen messages in my head to Linda Maine and played out her response back, which will hopefully include lots of exclamation marks and wild praise.

"Where are you scheduled tomorrow for camp?"

"I'm on concession duty."

"I'm pulling you to work with me tomorrow. We've booked Lindsey and will be grabbing content all day long for the Wildcats' social media pages."

"Oh my gosh. That would be amazing."

"Don't thank me yet. It's going to be a long day. Tomorrow afternoon they are going to the local library for story time. It's a way for us to give back, and the guys get a small dose of the required community service."

"That's great." My head is already spinning with the images of Johnny reading to small children. Swoon.

"Be here at seven," she says. Her gaze drops to my shoes. "I guess I don't have to tell you to wear comfortable shoes."

I click my heels together. "Forever a Kansas girl in my ruby slippers."

Before I head home, I send everything to Linda and cross my fingers and toes that she loves it.

I see Reese on my way out.

"Hey, how's working with Coach?" I ask him.

"I think I ran more than the players." He runs a hand along his forehead. His hair is disheveled, and his eyelids are droopy.

"Are you with him again tomorrow?"

"All week."

"Wow. You must be doing something right."

"Yeah." He chuckles. "The other guy with me today had to see a medic for a twisted ankle."

"Ouch."

We push outside, and he salutes me as he walks toward the parking garage.

Reagan calls as I'm getting to the apartment. Johnny's in the kitchen with an ice pack wrapped around his knee, shirtless (of course), and holding his phone to his ear.

"Why have you been avoiding my calls all week?" My best friend shouts in my ear. "And why did you decline the video chat? Where are you?"

I smile at Johnny and mouth *Reagan*, then sit on the couch while she continues to toss out questions to me without waiting for the answers.

"Well?" She pauses finally.

"I'm sorry. It's camp week, and I've been working crazy hours." I send her a request to start the video.

"You're forgiven. How are you?" She lies on her stomach on her bed, and man, do I miss her. I'd love to be in Valley right now so that I could tell her all about the crazy weekend and every detail of my job. It isn't the same over the phone.

I laugh at her quick mood change. That's Reagan. Quick to get riled up but also quick to forgive.

"Good." I glance at Maverick across the apartment. He's holding the phone between his ear and shoulder and twisting off the top of a giant jug of protein powder. The muscles and veins in his forearms pop and flex. "Really good."

Charli steps on my lap, waiting for me to pet her, which I do.

"Are you with Mav?"

I freeze. She knows we're roommates now, but not about everything else that's happened recently. "Uhh, yeah."

"He's on the phone with the guys." I can hear Adam's voice in the background and then Johnny's response from the other room.

"What have you been up to?" I ask her.

"Just hanging out with Adam mostly." She smiles. I can't see her boyfriend, but his hand comes over and pats her ass and then rests there casually.

"You two are adorable."

"Have you done any more online dating?"

"No. I haven't even opened the app," I say honestly.

"What about…" Her eyes widen.

I bite the corner of my lip and glance to the kitchen. Johnny and I haven't mentioned telling our friends, but I can't imagine he'd care if I tell Reagan. She must be able to read it on my face.

"Nooo?!" Her head pops up. "Really?"

"Shhh." I hold my finger up to my lips. "I'll tell you later."

"Oh my god," she squeals.

"It's been the wildest week," I say.

"I'll bet."

FRIDAY MORNING, JOHNNY AND I HEAD OVER TO THE ARENA together. He holds my hand as we go down the elevator, swinging it playfully and scrolling on his phone. "I heard you sent over the endorsement stuff. Hugh was happy with what you got."

"What about the Maverick Company?" I pull out my phone to see if Linda responded. She didn't.

"I assume they approved it. Hugh forwarded me an image and text that they want me to post on my accounts teasing the launch date." He tips his phone for me to see, and I take it, eager to see what they are using. They went with one of my favorites from the first shoot before he got under the shower. He's holding up the deodorant with a half smile that somehow comes off as confident and humble at the same time.

"That's it? Just one image? I sent hundreds. What about the behind-the-scenes stuff?"

"I don't know." He pockets his phone. "Maybe they're going to send more closer to the launch date."

I'm quiet as we step out into the lobby. I have an unsettling feeling that they weren't as happy with the shoot as I was.

"Are you okay?" he asks, shooting me a side-glance.

"Yeah." I shake my head. "Of course. I'm glad they're happy. I just thought they'd use more of the content. We got that image in the first thirty minutes."

He stops and tugs me closer to drop a kiss on my lips. I look around, but we're alone.

"Whatever they decided to use or not use is more about me than you. You did an amazing job."

"Yeah, so good they didn't use it," I mumble. "I told you that you should have gotten someone with more experience."

He laughs, the shake of his chest loosening the pit in my stomach. He tilts up my chin and forces me to look at him. "My slam piece has mad skills. Don't be hating on her."

"Oh my god." I smack his chest.

He laughs. "That's better."

"I don't think you can call me your slam piece when we haven't slammed."

"Could change that right now. I've got two minutes."

I roll my eyes and start toward the door.

"Orgasm buddy?"

I don't answer, and he keeps going. "Personal *ass*istant?"

Chapter Twenty-Six

JOHNNY

Coach divides us up into four teams to scrimmage. All week the guys and I have been looking forward to it. The workouts and the drills were necessary, but this is where it'll be decided. Everyone wants to prove they deserve to be here and no one more than me.

My team is resting while two others play. I catch Dakota and Blythe at the media bench with the photographer from my shoot, Lindsey. The stands are filled with people today, more than have been here all week. Diehards, mostly, who want to see what the future of the team looks like.

Statistically, most of us will end up in Iowa, where we'll continue to duke it out and try to impress the coaches to get our shot.

A couple of these guys I played against just a month ago at the Frozen Four. Morris from Waterville would like nothing more than to embarrass me and send me packing if his pissed-off stares all week are anything to go on. He's a great player, and I think he has a decent shot at staying. Either way, there's a good chance we're going to be teammates one day, so hopefully, a little shoving on the ice will make him feel better about the loss I helped deal at the college championships.

Coach blows the whistle. "Green and black teams. You're up."

"White and red, hit the bench."

I skate out and take a knee. Assistant Coach Peters puts us in our positions to start. Some of us will have to switch from where we're most comfortable, and that's kind of the purpose of this week. Yesterday we had to skate on one leg for thirty minutes, then switch for the next thirty minutes. Discovering weaknesses and knowing what to work on this week and beyond will, in the long run, make us all better pro players. Still, everyone wants to look good for the coaches and media watching our every move.

After getting our assignments, I skate into position, passing Dakota as I do. Lindsey and Blythe are looking elsewhere, and I can't help but wink at my girl as I do. I run my hand along my stick suggestively, and she rolls her eyes. I love doing dumb shit to make her laugh.

This week has been… honestly, even better than I could have imagined. And I imagined in vivid, pornographic detail. I had my own reservations about our relationship changing (not enough to stop myself, mind you), but the only thing that's changed is I get to feel her up and watch her orgasm on the regular.

I'm dying to have sex with her, but even if it's just handies and dry humping for the next month, it's going to be the best summer ever.

After scrimmaging, we hit the showers, then lunch, and then load up on the bus for our required community service gig.

Dakota's coming with us, and I pass her at the front of the bus, tugging the end of her red hair as I go.

I fall into a seat next to Tyler. He's coming from the junior league. The guy has a wicked slap shot.

"Nice goal today," I say.

"Thanks. You had a couple of good ones yourself."

"'Preciate you saying so, but that last one was ugly as hell."

"Ugly still counts," he says. "I haven't seen you at the hotel. Did you already rent a place?"

"Yeah, I'm at The Legends."

"You like it? I still haven't found a place. I'm waiting to make sure I'm not heading to Iowa instead."

"No chance, man. And, yeah, it's great. Come by sometime before you head out and see for yourself."

Before we get off the bus at the library, Blythe gives us instructions. "Split up, talk to the kids, read to them if you want, play puppets, just don't stand in the corner. I promise you, the more you try to hide, the more they will seek you out. They smell weakness." She laughs. "Have fun. Dakota and I will be around if anyone has questions, and Lindsey is with us for pictures, so smile pretty."

Morris smiles wide beside her, his front tooth missing, and the bus laughs.

The kids are a trip. Some of them rush us, and others eye us warily. I don't blame the ones in the latter group. We're a bunch of big dudes who don't know jack about kids or how to interact with them. Thankfully, some of the older guys came. Jack is great. He crouches down in front of one adorable little girl with pigtails, and four more kids crowd around.

Leo's got two kids fighting for a seat in his lap as he reads a book on space.

Blythe was right. The guys that try to hang back end up with kids seeking them out and shoving books in front of them. Some of the littlest children are with their parents. One woman has a tiny little thing strapped to her chest and a kid tugging her along toward Declan. The defenseman surprises me, kneeling and holding out a fist.

Kids don't scare me. I mean, I'm a big fucking kid myself, but I haven't had to carry a conversation with one recently. Tyler and I end up standing together. Neither of us makes a move, and Blythe encourages us, waving us toward some kids near the toy section.

"After you," I tell him, not really thinking he'll take the bait. Ty is a quieter guy. Besides the bus ride, he hasn't said much during our off-ice time, but he strikes up a conversation with two kids about dragons like he's an expert on the topic.

I stand behind him, listening to him debate if girl or boy dragons are stronger, like he's done deep thinking on the topic. He looks over his shoulder and hands me a pink dragon puppet. He slips the blue one on his hand.

"I don't know. Let's find out." He mock attacks me, biting my puppet on the neck.

It's short lived, but the kids laugh.

I catch Dakota's eye across the room. She smiles and lifts her phone like she's taking a picture of me. I wink, which makes her eyes widen and she glances around, looking for Blythe most likely. I already know where the boss lady is. I'm not stupid. I don't want to get Dakota caught any more than she wants to be caught.

She must come to the same conclusion I did—Blythe is too busy to notice us—because she glances back and gives me a haughty, sexy stare with pursed lips before turning on her heel and resuming her job.

I make the rounds, smiling tentatively at kids and saying hello to all the parents and staff, but every time I glance at Dakota, she looks up from what she's doing, and we share a heated stare that makes adrenaline and lust pump through my veins.

Leo's finishing a book as I near him. The kids he was reading to have lost interest and are jumping the carpet tiles. I take a seat next to him on a bright blue bean bag.

"Oh, fudge," I say. "I didn't think this through. Not sure I'm gonna be able to get up."

"Why do you think I'm still down here?" He laughs.

I look through the books on the floor in front of him. Space, US history, math, and finance. "Well, aren't you a barrel of fun?" I lift the one on finance that's as thick as a textbook.

"That one is mine." He snatches it from me. "I was hoping I could disappear and study for a test I have tonight. I'm trying to finish up my degree."

I nod. Leo came to the Wildcats after his sophomore year of college, like me.

"That's cool, man."

He shrugs it off, so I don't press. "Go." I tilt my head to the study room across the library. "I'll cover for you."

"Thanks, Rook."

All the kids are occupied for the moment, so I sit back and watch the chaos around the library. This is pretty cool.

I extract myself from the bean bag chair and circle around until I'm back with Tyler. He's still working those puppets hard. He tosses me one, and we slip back into action, acting out scenes from the books.

Dakota steps up next to me with her phone. She smiles as she aims it at me and takes a picture.

"Miss me?" I whisper, using the puppet as a decoy.

"I'm taking some behind-the-scenes pictures for the social media pages."

"Mhmm."

"I am," she insists and takes another.

"Then maybe you should take pictures of more than just me."

She rolls her eyes but doesn't try to deny it. "You're good with kids."

"Yeah, I guess. They're pretty cool."

"I can see you with a minivan full of them someday."

"Me? A parent?" I shake my head. "I'm more the fun uncle. What about you?"

"Do I want kids?" she asks.

I nod.

"Definitely. Not a whole minivan full, but a couple."

"You've got the death glare for it. No kid is sneaking out on your watch."

Tyler finishes the book, and the kids grab the puppets and entertain themselves. I step closer to Dakota. We're quiet, watching the kids around us.

"Seems like a lot of work." The mom with the baby and kid pulling her around looks exhausted.

Dakota leans down to say hello to the kid, and the mom gives her a thankful smile. "Do you like dogs?" She points to the book in his hand. It has a pug on the front.

The kid nods enthusiastically.

"You know who else does?" She turns to me. "Johnny Maverick. He's a big dog fan. Do you want him to read this to you?"

My palms sweat as his chubby little hand holds up the book.

She snaps another picture as I sit on the floor beside him. "Don't underestimate yourself, Johnny Maverick."

From the library, we're bused back to the arena. Tonight instead of getting to go home and rest, we've got scheduled team bonding time.

I catch Dakota as we're getting off the bus.

"Hey. I'm going to be late tonight. Can you let Charli out for me?"

"Yeah. I'll take her on a short run with me. I missed my run the last few mornings." She smirks and blushes.

"Sorry, not sorry." I say, remembering exactly how we spent that time. "Later, roomie."

One of the media rooms has been set up with video games and food. All the older guys that are in town stop by, but the coaches and staff are absent to give us time to talk and get to know one another without them.

I fill a plate full of grub and sit between Declan and Tyler.

"Boys," I say in greeting.

"What's up, Mav?" Dec says. "Knee holding up?"

"Yeah. It's a little sore after that slam into the wall earlier today." I give him a pointed stare.

He grins. "I had to make sure you could stay in one piece with a little check."

"Little?" He's one of the biggest guys in the league. I thought it was nice of him to stop by until I realized he was giving us a taste of what it'll be like playing against defenders like him.

Ty laughs. "It's been a fun week. I'm sad to see it coming to an end."

"The real fun will begin in September," I tell him and hold up my fist for a bump.

Chapter Twenty-Seven

DAKOTA

"Okay. Start at the beginning," Reagan says.

Ginny crowds in next to her. "Don't leave anything out."

They're sitting on Reagan's bed, and I feel a twinge of melancholy. I am loving my time in Minnesota, but I miss them.

"I'm leaving a few things out," I warn as my friends wait for details about Maverick and me.

Sienna joins our Zoom with a smile. "Sorry. I'm helping teach a figure skating class, and one of the kid's parents showed up fifteen minutes late."

"Poor kid."

"Poor me. What did I miss? Tell me everything."

"You haven't missed anything. She's holding out on us," Reagan says.

I huff a laugh. "I just didn't want to have to repeat myself."

"Well, we're all here now," Ginny says. "Spill."

"There really isn't that much to spill."

Reagan groans. "You're lucky you're so far away. I want to shake you."

"I could drive down and force it out of her," Sienna offers.

"Nobody needs to force anything out of me," I say. "We kissed and messed around a little."

It's the worst description ever for the amazing, hot, fun week of daily orgasms at the hands and mouth of Maverick. Threesome connoisseur wasn't on my dating must-haves list, but holy crap, maybe it should be because all that attention focused on me? It's mind blowing. My mind? Totally blown.

Ginny squeals. "Oh my god, I love it. Do the guys know? Heath hasn't said anything."

"I don't think so," Sienna says.

"No." Reagan shakes her head.

"Huh. I'm surprised that he didn't text them the second it happened to gloat."

"When has Maverick ever gloated about hookups?" Ginny shakes her head. "Not his style."

"Yeah, I guess you're right. Can we keep this between us? I don't want him to think that's what I'm doing either."

"So are you dating, or was this a one, or several times, thing?" Sienna asks.

"For the summer, I guess, or until we get sick of one another. The second may happen first." Though as I say it, I don't believe it. At least not on my account. Johnny is unpredictable and silly and just... fun.

"Then what?" Reagan asks.

"I'll come back to Valley, and he'll stay in Minnesota." I shrug. They don't look happy with my answer.

"We'll still be friends."

"I did not see this coming," Ginny says. "But I love it. You two are all sexy banter. I bet the sex is amazing."

They look to me for an answer with hopeful, eager faces.

"We haven't had sex. Just lots of other stuff."

"Stuff like..." Reagan's head bobs, indicating she wants more details.

"Let's just say he's very good with his hands."

Johnny doesn't get home until late Friday night, and I have to be at the arena early Saturday morning with the other interns for the last day of camp. I'm on floater duty and don't cross paths with him until it's all over. I'm helping break down tables and putting away displays and extra chairs.

I smell him before I see him. The Hailstone scent I told him I like is all he wears now. Maybe he's really into doing his due diligence for the endorsement, or maybe he just likes teasing me.

"I have an emergency," he whispers next to my ear.

"What's wrong?" I straighten, and he takes my hand and hauls me through a doorway into a closet that smells like dirty feet and cleaner.

His mouth descends onto mine, and his big hands frame my face.

"You said there was an emergency," I speak the words into his mouth, trying not to break the kiss more than I have to.

"There is." He takes my hand in his and rubs it over his crotch. "I woke up like this and can't seem to do anything about it."

"That sounds like a personal problem. Maybe you should see

a doctor."

He pulls my bottom lip between his teeth. "The problem is my hand is no longer doing it for me. I need yours."

"Such sweet talk," I say sarcastically.

"You want sweet words?" he asks, holding my face and looking into my eyes.

I don't know what I want, but my body likes everything he's doing right now.

I drag my palm down his length through his athletic pants.

"Mmmm. Sweetheart." He groans. "Baby. Ah, fuck. How does that feel so good through two layers?" He presses a soft kiss to my lips. "Baby doll. Bae."

"That's enough sweet talk," I say.

"I was just getting into it," he says. "Trying to find an endearment I like."

"What happened to slam piece?"

"You know you aren't just my slam piece."

"No?" I slide my hand under the band of his boxers and touch his dick. He hisses through his teeth.

"You can be whatever you want. Just don't stop touching me. Won't take long."

"Charming."

"Don't pretend like you don't love that I'm hard for you all day." His hand slides under my skirt, and he teases me through my panties. "You're so wet. Have you been this wet all day?" He shoves them to the side and wastes no time dipping his fingers inside of me.

I shut him up by covering his mouth with mine. Every word out of his gorgeous lips makes my head spin. We frantically rub and jerk as our mouths slant, and we suck and lick and play. I have been turned on all day missing him, but I missed being with him too, and that's a lot scarier thing to realize. I hope we're not screwing everything up by screwing each other up.

THE FOLLOWING WEEK IS MUCH CALMER AT THE ARENA. I'M WITH Reese today working the ticket office.

We make calls to past season ticket holders to see if they're interested in renewing. We send emails to businesses interested in booking suites or sponsoring games. Sponsors get signage around the ice and special callouts during the game.

It's way more involved than I thought, but I do not love being on the phone. So many people hang up or put us off. After four hours, I've only secured one deal.

"She didn't even let me get through the first sentence," I whine after another hang up.

"Come on," Reese says. "Maybe people will be friendlier after lunch."

In the hallway, we see Blythe talking to Wildcat President and CEO, Mr. Albert.

She smiles and opens her stance. "Brad, these are two of my interns, Dakota Lawrence and Reese Beck."

"Pleasure to meet you." Reese extends his hand first, and after they shake, I offer mine as well.

"I hear you've got the making of a great equipment manager," Mr. Albert says to Reese and then to me, "And you're the one that got the great behind-the-scenes content from the library outing last week, right?"

"Oh, uh. I got a few." Mostly of Johnny. He was right. Even though I was convinced I got an even number of photos of all the guys, half the photos I took had Maverick in them somehow.

"She has a great eye for what's trending on social media. The library has already asked us to come back."

I didn't know that, but it makes me happy it went over so well.

"Glad to hear it. The Stars have twice the following we have on social media. I'd like to change that this year. Maybe you can help."

"I'd love to. I'm only here for a few more weeks."

"You've both done a great job this summer," Blythe adds.

"Keep it up." Mr. Albert says. "And I hope the two of you will consider coming back to help us out once you've graduated."

Reese and I walk away, neither speaking until we're outside.

We turn to each other, smiling, and scream, "Ahhh!"

Sunday night Maverick and I are watching *The Office*. We've already made it halfway through season two, and it's become our nightly thing, followed by multiple orgasms. It's a good way to spend an evening, I have to say.

"What are you doing Wednesday night?" he asks. He lays with his head at the opposite end of the couch, Charli on his chest, and his feet are in my lap.

"At this rate? Watching season four."

"How about coming with me to a ball game?" He sits up. "I was invited to throw the first pitch at the Twins game."

"Seriously?" My lips pull up into a big smile.

"Yeah. It's a trip, right? Blythe cornered me and added so many events to my calendar. She's a hard woman to say no to."

"That's really cool."

"So, you'll come with me?"

"I don't think that's a good idea for us to be seen out together."

"Everyone knows we're friends. Besides, Jack is going too."

"Is he bringing a date?"

"No. He laughed when Blythe told us we got a plus-one." He slides his hands around my waist. "Come on. It'll be fun to hang out with you like a real date."

"If I come, it cannot be like a date," I say. "Just two friends hanging out at a baseball game." I bat at his hands. "I'm not shaving my legs or wearing deodorant."

"Do you really think that would scare me off?"

We both laugh. I know it wouldn't, and I won't go through with it anyway.

"One more date I need you to pencil in."

"Johnny," I protest.

"I ran this one by Blythe, but I asked if I could be the one to tell you."

Well, now I'm intrigued.

"There's a black-tie thing next weekend hosted by the Wildcats Foundation. I asked Blythe if you could come since you helped with the endorsement, and she agreed. She said you could grab some good behind-the-scenes images and content. That woman is going to be sad to see you go." He nips at my collarbone. "Me too."

"Black tie, huh? So you'll be in a suit."

He flashes me a sexy smirk. "That's right, and you in a sexy dress. Maybe the black one."

"I don't think that dress is black tie. It stops about two inches above my vagina."

"That's my idea of black tie."

He kisses my shoulder and collarbone while I consider it. "Are you sure it's a good idea?"

"Afraid you won't be able to keep your hands off me in public?"

"I'm sure there's a dark corner I can shove you in if needed."

He crawls onto my lap. All six feet of him wraps around me.

"What are you doing?" I ask through a grunt.

He attacks my neck with playful kisses and bites. The doorbell rings, and he stills, lips still on my neck.

"Expecting someone?" he asks.

"That's probably just Declan. I called him about a threesome," I say casually.

He's quiet as if he's giving my words deep thought.

"Oh my god, I'm kidding."

He jumps up to get the door. "I thought you'd be more into two girls with one guy, but two guys?" He bobs his head. "I can get down with that as long as we don't cross swords."

He opens the door, and when Declan's voice sounds from the other side, I have to slap a hand over my mouth to stop laughing. I grab a bottle of lube from the coffee table from our earlier activities and creep from my position on the couch toward my room in case Declan comes into the apartment.

"What's up, man?" Mav asks.

"Thought I'd see if you want to hang out. My internet's down."

"Oh, uh…" Mav sneaks a look at me. I nod, encouraging

him, then toss the lube in his room, and pop back out to say hi to Declan. I give them the living room and go to my room. One of the downfalls of us hanging out every night and keeping our relationship a secret is that he hasn't spent that much time with the guys, and I know he needs to bond with his new teammates.

I sit on my bed, smiling as I hear the guys talking in the living room.

It almost feels like we're really dating. Weird.

I'm not overthinking it. Johnny has a way about him that makes me not obsess too much about the details. Maybe it's his "it's whatever" personality rubbing off on me, or maybe I just have too much fun with him to dissect it. No matter the reason, I'm going to enjoy the hell out of the rest of the summer.

Chapter Twenty-Eight

JOHNNY

Heath: You and Dakota? Tell me it's true.

Adam: Oh, it's true.

Rhett: Yeah, congrats, buddy, but while we're on the topic of your awesome new relationship, I'm going to need you to take it down a notch. You're making me look bad, and I have plans that I need you not to fuck up for me.

Maverick: Kota told me she told them and that she told them NOT to tell you. Your girlfriends are all terrible at keeping secrets. And what the hell are you talking about, Rauthruss?

Heath: I'm a little hurt that Ginny knew before me. I want my BFF necklace back.

Adam: Seriously, Mav. Why are you holding out on us?

Mavericka: I wasn't sure if we were telling people. And unlike your girls, I'm an awesome secret keeper.

Adam: You're so fucked. You've got it bad.

Rhett: Dakota sent the girls a picture of the dresses you bought her. I can't compete with Oscar de la Renta and Valentino.

Heath: Who the fuck is Oscar de la whatever?

Adam: He bought Dakota a bunch of expensive dresses all Pretty Woman style.

Maverick: I wanted her to have options. Which one did she choose? She won't tell me.

Heath: I just asked Ginny, but she won't say.

Adam: Reagan either.

Rhett: Sienna's not here, but if Dakota swore them to secrecy, she won't tell me.

Maverick: Oh, sure. Now they're good at keeping secrets.

WEDNESDAY NIGHT, WE GET THE VIP TREATMENT AT TARGET Field. We meet some of the team, and then they show us to a room where we wait to go out on the field. Jack is chatting with one of the event coordinators in the hallway, leaving Dakota and me with a little privacy.

She's looking sexy as hell in cutoff jean shorts, a white tank top that stops an inch above her belly button, and an open Twins jersey over it. Her red hair is pulled back in a ponytail, showing off her neck, and all I can think about is sucking on it.

She sits about a foot away from me, insisting on playing this off like we're just friends, even though Jack pretty much already knows something went down between us in his bathroom.

I walk my fingers across the leather couch toward her. She arches a brow as I reach her smooth legs.

"Johnny," she admonishes.

"You're so far away," I whine. "I sat closer to Jack on the ride over than I did you. Not that I minded, he smells fantastic."

"He really does," she says.

"Maverick." Jack steps into the room, and Dakota stands so quickly you'd think the couch caught on fire. "They're ready."

As Dakota and I follow him down the tunnel to the field, she brushes her fingers against mine and gives me a slight smile. "Good luck."

She's led to our seats, and Jack and I go out on the field to get a few practice throws in. I played baseball as a kid, so I'm not too worried. I would like to impress a certain redhead in the crowd, though.

I find her in her seat, eyes glued on me, and I give her a little hat tip. I can't believe she's with me, even if it's only for the summer. Luckiest. Guy. Ever.

Tossing a baseball in my hand, I stand next to Jack, watching the teams warm up from behind home plate.

"So, you and Dakota… are you two a thing now? Because I feel like I should warn you, being in a relationship your rookie year will be hard. Especially if she's planning to go back to Arizona at the end of the summer."

"We're just having some fun," I say. "We're friends. She's cool."

He doesn't look like he believes me, but I don't need him to. I know no matter what, Dakota and I will be cool. We have to be. I can't imagine any scenario where we end on bad terms. I'd do anything for her.

Throwing out the first pitch is wild. I manage to get it over the plate, but I'd say about half the crowd isn't even paying attention. They're getting beer and hot dogs, finding seats, and anxiously waiting for the game to start. But as I wave to polite applause, I can see Dakota standing, hands up to her mouth, screaming for me like I just hit a grand slam.

I can't wait to sit down beside her and watch the game, almost like we're on an actual date, but the media are waiting for pictures and sound bites, then there's a lot of hand shaking.

When Jack and I finally make it to our seats, it's already the bottom of the second inning.

Dakota stands, hesitates, and then hugs me. "That was amazing."

"Thanks. I didn't want to embarrass my girl."

She looks at Jack like he might be listening in on our every word. We take our seats, Dakota sitting between Jack and me. The game is good, the beer is cold, and the three of us have a good time cheering and chatting.

It's more difficult than I imagined keeping my hands off her. I keep finding myself absently reaching for her or wanting to lean over and kiss her. I'm gonna go crazy before the end of this game. I stand. "I need another beer. Does anyone else want anything?"

"I'm good." Dakota lifts her mostly full cup.

Jack tips up his head. "I'll take another."

I wander around the lower deck, scoping out merchandise. I grab some souvenirs for Dakota and then the beers.

I'm walking back to our seats between innings. The kiss cam is going, and I slow my steps to watch the monitor. They stop on an older couple in matching Twins jerseys. The husband plants a big ole kiss on his wife, hands on her cheeks, not letting her go until the stadium erupts in cheers.

Old people still hot for each other? Yeah, I want a little of that. I pull my gaze from the screen to Dakota. She's watching the old couple like I was, with a big smile on her gorgeous face. I have a flash of Dakota and me with gray hair still unable to keep our hands to ourselves, and my chest tightens.

I slide into my chair and lean forward to deposit everything on the ground.

Dakota squeaks beside me. I sit tall, beers in hand, ready to hand Jack his, but the look on my girl's face stops me short.

"Wha—?" I don't even get the question out of my mouth when I spot Dakota and Jack on the kiss cam screen.

She ducks her head and blushes, which only makes the announcer and crowd more determined. Jack wears an amused smirk, arm casually resting on the armrest between them. They look great together. Well, she looks great. She could carry any guy to couple goals.

Dakota manages a side-glance at me as the people around us chant, *Kiss! Kiss!*

I don't have a lot of options. I could push Jack out of the way and kiss her myself in front of all these people or drag her all caveman-like out of the stadium. I doubt Dakota would like either of those options.

I'm frozen watching the two of them, just like everyone else. Finally, Jack leans over, puts a hand on her face, shielding most of her from the camera, and brings his mouth to hers.

Every cell in my body pulses with waves of anger and frustration at the roaring applause as their kiss is captured on the big screen for everyone to see. No. Just... fucking no.

Her lips are wet and shiny, and her face has that just-kissed flush. The only time she should look like that is after *I* kiss her.

Goddammit. I should have pushed Jack the fuck out of the way.

Chapter Twenty-Nine

DAKOTA

Maverick and I leave before the game is over. We all took an Uber together on the way here, but Jack said he was going to stay and get his own ride back. Really, I think he's graciously bowing out after the kiss-cam fiasco.

Once we're away from the stadium, Johnny pulls me over into the middle of the back seat so that I'm sitting next to him. "Gonna have to keep you glued to my side from now on."

He wraps a hand around the back of my neck and drops his mouth to mine. No warm-up, no tenderness. His kiss is hard and demanding, and I am here for it. Sitting next to him all night and not being able to touch him was frustrating. A lot more frustrating than I thought it would be. Years I've hung out with him and not thought about kissing him, and now I can't do it for five minutes without wanting to jump him.

"Did you like it when he kissed you?" He pulls my bottom lip between his teeth while I shake my head.

Jack and I barely kissed. His lips brushed mine like a whisper. But even from that soft touch, I know kissing Jack, *really* kissing

Jack, wouldn't feel like this.

"You looked good kissing him, and I didn't like it. You're mine. If you want to kiss another guy, it's on my terms."

"Like a threesome?" I ask as his lips skim down my neck. Liquid heat pools in my lower belly at the idea.

"Mhmm," he murmurs against my collarbone. "Whatever you want as long as I'm a part of it. I don't want to miss out on a single kiss or orgasm."

The Uber driver stops at the curb outside of the apartment complex. Johnny thanks him, and we step out onto the sidewalk in front of the arena. It's quiet on the street in front of our building, but up ahead, I can see people walking to and from the bars and restaurants.

My arms are full. Between the things the Twins gave us and all the extra stuff Maverick insisted on buying me, I'm flush with merch.

Inside the elevator, he pins me against the wall and keeps showing me just how much he wants me.

"I'm so hard thinking about you in a threesome."

I can feel just how hard. "I don't think I could go through with a threesome."

"But you like the idea, I can tell."

I do, but not for the reason he thinks.

I lean forward, stopping when my lips hover near his. "Right now, I like any idea that includes sex with you."

He stills, face searching mine. "You mean…"

I close the distance and place a kiss on his lips, then softly whisper, "Fuck me, Johnny."

He says nothing for too long, and I think maybe he's going to tell me no. The elevator dings, and the doors open on the eleventh. The doors start to close, and he's still staring at me, unblinking.

"We don't have—"

"Fuck yes!" He hauls me out of the elevator and to the apartment.

"I think I dropped a foam finger back there," I say, giggling as he shuts us inside.

"I'll buy you five more." He takes everything else from me and drops it all to the floor, then scoops me up, tosses me over his shoulder, and heads for his bedroom. He smacks my ass. "It's go time, Kota."

I'm laughing when he lays me down, but then he begins undressing me, and everything shifts. He starts at my shoes, kissing my calves and knees as he does it, then working his way up. He's slow and deliberate, dropping more kisses and murmuring how gorgeous I am and reminding me I'm his over and over again.

As if I would be anyone else's. Not when this is an option. I'd trade away everything else for another few weeks just like this. Summer is blazing by, and I am through denying myself anything.

My heart rate skips as he covers me, adoring every inch of skin. By the time his lips skim over the heated skin at the apex of my thighs, I'm trembling. His big shoulders push between my legs. He hooks an arm around one and brings his mouth down, kissing me softly on the mound of my pussy. He groans, the sound vibrating against my sensitive flesh.

"Johnny," I whine. I need more, and I need it now.

"Patience, slam piece." He chuckles, and his tone softens. He runs a finger along my swollen slit. "Fuck, baby, you're so wet. Tell me what you want."

"You. Just you." The honest admission slips from my lips. "And, uh, shirt off, obviously."

He leans back on his knees and pulls the jersey over his head. He really does have a great body.

"Better?"

"Keep going?" I stare at the bulge in his jeans.

He shakes his head side to side. "Uh-uh. Not yet. I need to make sure you're ready for me."

I feel pretty damn ready, but before I can voice it, his mouth covers my pussy, and I can't form words. He licks and nips while dragging the pad of his thumb over my clit at a slow, torturous pace.

I grip his shoulders, digging my fingernails into his skin until I'm certain he will have tiny crescent moons indented on his flesh.

"That's it, baby." He tightens his grip on me, latching on as my orgasm rocks through me.

I've barely melted into the mattress when he places a kiss at my belly button and says, "Turn over."

I comply, boneless and satiated but excited for more. I can hear him undressing behind me. I glance over my shoulder, slightly turning so I can appreciate the view. He catches my gaze as he stands at the end of the bed naked, stroking his dick.

"I thought I told you to turn over," he says with a sexy smirk.

"The view is better this way."

"You've been staring at the one-eyed monster for weeks, baby."

"I don't want to miss any of this," I say.

He gives my ass a smack that's just above playful and places a kiss on the same spot. "On your stomach. You're not ready for me yet."

I am, but I fall back to my stomach anyway. His body covers mine. He runs a hand down my ponytail and then wraps his hand around it until my scalp pricks. He kisses my neck and down my spine.

He's a heady mixture of playful and bossy. Commanding me to get on all fours one minute and the next blowing raspberries on my ass.

He gives me another smack and then slides his hand between my legs. I'm slick, and his fingers glide easily through my folds.

My shoulders sag as the next orgasm builds.

"Johnny," I whine as his hand disappears. I'm so close.

His laughter caresses my skin. "What, baby?"

"You know what." I push my hips back until his dick pokes my ass.

He groans and bites my neck, then kisses it. Playful and bossy. "I need another orgasm out of you before I know you're serious."

"What?" I'm deciphering his meaning as he rolls us, so he's on his back, and I'm straddling him.

"Ride my face, baby." He wriggles down and smacks my ass to get me into position. My muscles clench as I lower onto his eager mouth. I hold still, letting him lick and suck.

"I said ride my face, baby. You want my dick? Show me what you're going to do with it."

My face flames, but I roll my hips and rub myself on his mouth. My second orgasm hits with barely any warning. Johnny holds my ass in his palms as he sucks hard on my clit while I ride it out.

I cry his name as I slump against the headboard.

"Fuck, that was hot," he says as I lift my leg to fall onto the bed beside him.

"Fuck hot?" I ask, trying to catch my breath.

"Everything about you is fuck hot. Are you sure you want to do this? I can get you off about a thousand more ways with my hands or mouth."

"The MacGyver of orgasms," I joke. "I'm ready."

He reaches over to the nightstand and grabs a condom. I lean forward and place a kiss on the head of his dick before he can cover himself. His head falls back, eyes closed. One hand caresses my face and then tangles in my hair, bringing me down on him until he hits the back of my throat. Tears prick my eyes, and he lets go, stealing my hair tie from my ponytail and letting my hair spill free.

"On the bed. Hands above your head."

He finishes covering himself with the condom and then loops the tie around my wrists, keeping them together over my head, resting on the mattress. He frames my face in his big hands, kissing me deeply as the head of his cock nudges my entrance. He rests his forehead on mine as he slides inside.

"Fuck, Kota. You're so goddamn tight and perfect and fucking *mine*." He growls the last part as he pounds into me, finally hitting the spot deep inside of me that's been aching for him.

I bring my arms up and loop them around his neck. He bites my bicep and then kisses it before finally giving all his attention to my mouth, kissing me so hard and stealing all the air from my lungs.

I come with tears welling behind my eyelids. Too many orgasms and too many emotions. I'm overloaded on Johnny Maverick. He groans, sliding his mouth down and clamping onto my neck, sucking hard as we come together.

I'm going to have a mark for sure. *His*. And I like it a little too much.

I silence my alarm and try to sit up. Johnny's arm at my waist weighs me down, and even through his light snores, he's holding on tight. Charli is curled up between our legs, and I encourage her to come closer by patting the comforter lightly. She wiggles as if she's too lazy to walk, and I pick her up and put her in my spot, then lift Johnny's arm around his dog.

"The sneak out, huh? Are you gonna at least leave some money on the nightstand?" He opens one eye.

"Ha! Ha!" I pull my tank top over my head. "I need to shower and change. I smell like sex and Hailstone."

"Look and smell pretty fucking good to me." He rolls onto his back, lifts his arms, and makes a window with his thumb and pointer finger on each hand, then looks at me through it.

I finish dressing and lean over to place a kiss on his lips. He captures my legs and pulls me on top of him.

"I have to go," I insist, but don't try to pull away just yet. "Thanks for last night, slam piece."

He grins and rubs a finger along my neck. "I'll be your slam piece any fucking time."

I can't stop smiling as I get ready and head to work. The more I replay last night, the more details I remember, and wow… I want to do it all again.

I consider going straight to Blythe's office and faking a stomachache to spend the day in bed with Johnny, but there are only two and a half weeks of the internship left, and I guess I actually like my job because it's a close second to spending the day in bed.

Quinn and Reese are at their desks when I get to our area in the intern pool.

"Morning," I say cheerily. I come up short when I see the big flower arrangement sitting on my desk. Twelve stunning red roses. "Are those for me?"

My face heats. I'm going to kill Johnny. And how exactly did he pull this off so fast? The card mocks me, but I don't dare reach for it.

Reese leans back in his chair with a pen poised in one hand up near his mouth.

"Morning."

Quinn stands and comes to sit on my desk. Reese rolls his chair closer.

"What's going on?" I remove my laptop from my bag and set it on the desk, avoiding their stares.

"Are those from Jack?" Quinn asks. She makes like she's going to take the card, and I block her.

"Jack?"

"Jack Wyld. The guy you made out with on national TV. Ringing any bells?" Quinn raises one accusatory eyebrow.

Right. The kiss cam. I'd all but forgotten it. Who would have thought that'd be the least interesting part of last night?

"No, they aren't from Jack. That was nothing."

"It didn't look like nothing." Quinn holds up her phone to show me.

I take the device and my stomach twists at the photo evidence of Jack and me kissing. It really was nothing, but I can see how it looks. Especially knowing Jack's history. "Where did you find this?"

"There are a bunch more. People tagged Jack and the Wildcats. You're everywhere." Her gaze drops to my neck. "Nice hickey."

My hand shoots to my neck, and I brush my hair over my shoulder to cover it.

"It isn't what it looks like."

Quinn shrugs. "Okay. What is it?"

"I went to the game with Jack and Maverick to watch Johnny throw the first pitch. That kiss lasted all of a second, and it was nothing. I'm not hooking up with Jack."

Neither speaks.

"I'm not."

Quinn stands and her gaze lifts over my shoulder. "Look less guilty."

"Good morning, everyone." Blythe, stunning as always, steps into our area. Her body language gives nothing away, but I stand in front of the flower arrangement on my desk.

"Morning," we say in unison.

"Before you head off to your work assignments for the day, I wanted to make sure you all got the invite for the charity gala next Friday night?"

I breathe out a sigh of relief that she isn't here for me. Also, another point for Johnny. I told him I'd only come to the gala if he made sure Quinn and Reese were going too. It'd look too suspicious if I were the only one.

"I already bought my dress," Quinn says.

"It will be a great opportunity for you to see another aspect of the job and…" She pauses. "It's a small way for me to thank you for all the hard work you've done this summer. I'll pull you three from your rotation next Friday to help me set up."

We groan. I've lifted enough tables and chairs this summer to last a lifetime. She laughs. "Everything will already be in place. No heavy lifting required. Great job, everyone. The reports from your rotations have been wonderful. You make me look good." She takes a step closer to my desk, her smile never faltering. "Dakota, before you head to your rotation, can you stop by my office? It'll only take a minute."

Heat creeps up the back of my neck. "Sure. I'll be right there."

With a nod, she leaves, and I let out a shaky breath. *Oh shit.* Quinn shoots me an *I told you so* look. I grab my stuff for rotation and snatch the card from the flowers to read later.

Blythe is standing in her office next to a fancy-looking espresso machine fresh out of the box.

"Come in," she says when she sees me. "Shut the door."

I gulp and force a smile as I close the door behind me and take a seat.

"I went to the store to buy an electric kettle and ended up with this," she says and holds up some sort of attachment. "What do you think this is?"

"I don't know. I'm not much of a coffee drinker unless it has a whole lot of cream and sugar."

"Do you like tea?"

"Yeah. Sometimes." Oh my gosh, why am I here? I can't seem to relax, and I'm afraid I'm going to blurt out I slept with Johnny Maverick any second if she doesn't get to the point.

Someone knocks on the door, and she looks up and waves. Katherine from HR walks in, and I feel like I'm going to throw up.

"Hi, Dakota," Katherine says.

"Hi." I look between them. "Am I in trouble?"

"Sorry, I should have explained," Blythe says as Katherine takes a seat beside me. "We saw the photograph of you and Jack last night at the Twins game."

I'm silent, forcing her to say it.

"The kiss cam?"

I nod. "It wasn't what it looked like."

"Jack said the same thing, but we had to talk to him and you per protocol." Blythe gives me a reassuring smile.

Katherine angles her legs toward me. "It's just a reminder that while interning with the Wildcats, any relationships with players or coworkers need to be disclosed."

"I thought we weren't allowed to have relationships with players." My brows pull together.

"So you are having a relationship with Jack Wyld?" Katherine asks.

"No." I shake my head. "Definitely not."

"*If* you were involved with a player, you would be reassigned for the duration of your internship." In other words, moved somewhere I can't do any damage to the reputation of the company.

I curl my fingers around the card from the flowers. "I am not involved with anyone."

"Great. That makes my job easy then." Katherine sits tall. "If you ever need to talk, you know where to find me." She and Blythe stand and walk me out.

"Thanks, Dakota," Blythe says as I move down the hall away from her.

Only when I turn the corner out of view, do I finally pull the heavy cardstock from the tiny envelope. My stomach flips, and a smile tugs at my lips.

Mine.

-Yours

Chapter Thirty

DAKOTA

I'm crossing the street to the apartment after work when a motorcycle catches my eye. It idles in a no-parking zone right outside of the building. The driver has on a helmet, but I can almost feel him watching me. I pull out my key card and phone as I approach, but then he lifts the helmet and shakes out his dark hair.

Johnny.

Johnny on a motorcycle. That's a fantasy I didn't know I needed in my life.

He rests the helmet on his thigh and flashes that Maverick smile that makes me want to roll my eyes and kiss him in equal measure.

"Want a ride, baby?" His tone is all sorts of innuendos.

"Where did you get this?"

He swings a leg over and stands in front of me. "Declan is letting me try her out. I'm thinking about getting one. What do you think?"

"I think they're dangerous."

"Worried about me?"

"Worried about the bike. It's so pretty."

"Come on a ride with me."

"Where are we going?" I move the strap of my purse, so it's across my body.

"Don't know. We'll just see where the night takes us." He lifts the helmet carefully onto my head, then stands back and looks at me through a window he makes with the thumb and pointer finger of each hand. "Sold."

He gets on, and then I do, tucking the hem of my dress under me so it won't blow up, and then wrapping my arms around his waist. A thrill shoots through me as he starts it up. I tighten my grip, and he takes off. Johnny navigates through the busy city traffic, and then I lose track of where we are and what direction we're heading.

On a quieter road, he turns his head and yells, "Hang on, baby."

Then, the bike accelerates, and we're moving fast. The wind whips my hair around, my heart hammers in my chest, and the smile on my face never leaves. At one point, one of his hands drops from the grip to stroke my leg, then rests on top of mine clasped around his chest, and I think *I could get used to this*: the spontaneity, the fun, spending evenings with Johnny.

There's good and bad to knowing the end point of a relationship. On the one hand, it forces you to really appreciate every moment, but on the other, each moment feels bigger than it might if you didn't know it could be the last. I guess it's just that summer is coming to an end, and I'm sad about leaving my friend.

Johnny slows inside a little town and pulls off into a parking lot, and kills the engine.

I remove the helmet and stand on wobbly legs.

"What'd you think?" he asks, taking the helmet and setting it on top of the bike.

"I think you're going to pick up a lot of girls driving that thing around." It's the first flash of jealousy I've had, thinking about him doing this with someone else when I'm gone.

He laughs it off. "Come on, let's grab dinner and have some fun."

When he walks into the restaurant and gives his name, it's clear that this was not just a joyride. It's a small, cozy place, but it's packed and obviously by reservation only. We get a table for two in the back corner, and Johnny stretches out his long legs in front of him, circling mine.

He stares across at me with a smirk.

"What?"

"You've got sex hair. Another plus for the bike."

I run a hand along my knotted hair. I don't think there's any fixing it without a brush. I have a serious rat's nest. "This is a plus?"

"Hell yeah. Just fucked is my new favorite look on you."

My body tingles, and thighs clench. Umm, check, please? Why are we so far from the apartment where I can kiss him? The bike suddenly seems like the worst idea he's ever had.

AFTER DINNER, WE GET BACK ON THE MOTORCYCLE, BUT INSTEAD of heading toward the apartment, he heads farther in the opposite direction to a bowling alley.

"Seriously?" I ask. "You bowl?"

"This place is supposed to be fun." He slips on a baseball hat, pulls it down low on his eyes, and then takes my hand.

I'm touched that he put so much effort into this, but I really shouldn't be surprised. Johnny is a considerate guy and also, as it turns out, an awesome date.

Again, inside he gives his name at the desk because every lane is booked. It's dark with neon lights, and upbeat music plays loudly over the sound of bowling balls knocking into the pins. A concession serves food like pretzels and pizza, and there's a full bar.

We get shoes and pick out our balls, and then Johnny leads me to the bar where he orders me a Pop Rocks cocktail. It's bright blue and served in a tall glass with the candy around the rim. I take a hesitant sip. It's sweet and bubbly and delicious. He kisses me while the rocks pop in my mouth, making us both laugh.

"You're good at this," I say as he punches in our names to start the game.

"Bowling?"

"No, *this*." I motion between us. "This is the best date I've ever been on."

I feel the instant need to correct the word date because I'm not even sure that's what this is. Do you go on dates with your slam piece? But Johnny's smile lifts slowly. "Yeah?"

I nod. "How come you don't date more?"

He shoots me a look and laughs it off.

"I'm serious. In the two years that I've known you, I've never heard you talk about going out with a girl and doing something like this."

"I haven't. Not really. I was pretty content hanging with my boys in Valley." He smiles. "And you and the girls."

I wonder how things will change now that he's left the college atmosphere behind. After I go, he'll spend more time with his team and meet new people. New girls. Lots of girls. I'm getting to see this side of him he hasn't shown anyone else yet, and I feel fiercely protective over it.

"You're up first," he says and leans back. "Show me what you got."

What I have isn't much. I'm a terrible bowler but too competitive to give up after the first game where he destroys me.

We start the second, and I decide to go with distraction and frustration to beat my opponent. It's my turn, and I walk in front of him, sticking out my butt in exaggerated form.

I only manage to hit three pins, but when I turn around, he's chuckling, brows raised.

"It's going to be like that, huh?"

"Like what?" I play innocent as I take a seat next to him and reach across him, brushing my boobs against his arm as I get my drink. It's my third. They aren't very strong, but the Pop Rocks are fun.

He licks the side of my drink and then kisses me. His tongue sweeps in and tangles with mine. The sweet candy pops and tingles. I'm breathless when he pulls back. His voice deepens, and his gaze pins me in place. "Two can play that game, Kota."

Neither of us moves. The air between us feels thick. He cups the back of my neck and kisses me again. His hand travels over my shoulder, down my arm, and to my thigh, where he inches along the hem of my dress. I hold my breath as his fingers disappear underneath and brush against my panties.

It's dark, and we're sitting so close that I'm not worried about anyone seeing, but I glance around to make sure no one is looking this way, anyway. His thumb makes a slow circle over my clit. My body shakes as he pushes one finger under the lacy material.

"You should have worn a dress," I say as I dig my fingernails into the denim covering his thighs.

"No fucking kidding."

I slide my hand higher, and he groans. My panties fall back in place as he stops what he was doing and stands.

"Let's go." He takes my hand and heads off. I think we're leaving and grab my purse, but he leads me down a hallway to the bathrooms. I try to drop his hand as he enters the one labeled MENS, but he pulls me through and shuts the door.

As soon as I'm inside, he backs me against it and kisses me hard. Then, he lifts me by the waist, and I wrap my legs around him. His bulge hits at the perfect spot. My eyes fall closed as he grinds into me. When my orgasm is close, I scramble to undo his pants, and he pulls a condom from his wallet and then helps me push his jeans and boxers down far enough that his cock springs free. Every move is frantic. He covers himself, shoves the soaked material of my panties aside, and pushes inside of me.

We both cry out with such relief. I hang on to his neck, burying my face and breathing him in as he fucks me against the bathroom door. He murmurs quietly, "You're mine. I can't believe you're really mine."

And I relish in the feeling of being his, even if it's only for a short time.

The next week goes by in a blur of orgasms and laughter. We hit happy hour with Jack and Declan one night, and another night we video chat with our friends from Valley. It's a happy little bubble. Friends in public and then kissing every second we're behind closed doors.

I know it can't last much longer, but I've done an impressive job not worrying about it and just enjoying the time together.

Friday evening, I'm getting ready for the gala while talking to Reagan, Ginny, and Sienna.

"Your makeup looks A-plus," Ginny says, giving me a thumbs-up.

"I learned from the best," I tell her. She is the makeup queen. "Reagan? How's my hair?"

"Big and badass."

"Put on the dress!" Sienna says.

I smile at their eager faces on the screen of my phone. I miss them.

"Okay. One second. It's hanging in the closet. Maverick has been trying to sneak a glance at which dress I picked all week."

He had so many options sent over I was a little overwhelmed. All different colors and cuts. All my size. I think he's going to be surprised by my selection.

I slide the silky material over my head and ease up the zipper on one side.

I walk back to my bedroom, where my phone is propped up on my bed. "What do you think?"

Ginny gasps, and Reagan's jaw drops.

"Damn, Dakota," Sienna says, finally.

"Not too much?" I smooth my hand over the skirt. It's lacy and sort of poufy and girly and nothing that I ever would have picked out.

"It's perfect. You are stunning."

"Are you wearing your red Converse?" Ginny asks.

"Nope." I kick up a foot to show her the red strappy shoes I bought. Still red, just a little sexier.

"It's like I don't even recognize you." Reagan holds a hand over her heart. "I knew there was a vixen in there dying to dress up for the right guy."

"Maverick prefers me undressed," I say, and then my face goes hot. I've been careful to draw a line between how much I tell our friends. When I go back, I don't want it to be weird for anyone.

"I should go. He's probably waiting."

"Take pictures!" Reagan yells. "I want to see you two together."

"I'll see what I can do. We're still walking the careful line of being friends in public but not making it obvious we're…" I grapple with how to describe our relationship.

"Tearing into one another on the regular?" Sienna asks with a smug grin.

"Something like that." I pick up my phone and my clutch for the night.

"I'll call you guys later." I kiss the air and end the call.

I glance in the bathroom mirror one last time. I hope I didn't overdo it.

"Kota, you ready?" Johnny calls from the living room, right on cue.

"One second," I yell, blow out a breath and walk my vixen badass self out to the living room.

Chapter Thirty-One

JOHNNY

I'm staring down at the text my dad sent an hour ago, trying to figure out how the fuck to feel about him showing up tonight for the gala. On the one hand, he paid the ridiculous plate fee and supported the cause, which, tonight, is underprivileged youth. Still, it doesn't escape me that his travel plans include rolling in an hour before the gala and leaving first thing tomorrow morning.

Distracted and annoyed, I've nearly forgotten that I've been dying to see which dress Dakota picked out for tonight until she steps out into the living room. The fucking world stops. At least my heart does.

Her red hair is curled, and her makeup is heavier than normal. Bright red lipstick that I'm definitely hoping to have all over me tonight coats her lips and contrasts with the black dress.

"I was hoping you'd pick this one," I say, walking slowly toward her.

"You were?" She runs a hand along the fluffy skirt. "It's like nothing I've ever worn before."

"It has the same straps as that little black dress you wore to the

Frozen Four party."

She smiles. "I wondered if that's why you chose this one."

"You'd have looked killer in anything."

"What about you?" She rests a hand on the lapel of my maroon jacket. "This suit is… well, it's something. You clean up nice."

"Don't worry, baby. Still the same dirty boy underneath. Respectable on the outside, little less so on the inside."

"I like you the same either way," she says, and it means more than she could know. I never feel like I have to be anything but myself around her. Sure, she might roll her eyes or whatever, but the next second she's smiling and staying despite whatever dumb shit I said or did.

"Should we go?"

"In a minute." I take her hand and force her to do a spin for me. "Damn. I feel like the luckiest guy alive showing up with you and getting to come home with you. Maybe even sneaking into a closet somewhere during dinner." I bring her body against mine and let my hands wander.

"Three feet of distance," she warns. That's her new rule any time we're at the arena together or out with friends. We can be close, like friends, but not so close we can touch. I may have been the one that needed that rule. I can't help it. When she's standing next to me, I want to touch her.

"Maybe we should just walk in hand in hand and march right up to Blythe and tell her we're together."

"You're kidding, right?" Her blue eyes widen, and she studies my face to gauge my seriousness.

I shrug a shoulder. "Summer is almost over, and you said they were cool about the whole Jack thing."

"Because I swore I wasn't dating him."

"Yeah, I guess so."

"Johnny, I get it. I would love to be able to hold your hand all night, but we cannot tell them. Two more weeks. That's all I have left." I don't know if she means with the job or me.

"Okay. If that's what you want, but the second we get home tonight." I wrap one of her red curls around my finger. "You're all mine."

Maverick: Sorry, boys, I snagged the hottest date. <attached picture of Maverick and Dakota. Dakota's pressing a kiss to his cheek.>

Payne: Looking sharp, buddy.

Scott: Thumbs up emoji.

Rauthruss: You're definitely dating up.

Maverick: Oh, like you're one to talk, Rauthruss.

Rauthruss: <picture of Sienna lying on his chest smiling at him> Noted. Don't care.

Rauthruss: Also, we're coming up next weekend before Dakota heads back. Dinner? Somewhere nice.

Maverick: Sounds good. I know a place. Send me your travel

deets. You can stay at my place and crash in my room. I'll bunk up with Kota for a night or two. It's a *real* inconvenience. 😉

"My dad is coming tonight," I say as we cross the street to the arena.

"He is?"

I nod and adjust my cuffs. "I just found out about an hour ago."

"What about your mom?"

"Nah, she's in Italy for the next month. She has a sister there. My aunt, I guess, although I don't really know her."

"Did she come to the Frozen Four or the party at Valley after?"

"No. She was in..." I think back. She's always traveling somewhere. "Fuck. I don't remember."

"You don't talk about them a lot."

"Not much to say. They live their life in Chicago and traveling the world, and I'm here. Occasionally they drop in, usually when it benefits the company somehow." I don't mean to sound bitter, but I guess I am.

She takes my hand and squeezes. "I'm sorry."

I lace my fingers with hers, wishing I could hold on all night long. "It's fine. They're busy running an empire."

The gala is held in a suite at the arena that's been transformed for the event. Cocktail tables are set up around the room's perimeter, and a live band plays in one corner. I spot Dec near the bar, and Dakota and I walk toward him. She's serious about her three feet rule. Every time I step closer, she moves another step away.

"Two feet?" I turn my head and whisper.

"Three feet." She smiles. "You're terrible at following the rules."

"It's a stupid rule."

"Hey, you two," Declan greets us. "Got roped into suffering through this tonight, too, huh?"

"It isn't so bad," I say.

He grunts. "They all start to look the same after a while."

"I see some of the other interns," Dakota says. "I'll see you guys later."

She walks off, and I watch her go, not even trying to hide it.

When she disappears behind a crowd of people, I turn my attention back to Declan and find him grinning at me.

"What?"

"The whole kiss cam thing moved you to action, I see."

"I don't know what you mean." I get a beer from the bar and take a long drink.

"Oh, please. You've been circling each other all summer."

I don't confirm or deny it, but he huffs a laugh and says, "Relax. I don't care, and I won't say anything."

"What about you? I haven't seen you with anyone. Do you have a girlfriend you keep chained to the bed in your apartment? Or boyfriend?"

"Nah. Too busy right now. It's the last year on my contract. The next one I sign needs to take me into a nice retirement."

I lift my beer. "Cheers to that."

There's no dancing, which is a real shame because I'd love to have an excuse to wrap my arms around Dakota. I convince her to sit with me during dinner, but she's mingling around the room until then, and I'm avoiding my dad.

As soon as he walked into the room, he started chatting up Coach Miller and Brad Albert, the president and CEO.

I'm with some of the guys on the team, smiling for photos when he finally decides to approach me.

I thank the photographer and walk over to where he stands, waiting for me.

"Hey, you made it," I say, adjusting my cuffs.

He shakes my hand. "Just got a tour. Not a bad arena here. It's a little smaller than the one in Chicago, but not bad."

"Sorry it doesn't live up to your expectations." I grit my teeth. One sentence out of his mouth, and already I feel like I'm bracing for a puck to the face.

He laughs it off and squeezes my shoulder. "Let's get a drink."

My dad has this way about him where no one is a stranger, and he's totally at ease in any situation. He works the room like he's the most important person here. I plaster on a smile and keep a fresh beer in my hand at all times.

When they start to bring out dinner, we take our seats, and I let out a long breath. Dad's on one side of me, and Dakota is on the other. I've never been happier to have her next to me. She brings Quinn, ever eager to look like just another intern, and Jack joins us too.

"Dad, this is Dakota. She worked on the endorsement." I make the introduction, placing my hand on her elbow and thankful for an excuse to touch her.

"Ahh," he says, nodding politely. "You're responsible for the photos of my son taking a shower." He makes a face—one I've seen often, disapproval dripping from it.

She inhales sharply, and her cheeks dot with pink and I want to punch him in the jaw.

"They are hygiene products," I say.

"Yes, yes, I know. We're looking to go in a different direction, something a little classier. Upscale." He waves a hand and picks up his scotch. "Something like that ad you did for Givenchy, Jack. Now that was a good ad."

"That was for a clothing company," I say. "It isn't anywhere near the same thing."

He makes a dismissive humming noise.

"I like the photos we got. Dakota did a good job. Even the head of publicity here said so."

"It's fine." Dakota shoots me a wide-eyed glare, and her lips pull into a brittle smile. "The campaign should fit the brand."

"See? She gets it." Dad winks at her. "I brought a couple of suit options with me tonight. Maybe after dinner, we can snap a few pictures. See if we can get something nailed down."

Is he for real? Well, that explains the sudden desire to see his son. He needed something for his company.

I push back my chair with a loud scrape against the floor. "Excuse me. I'm going to get another drink."

Dakota's heels click-clack behind me as she tries to keep up. She whisper-hisses my name, "Johnny. Johnny."

I don't stop until I get into the hallway.

She starts to reach for me and then stops herself, which just further pisses me off. I don't want any rules on when and where I can touch her. Especially not right now.

"He wouldn't know a good campaign if it hit him upside his head. It's bullshit."

"Johnny, it's fine."

"You worked your ass off on that campaign, and it's good. I'm not just saying that."

"I should have listened to what they wanted. I had my own vision, and it didn't meet the clients' expectations. That's on me."

She might be playing it off like it's fine, but I know she's upset.

"I want to kiss you right now," I say, bringing my hand up to her cheek and grazing it with the back of my fingers. "I want to kiss you always."

"Johnny." She leans into my touch and then steps back. "We should get back inside."

"I'm not reshooting the campaign. It's bullshit."

"You signed a contract."

"Fuck that."

She laughs quietly. "Don't be pissed on my account. Seriously. I am proud of that shoot. Do I wish they loved it as much as I did? Of course. But they didn't, and it's their call."

"It's fucking bullshit."

She takes a step in.

"Three feet, young lady," I joke, wrapping an arm around her waist and pulling her flush against me.

She drops a quick kiss to my lips and wiggles out of my hold. "I'll see you inside."

The rest of dinner goes by smoothly because I keep my mouth occupied with food and alcohol. I answer direct questions from my dad in grunts and focus on Dakota.

As soon as the dishes are cleared, he stands and rests a hand on my shoulder. "Shall we, son?"

I grind down on my molars, but Dakota places a hand on my thigh under the table and squeezes.

I follow him, downing the rest of my drink on my way to a room down the hall. It's set up with a backdrop and lighting, and the photographer is waiting for us. I'm pissed that he made it seem like he was coming to see me when really he was dropping in to get something for his company—something I don't want to give him.

Blythe smiles at me as I step into the room. "If you need anything, let me know. I'll be right outside."

Dad thanks her, and I shrug out of my jacket and untuck my shirt. There is a row of shirts and jackets hanging on a rack—traditional cuts and expensive fabrics. Each one looks exactly like something my dad would, and does, wear. They reek of money and importance. They're nice, but I don't see how they're going to sell body wash.

I dress and stand in front of the backdrop. The photographer snaps a couple of photos, and I blink back the flashing dots. I tug at the collar, wishing I could rip off the bow tie, lose the jacket, and roll up my sleeves. I can do formal, but right now, my skin crawls. This whole situation just pisses me off.

I catch Dakota standing in the doorway with Blythe. She smiles at me, twisting her fingers in front of her. She's so goddamn beautiful and fucking perfect.

I want her. Not just for the summer. Longer. So much longer. And I'm tired of not being able to tell the world. How much better would tonight be if I could have her by my side for everyone to see?

"Little bit less of a smile," my dad says, wiping whatever smile was there off my lips. I didn't even realize I was smiling, but I guess staring at Dakota does that to me.

"Can we Photoshop his hands later?" my dad asks. "The tattoos are distracting."

I glance down at the small amount of ink visible. That's it. I've reached my limit. I stand and undo the bow tie, unbutton the shirt.

"I'm not doing this," I tell him.

"Doing what?"

"This." I pull off the jacket and toss it toward the rack. "Pretending to be this guy you want me to be."

Someone rushes to pick it up and place it on a hanger, and I feel like a dick for throwing a tantrum.

My dad sighs and lowers his voice. "What the hell does that even mean? Sit down."

"You don't want me in this campaign. You want some version of me that doesn't exist. Someone who wears suits every day and doesn't have tattoos, someone like you."

"Don't be ridiculous. The campaign—"

"Was great. Dakota's ideas were amazing, but you can't see that because they highlighted too much of me."

"It isn't the direction we want."

"Why? Because it showed the real me? Highlighted all the things you don't want me to be and are embarrassed to be associated with? I'm a tattooed hockey player who prefers being shirtless to wearing suits. That's who I am, and you're not going to change me to fit your agenda. You don't want me in your campaign, and I don't want to be, okay? Find someone else to be the face of Maverick Corporation's sack spray."

I'm tired of apologizing to him for who I am. I spent the last two years finally feeling free of those expectations with people who accepted me. I'm not wasting another second trying to be anything but who I am. A hockey player. A joker. A guy who thinks tattoos are badass. Someone who thinks life shouldn't be taken too seriously.

And a guy falling in love with a girl who makes him feel like all of that is okay.

Chapter Thirty-Two

DAKOTA

We say hurried goodbyes and walk back to the apartment. Johnny's quiet as we ride the elevator. I don't know exactly what was said between him and his dad, but I know that it resulted in Johnny storming off the photo shoot and that alone makes me want to scream at John Maverick Sr.

Since I can't do that, I hug Johnny's side. "Are you okay?"

He nods and presses a kiss to my temple. He takes Charli for a quick walk while I pace the apartment, brainstorming how to cheer him up.

I grab every bottle of lube he owns, more condoms than any two people could possibly use in a single night, my vibrator (that has seen little action this summer thanks to Johnny), a bottle of Mad Dog from the kitchen, and my laptop.

I'm browsing porn when he gets back, and at the sounds coming from my computer, he lifts a brow. "Whatcha got going on over there?"

I wave a hand in front of the coffee table. "I thought to myself, how does one cheer up Johnny Maverick."

He drops onto the couch beside me, chuckling, and slides his arms around my waist, holding me close to him.

I lift the hem of my dress and straddle him. The video playing is of a couple taking a vacation and, according to the very succinct description, having a threesome with *gasp* the maid. Not very original, but it was the best I could find on short notice.

"We should go on a day trip tomorrow. Drive out to the lake or somewhere. Just the two of us, and Charli, of course." I start on the buttons of his shirt, and he leans back into the cushion.

"Okay." His expression is still broody, but he shifts to pull out the hem of his shirt and groans as I glide my palms along his chest.

I lean forward and kiss the spot over his heart and then unbutton his pants. Scooting back, I drop to my knees in front of him and grab the tingling lube. I finally get another light chuckle as I free his dick and gasp in exaggerated porn-worthy fashion.

The video is past all the cheesy talking, and the couple starts having sex. Feminine moans fill the apartment. Johnny's gaze flits to the screen, but instead of holding there while I take him into my mouth, he uses his foot to close the lid of the laptop, and then he threads his fingers through my hair gently.

"Not doing it for you? You can pick another video."

"Right now, the only sexy little sounds I want to hear are the ones coming out of your mouth. Come here." His hands lift me gently by the neck until I'm back straddling him. He covers himself with a condom and then guides me down onto him.

"Johnny." His name comes out with a whimper. We both go still. I drop my forehead to his, feeling so full of him I can't breathe. He lifts my chin with a thumb, staring into my eyes with an expression that makes my heart race and my pussy clench around him.

"Thank you for wanting to make this shitty night better, but it already is just being here with you." He places a soft kiss on my lips, and his voice softens and comes out gruff. "This is perfect. You're perfect."

A lump forms in my throat, and the back of my eyes burn. I don't know what to say, so I lavish him with kisses and then bite his bicep playfully to lighten the moment. He responds by slanting his mouth over mine and holding me hostage with the sweetest, toe-curling kiss. He holds me close as he continues to slowly lift my hips and drive into me from below at a pace that's unhurried and savoring.

Sex with Johnny is always consuming in a way it never has been with anyone else, but tonight is different. It's intimate and real.

I moan into his mouth as I fall apart around him, and he whispers, "Perfect."

I WAKE UP EARLY, NAKED AND SMILING, TO JOHNNY'S DEEP VOICE.

"Morning, baby." The bed dips, and he drapes an arm across my waist. "Wake up, gorgeous."

"It's Saturday," I murmur, snuggling Charli closer to my chest. "We want to sleep in."

"No can do. Charli's got a hot date, and so do you."

I pry my eyes open, ready to joke about not seeing a hot date anywhere, but that would be a lie. Johnny's shirtless, and well… he's hot.

"Our day date?" I ask, a wave of excitement washing over me to get out and spend the day with him. "Can I wear what I have on?" I ask, dropping the sheet to flash him my naked body.

He drops a kiss to each nipple. "Cover these up." Then he places a tender kiss on my lower stomach. "And this. They're mine."

He stands, lifts his arms, and pushes his thumb and pointer finger together to make a window, then looks at me through it like he's memorizing the moment. I love when he does that. "You're a hard woman to resist, but I have a surprise. I'm going to take Charli upstairs. Declan is going to watch her for the night."

"Why? Where are we going?"

He grins and rubs his hands together. "Pack a bag, little lady. We're going to Vegas."

We take a midmorning flight, arriving in Las Vegas a few hours later. Johnny dons a Twins hat instead of the usual Wildcats one he wears and sunglasses. He might be trying for incognito, but people still stare at him like he's someone famous. I guess he is.

Inside our suite, I gape and walk around, taking it all in. A living area with couches and a dining table and small kitchenette, and a separate bedroom that's as large as my apartment with Reagan and Ginny back in Valley.

"Johnny Maverick, what did you do?"

He chuckles. "Like it?"

"Like?!" It's amazing. I walk to the window, where a view of the strip lies below. It's going to look incredible at night with all the lights.

"What do you want to do first?" he asks, joining me by the window and wrapping his arms around my lower back.

We only have one day, and I want to see it all. And leave plenty of time to enjoy this room later.

After walking through the casino downstairs, we head outside and cruise the strip and malls. We go into stores where Johnny insists on buying me things no matter how much I try to protest. I get new shoes, sunglasses, a blinged-out trucker style hat that made him laugh, and a necklace with a star charm on it that he surprised me with. I didn't even see him buy it. It's gold with what I hope aren't diamonds in the center, but knowing Johnny, I'm sure they are.

"Oooh, we gotta get one last thing." He's wearing my many shopping bags around his arms.

"No more," I say. "I don't need anything else.

"Need and want. Totally different things." He winks. "You need and want this one, though. Trust."

Somehow, he fishes out his wallet and gets us two large drinks the size of my arm with bright yellow, crazy straws.

"Well, that looks dangerous," I say and taste it. "Oh, wow. Hello, I'm drunk."

He laughs and takes a sip of his. "Sweet and strong. Like you."

We continue strolling through the city, drinking and laughing until the sun starts to fall. Back at the hotel, we shower together, and then I shoo him out of the bathroom to get ready. It's been a day of him surprising me, but tonight I have one for him.

I peek out of the bedroom into the living area. He's parked in front of the TV, looking seriously hot in a white button-down with the sleeves rolled up his forearms. His dark hair is styled and free of the hat he wore all day.

I'm silent, but his gaze slides over to the doorway, and he sits up.

"Ready?" I ask.

"Always." He stands as I walk out, moving toward me in slow, measured steps while his gaze rakes over me. "The black dress finally makes another appearance."

It's a simple dress. I think I paid all of forty dollars for it, but it's short and tight, and well, the way he looks at me, I feel like a million bucks. I paired it with my red Converse because they just felt like me.

"Fuuuck, Kota." He makes a circle around me. "I had big plans of showing you off downstairs, but now..." He stretches his hands out around my waist. "Maybe we should stay in."

"Or maybe a little delayed gratification will make it hotter."

"Hotter?" His brows raise. "Baby, I don't know if you've noticed, but I run hot."

"I might have noticed."

"And you." He cups my ass and takes my mouth, pressing a far softer kiss on my lips than his grip and words suggested. "You're a rocket, and I just want to hold on tight and let the flames melt my face off."

I laugh at his ridiculous words. He moves to the dining table and pulls a bottle of champagne out of a bucket of ice. "Do you want a drink before we go?"

I bite my lip. "Maybe we save it for after?"

His eyes darken. "You're killing me."

"I'll make it up to you later," I promise.

He doesn't drop my hand all night. We play a few games, but mostly we drink and engage in public displays of affection that have been so limited in Minnesota. Being his date or girlfriend or whatever I am is fun—so much fun.

Having all of Johnny's attention for the world to see is not something I think I'll ever get enough of. I do have a niggling worry in the back of my mind that someone might recognize him and post a picture of us, but I push it away and just enjoy our time away.

Once we get back, I only have two weeks left of the internship, and then goodbye Wildcats and Maverick.

I'm happily drunk and enjoying his big hand splayed out on my lower back while we sit at the bar on the lobby level of our hotel.

"I feel like doing something crazy," I say. "It must be the Vegas air."

"I think it's the alcohol. We should feed you."

"I'm not hungry." I drag my fingernails across the top of his thigh.

He groans and throws back the rest of his drink.

"Can I get you another?" The bartender is quick to take the empty glass.

"Two shots of Rumple Minze," Johnny says.

"That's my favorite shot," I squeal.

"Almost like I ordered it on purpose." He chuckles, and I realize I'm definitely drunk. My face is hot, and I feel so free and happy.

"Four shots!" I call out.

Johnny's mouth twists into an amused smirk.

The bartender sets the four shots of the clear liquid in front of us. Johnny picks up one and hands it to me and then takes the other. His knees close my legs in on either side, and he leans forward.

"To getting to spend the day with you and touching you any time I want." He places a kiss on my lips and then takes the shot. I do the same, enjoying the minty liquid on my tongue.

On the opposite side of the bar, a man with gray hair walks up, a girl on each arm. They are young and beautiful, and their combined age probably doesn't equal his, but the three of them look perfectly content as he orders drinks, and the women hang on either arm like accessories.

"Look, it's you in forty years," I joke.

He laughs it off.

"What's the craziest thing you've ever done?"

He gets a deer in headlights look, like maybe he doesn't want to tell me.

"Threesome? Foursome?"

"Three is plenty of people. After that, it starts to feel a little gang bang-y for me." He juts his chin. "What about you? What's the craziest thing you've ever done?"

"I don't know." I'm a little embarrassed to tell him it's probably one of the many times he's gotten me off in public. My sexual experiences have been far less exciting than his. And for reasons I refuse to think about, I want him to think of me too when he thinks about all the crazy, fun times he's had. I want to be his number one.

"I have an idea," I say, heart racing before I've even told him.

"What's that?" His lips caress my shoulder as he waits for my answer.

"Let's do something crazy. I mean, we are in Vegas. If we can't top both of our lists tonight, then we're not trying hard enough."

His deep laughter boosts my excitement.

"Think of the possibilities. Sex in public, or maybe a sex club. Are those really a thing? Ooooh, what about a threesome? We'll have to figure out how to make that crazier than a foursome, but I believe in us."

His head lifts slowly, and he studies my face. "You're serious? *You* want to have a threesome? I thought you weren't into the whole idea."

"And I thought you'd jump at the chance to add another person to our sexcapades." Seriously, I thought Johnny would be all about a threesome. Especially with me after I've given him so much crap about it. "Do you not want to?"

"You should do it if it's something you're curious about, and, of course, I'd want to be there to experience it with you."

"You're a pretty great guy, Johnny Maverick."

"Agreeing to a threesome doesn't exactly make me a saint."

"You underestimate yourself a lot." I rest my hands along his forearms. "This summer, hanging out with you, the fun, the sex…" I start to choke up. Jesus, I must be drunker than I thought. "It's meant a lot to me."

"Same. I don't want it to end. Be mine after the summer." His arms circle around my middle and squeeze until I'm basically in his lap.

"What?" My heart races. "But I'll be in Valley, and you'll be in Minnesota."

"So what? I could be a baller long-distance boyfriend."

"Johnny, I—" My head spins.

"Just think about it, okay?"

I nod, pick up the last two glasses, and hand him one. "To doing something crazy."

We leave the bar drunk and giggly and go up to the club on the top floor. The music is loud, and we get lost in each other, moving to the rhythm, hands roaming. I'd call it dancing, but if there wasn't music, it'd just be called foreplay.

"Ready to get our crazy on?" I ask him.

"All right. A threesome for the lady. You're sure you want to do this?"

"Yeah, it'll be fun. I want to know what the big deal is."

"Okay, then. What's your type, baby?"

"I don't know." I look around at all the beautiful girls. I'm easy, apparently, because I can picture kissing any number of them, but the second I picture their grubby paws on Maverick, I'm rethinking this idea.

"Take your time. The night is young. There's another club next door. Maybe we can find some other ways to make this night the craziest yet. Want to take a walk?"

I lace my fingers with his, and we leave the hotel. Heat radiates off the sidewalk. From inside me too. I'm bubbling with energy and lust and so many emotions I feel like I might burst with it all.

We get in the back of a line for a dance club. We're waiting outside, neither of us really caring that we're not inside.

I'm turned around, not paying attention to the line as I kiss Maverick. I have never been a clingy partner, but I'm flush against him and still can't seem to get close enough.

The girl in line behind him clears her throat, and I look up to see the people in front of me have moved, and we're holding up the line.

"Sorry," I say.

"It's okay." She smiles and tosses her shiny, black hair over one shoulder. "If I had one of those, I wouldn't need to go inside the club."

Johnny ducks his head bashfully, playing it off with a small grin.

I bite my lip and look at him to see if he's thinking what I am. She's beautiful and curvy, and knowing how much Maverick likes boobs, he'll be able to dive right into the double Ds she's sporting. I feel a little ragey about the two of them touching, but fair is fair. I know how a threesome works. Maybe it'll be hot watching them together. Then again, perhaps I'll toss her out—game-time decision.

"Why don't you go ahead of us," he says. "Need to chat with my girlfriend." He pulls me out of the line.

"Where are we going?" I ask, stretching my legs to keep up with him. "She was perfect. Don't you think so?"

He runs a hand through his hair. "She was gorgeous, yeah."

"Let's ask her to come back to our room."

"That's what you want?"

"Yes." I laugh at his resistance.

"You want me to kiss her? Fuck her?"

I ball my hands into fists at my side. "As long as I get to be a part of it."

He takes my hand and places it over his heart. "I'd do anything for you, Kota, but don't ask me to do this. You don't want to any more than I do."

"Boring Dakota didn't, but drunk, fun Dakota does. You've had threesomes. I want to know what it was like."

"It was impersonal and…" he struggles for words.

"Hot?"

"Yeah, sure, that too, I guess, but it wasn't anywhere close to being as amazing as it is with us. What you and I have is special."

I try to laugh it off, but he won't let me. "I'm serious, baby. If you need to do it, so you understand, then I want to be there, but not tonight. Today is about us. I just want you."

I throw my hands up in the air. "We're supposed to be having a wild and crazy summer."

This all feels too heavy right now, and that isn't what we signed up for. Fun, casual, and fleeting.

"Best summer of my life. I wouldn't change a thing about it."

Relief washes over me, and I know there'll be no threesome happening tonight. Maybe someday, but not when I'm holding on to the days left with him like sand slipping through my fingers. He's right. Tonight is just about us.

He kisses me and then leans his forehead against mine. "I do have another wild and crazy idea, though, if you're up for it. It would top the list for sure."

"Does it include sex because this day has been one big cocktease?"

His laughter tickles my face. "It sure does, but first… wanna get hitched?"

Chapter Thirty-Three

JOHNNY

Dakota laughs.

"Okay, not the reaction I was hoping for."

"You're serious?" Her cheeks are flushed from the hot Vegas night.

"Yeah, let's get married in Vegas. It'll be awesome, and then I can fuck my hot wife upstairs in our room."

"You can fuck your hot *slam piece* any time you want. No paperwork necessary."

"Wild and crazy, remember?"

She keeps looking at me like she thinks I'm going to change my mind. I'm so serious. She grins. "I don't know."

"Be mine, Kota. All mine."

She glances back at the chapel. "This is crazy."

"Exactly," I say. "Sex against the window in our hotel suite as Mister and Mrs. I'm not sure it gets crazier than that."

"You're insane."

"Probably," I agree. "Marry me anyway?"

She shakes her head side to side, and a slow smile spreads

across her face until she's grinning up at me. "Let's do it."

"Really?" My chest expands.

"Yeah. When in Rome." She waves a hand. "Or, in this case, Vegas."

We giggle all the way to the chapel. It's busy, but I'm able to slip some extra cash to the lady at the desk and get us to the front of the line. This might have been my best idea yet.

"Do you have a ring?" she asks as we're picking out packages. They have everything: dresses, flowers, photos, the works.

Ah shit. A ring.

"I don't need one," Dakota says. She steps closer. "Absolutely do not buy me a ring for a fake wedding, Johnny Maverick."

I pull the hair tie from her wrist and loop it around her ring finger three times. "That'll do for now, and it's a *real* wedding. Last chance to back out."

"No way. This place is amazing. I wish I had some white Chucks." She kicks the heels of her red Converse together twice.

It's gaudy and smells like cigarette smoke in here, but I don't care.

Dakota opts for no flowers but picks out a veil that clips into her hair and drapes down to her shoulders.

"You never dreamed of having a big wedding?" We wait at the back of the chapel for the couple in front of us to finish their ceremony.

"No." Her voice is quiet. "When my mom died, I struggled to picture a wedding day without her there with me, you know?"

"I do in a weird sort of way. Can you imagine what my dad would say if I called him and told him to hop in his jet for a Vegas elopement?"

She cups my cheek. "It's his loss. You're a good man."

When it's our turn, Dakota and I walk up to the front and stand looking at one another as the guy talks about love and marriage. I'm only half listening because I'm lost in her. She's gorgeous. The black dress of my dreams and that white veil clipped into her red hair. Her cheeks are flushed, and she smiles at me so big that my heart thumps loudly in my chest.

Mine. One word that sums up exactly how I feel about her. Mine, not because I want to keep her all to myself (though for the rest of the night that's exactly what I plan to do), but because there's no piece of her that I don't want to know. I want all her words and every inch of her body. Her thoughts, her dreams, all her fantasies. I want to know them, and I want to make them come true for her.

The man stops talking and looks at me. Oh, right, that's my cue.

"I do." I wink at my bride.

He starts in on his spiel again, this time facing Dakota. I hold my breath. This is it. It didn't occur to me until right now that this summer might not have been as epic for her as it has been for me. Maybe she doesn't want to be mine and everything that comes with it.

"I do," she says and bites her lip like she's trying to keep herself from laughing.

I kiss her before the guy finishes pronouncing us husband and wife, then pick her up and carry her out of the chapel to recessional music.

Outside underneath the lights of Vegas, I place her feet on the ground. My chest feels so full staring at her and seeing her mirror back everything I'm feeling in her expression.

I lean down and whisper, "So much better than a threesome."

She throws her arms around my neck and kisses me. Neither of us seems to be able to stop. We're a smiling, giggling, kissing spectacle as we hurry back to the hotel.

"Oh my god, did we just do that for real?" she asks when we get into the room, and she sees herself in the mirror.

"Yep, wifey." I drop a kiss on her shoulder.

"Husband." Her fingers work the buttons on my shirt, and she slides it off my shoulders. I hold still as she undresses me at a slow, torturous pace. She runs her fingernails down my stomach and cups my balls. They're heavy with lust, and my dick leaks as she starts to get on her knees.

"Uh-uh," I say. "Turn around and place your hands on the window."

Her eyes spark with desire. She does as I command, and I make her wait, popping the champagne and bringing the bottle with me.

"Open," I say as I get close. Her perfect red lips part. I take a long drink and then spit it into her mouth. It drips down her face and onto her cleavage.

I push up her dress until the black material bunches at her waist and drop to my knees to place a kiss on her ass while I work down her panties. I cover myself with a condom and stand tall.

"Can I borrow your wedding ring, wifey?"

She giggles and pulls the hair tie off her ring finger.

I place the tie around her wrists, smiling at the red rubber band. "Hands together on the window."

A fucking hair tie as a wedding band. Yeah, she's definitely going to need something a little flashier, but it was the perfect solution at the moment and fits us somehow. That little hair tie has seen some *things*.

She moans as I push inside of her from behind.

"All mine." I nip at her neck around the lacy veil, enjoying the feel of its cheap, scratchy material as I pump in and out of her.

It may have been a drunken decision, but it feels like the best one I've ever made.

I WAKE WITH A CHAMPAGNE HANGOVER AND A SMILE ON MY FACE. Dakota is wrapped around me, her red hair fanning out on my chest. Her dress never made it all the way off. Neither did her shoes. We were a fucking mess last night.

I grab my phone to check the time and then snap a picture of her long legs tangled up with mine and her hand, complete with new finger accessory, in view on my chest.

She stirs with a cute little groan.

"Wakey, wakey, wifey." I place a kiss on the crown of her head. "Gotta leave for the airport soon."

She curls into my chest.

"Oh, my head is pounding." Her voice is husky with sleep. "What the hell did we do last night?"

"Just the usual." I slip from bed and grab some Tylenol and water for her as she sits up. "Drank our asses off, almost had a threesome, and then decided to get hitched instead."

I kiss her and drop both medicine and water on the bed in front of her. Her lips don't move under mine, and when I stand tall she's staring at me with a weird expression.

"Did you say got hitched?"

I point at her head, and she runs a hand over the veil as if she can't believe what she's feeling. She gasps audibly, rushes to her feet, and goes to the mirror.

"You don't remember?" I sit on the edge of the bed as I pull my T-shirt over my head.

"I remember drinking Rumple Minze, then dancing, and standing in line at another club…" She trails off, rubbing the lace of the veil as she studies the floor. "I wanted to bring that girl back for a threesome, and then…" She looks at her finger and the red rubber band on it and squeezes her eyes shut.

"Oh my gosh, Johnny." She pulls the veil from her hair. "How are you not freaking out."

I shrug because I don't know how to answer that. I knew she'd been drinking, but I guess I didn't realize how drunk she was. I was drunk, but I knew what I was doing. I'd do it all again, too.

"Last night was incredible. I wouldn't change any of it."

"You want to be married to me? We aren't even together. I mean not really. This was supposed to be a summer fling."

"I told you last night. I want you to be mine."

"I think we skipped a few steps. I could be your girlfriend, for starters."

"Girlfriend, wife." I shrug.

"Seriously, Maverick. What are we going to do? You are a professional hockey player who has assets to protect, and I'm…. Oh god, my internship."

"Breathe, baby." I rub her shoulders. "I'm not worried about my assets. You wouldn't even let me buy you a real ring last night.

I doubt you're going to clear out my bank account when I'm not looking. And this actually helps your internship. They can't fire you if you're married to a player."

She kneads her forehead with two fingers. "I know this is hard for you to understand, but I need them to believe I'm the right person for the job because of my work and not because I tricked some hot hockey guy into letting me work his endorsement and then married him to keep my job."

"You and I both know that isn't how it went down."

"But that's what they'll think."

"I've never cared much what other people think."

Her eyes fall closed again, and her chest rises and falls with a deep breath. "We should keep this between us until we figure out what to do."

"All right." Little bit of a kick in the gut to see her second-guess being with me. "When we get back, we'll figure it out together, okay? Let me bask in my newlywed glow a little longer."

"I can't believe you'd want to be married to me." She melts in my arms, and I hold on tight.

"Easily the best decision I ever made."

WE GET BACK SUNDAY AFTERNOON AND LIE AROUND THE REST OF the night. Monday morning, Dakota is up with the sun, lacing her sneakers and taking Charli for a run. She hasn't said anything else about our Vegas wedding, but I know she's still spinning.

I'm making her smoothie when she walks through the front

door, sweaty and red-faced. She lets Charli off the leash, and my girls move toward me.

"For you." I hand her a glass and then set Charli's food bowl on the floor. "And for you."

"Thanks." She sets it on the counter. "I need to catch my breath first. I'm out of shape. It hurts."

"When you ran track, what distance did you do?"

"The eight hundred was my best event. High school state record."

I grin. "How come you quit?"

She shrugs, picks up the glass, and moves into the living room to sit in the leather recliner. Avoiding. Interesting. I always assumed she quit because being a college athlete is a lot of fucking work.

"Kota." I sit across from her on the couch and kick up my feet on the coffee table. "Wifey."

She glares at the last endearment.

"Come on, tell me. I've never heard you talk about it, but you obviously still love to run. Was it too much with school? Bad coach?"

She meets my gaze on my last guess.

"Bad coach?" I repeat.

"Good coach, bad human."

I raise my brows, waiting for her to elaborate.

She sighs. "If I tell you, you have to promise to never mention it again. Ever."

Charli trots in and lies at her feet.

"We'll see." I'm not promising anything until I know the details.

"When I was in high school, I had a close relationship with

my track coach."

Adrenaline starts coursing through me. I don't know where this is going, but I already know I'm going to be pissed.

"He was good to me. He stayed late and came in on weekends to help me improve. He was young, in his midthirties, and all the girls thought he was hot. We called him Coach Hottie. God, we were so young and naive." She stares into her lap.

I stay quiet, grinding down on my molars.

"One night after the last track meet of my senior year, he asked me to come to his office. Up until the very minute it started, I convinced myself that any romantic vibes I was getting from him were just my overactive teenage brain. Once he started undressing me, I don't know; I can't explain it. I was horrified and realized how stupid I'd been."

My jaw feels like glass, and rage like I've never felt before builds in my chest. "The fucker raped you?"

"No." Her voice hardens. "I stopped him before it went that far, but I was so ashamed. I totally flirted with him and was inappropriate, so I don't blame him for thinking I wanted him, but you have to believe me when I say I never thought it would go anywhere." Tears fill her eyes. "After my mom died, I was lost for a while. I didn't even realize how lost I was until that very moment when I was confronted with how far I'd go to feel that type of attention from someone. Anyone. He made me feel special. I thought that he saw something in me. I was an okay runner at best when I started. Without him, I'm not sure I ever would have won any races. He even helped me get into Valley. My dad didn't know anything about applying for colleges or financial aid, and he was still a mess too."

"Of course I believe you. What happened was not your fault."

"I know." Her voice is too quiet, and she still doesn't look at me. "Bullshit."

"Okay, fine, I'm working on it. I know that he was wrong, but what I did wasn't right either."

"And so you quit because you didn't feel like you earned it?" I'm starting to get a feel for Dakota, who she is inside, why she's so adamant that she prove herself with the Wildcats internship, and her desire to always be on an even playing field with her peers.

"I know it doesn't make sense. I won those medals fair and square. I trained my ass off, but would I have done all of that if he hadn't taken a special interest in me? And did he only do that because he wanted to sleep with me? I'm so embarrassed that I let it go that far. I didn't want anything that he'd been a part of or that reminded me of how dumb I'd been. I thought when I got to Valley, I could put it behind me, but I couldn't shake the feeling that I didn't deserve any of it."

I sit with her in the chair, pulling her into my lap and smoothing a hand down her ponytail. She's still slick with sweat and sticks to my bare chest. "I'm so sorry, baby."

"Thank you."

"I want to kill him. I hate that you quit something you love. I don't even have to know you broke the state record to know you deserved it. You give your all to everything."

"It turned out okay. I stopped running altogether for a while, then when I realized that just made me more miserable, I picked it back up. I still run almost every day, or I did until recently. I can't seem to pry myself out of bed as easily these days." Her lips tip into a half smile.

A memory floats back to me. "That was the prick we ran into when we were out running by your dad's house." I clench my hand into a fist.

"Yeah, that's the first time I'd seen him since I graduated. They've been trying to get me to come back and be inducted into the Hall of Fame, and I just can't bring myself to do it. I don't want to face him."

"As your husband, I will happily drive to Kansas and beat him with my hockey stick."

"As my slam piece, I'm going to need you to play it a little cooler."

"I'd run through hell and back for you, wifey."

"I know." She cups my cheek. "How about showering with me instead?"

Chapter Thirty-Four

DAKOTA

I'm assigned to tours at the arena with Reese for our second to last week at the Wildcats. We're a good pair—him with tons of history about the team and me with experience leading groups. It's good to be away from my desk, and I have very little time to overthink everything going on.

Namely, I am Mrs. Johnny Maverick. How weird is that? I haven't told a soul. Not even Reagan.

Johnny plays it off like it's no big deal. He asked me to give it a week and think about it, but what's there to think about? We've been messing around for a month. We haven't even said I love you, and he wants to be married?

I think a threesome might have been a saner choice. What's the worst way that could have gone?

On Friday, Rhett and Sienna come to stay with us.

"It's so good to see you." I hug my friend.

"I can't believe you've been this close all summer, and I'm just now seeing you." She's positively glowing. She's so happy.

"We're going to make up for it tonight." I glance at Rhett.

"Girls' night."

"Always stealing my girl away."

"You've had her all to yourself for weeks."

He smiles and looks at Sienna with hearts in his eyes. I love their love.

"Go drop off your stuff. I can't wait to catch up," I tell her.

She and Rhett take their stuff to my room, where they're staying for the weekend. We were going to have them stay in Johnny's room, but mine is cleaner since it's used less. I guess we did only need one bed this summer.

My guy lies on the pink couch, something he only does when he's trying to get my attention, and holds his arms out for me to join him. "Maybe you should repurpose this couch into a throw pillow or something."

"I have to get ready. I'm taking Sienna to Wild's, and I want to get there before it's too busy to find a table."

"That's where I was going to take Rauthruss," Johnny says, still wiggling around on the couch, trying to get comfortable.

"Called it." I walk over to him, and he takes my hand in his, closing his eyes and smiling.

"Are you going to tell Sienna about…" He runs his thumb over the hair tie on my ring finger. His dark eyes open while he waits for my answer.

"I don't know," I admit. "Probably not. I don't want everyone to get in the middle of it when we haven't even figured it out ourselves. Are you going to tell Rhett?"

"Not if you don't want me to."

"But you want to?"

"Yeah." He shrugs. "It's pretty epic news."

He's so all in with this, and I don't understand it.

"You can tell him, but make him swear he will not tell Adam. If Reagan finds out from someone that isn't me, she will show up here and beat me to death with a shoe."

He chuckles. "She'd have to get through me."

"Please. You're the biggest softy ever." I let him tug me down onto the couch with him. "She'd fake tears, and you'd be a goner."

"I'm no softy," he says, rolling his hips into me to show me how not soft he is.

SIENNA AND I WALK TO WILD'S, LINKING ARMS AND CHATTING A mile a minute.

"Are you loving Minnesota?" she asks as we slide into a table with our drinks.

"I am, actually."

"I'm so glad. Now you can move here, and I'll have a friend."

"A friend you haven't seen in almost two months even though she's been forty-five minutes away."

"I know. I'm sorry. We have been so busy at the rink and…" She smiles. "Just hanging out at the new apartment."

"How's living together?"

"Amazing." She gets that dreamy look on her face. They're so in love.

"I'm happy for you."

"Thanks." She leans forward with her elbows on the table. "Now. I've waited an appropriate amount of time before harassing you for details, but spill! What is going on with you and Maverick?"

My eyes fall to the red rubber band looped around my finger, and I curl my hand so it's out of view. "We're hanging out."

"Is it still just for the summer, or are you thinking it could be more serious?"

"I don't know," I answer honestly. I consider telling her about the wedding, but I just can't bring myself to say the words. *Oh, hey, Johnny and I got married on a whim in Vegas.* Seriously, who does that with a guy she's just hooking up with for a summer?

"He's totally smitten. I could see it all over his face."

"He does seem to be, but, come on, it's Johnny. He lives in the now."

"You don't think he could do a real relationship?"

"I don't know, and if I asked him that, he'd be like, this is real, baby." I roll my eyes but smile. "Everything is real to him. He's unconventional and spontaneous, and I love that about him, but I'm not. I like traditional. It's how I always pictured it. Plus, I'm going back to Valley, and he's going to be here and traveling. It would be hard."

"But not impossible."

"You were supposed to be the other levelheaded one of the group," I tell her. "You're as bad as the other two now."

She grins. "I can't help it. Love—"

"Changes people?"

"I don't think we change so much as we realize what it is we really care about. Everyone has their quirks. You have to figure out your deal breakers." She tips her drink toward me. "You like traditional, but is spontaneous and unconventional enough to make you walk away from someone you love?"

"Apparently not," I mutter as I turn the glass in my hands.

"So you do love him then?"

"He's Maverick. Everyone loves him. You should see the people at the Wildcats. Most rookies walk in needing to prove themselves, or that's what my friend Reese says, he's another intern, but Johnny just stepped right into a team that is so excited to have him. He has this effect on people where they change their expectations for him. Without even meaning to, I think. He's charming and fun, and people want to like him and be near him. Me included."

"And we all thought you were immune to the Maverick charm."

"He chipped away at my better judgment."

"Or maybe you realized that your better judgment was getting in the way of you being deliriously happy?"

"It was a fun summer. Let's leave it at that for now."

"Okay. But I'm rooting for you two, just so you know."

Johnny and Rhett join us a few hours later. Rhett and Sienna go to the bar to get drinks, and Johnny crowds in beside me, resting an arm around the back of the booth. It's weird not touching him in public after letting our guard down so much in Vegas, but in here, people would definitely notice if we showed any signs that we're together.

"Did you tell her?" he asks.

"No." I shake my head, expecting disappointment to be etched in his features, but instead it's relief.

"Oh, good."

"Good?"

He chuckles. "I didn't tell Rauthruss either, so if you told her I was about to get an earful."

"Yeah, probably better we don't tell anyone. None of our friends can keep secrets from each other. It'll be around the group faster than you can say holy elopement."

"Holy elopement," he says, grinning. "I know we're supposed to keep things on the low, but can I convince you to be my date tomorrow night? Rauthruss wants to take Sienna to some fancy-ass restaurant downtown. I had to make a call to get us in."

"Throwing your name around in this town, huh?"

"Just for a good cause."

"I think it's sweet. And yes, but three feet rule." I look at the small space between us. "Scooch."

"Yes, wifey," he whispers and moves down the wooden bench.

THE NEXT NIGHT WE'RE LED THROUGH AN ELEGANT RESTAURANT where the sound of wine being poured into glasses overpowers that of the polite conversation around us. I feel like I need to whisper. As usual, Johnny fits right in. He stands behind me as I take my seat and then takes the chair beside me.

He looks too good to be true. He skipped the suit jacket and wears gray dress pants and a black dress shirt that's open at the collar and rolled up over his forearms.

Rhett looks nice too, but his nervous expression tells me he isn't as comfortable in this place.

Johnny orders a bottle of champagne which makes me laugh. Yeah, he fits in just fine here.

"I hear congrats are in order," I tell Rhett after we have drinks in front of us.

His eyes widen, and he looks from Johnny to me. I feel like I'm missing something.

I try again. "Sienna told me that your hockey camps this summer were fully booked, and you already have a waiting list for next year. That's so exciting."

"Oh, that. Yeah, it went really well."

"I guess having a national champ running it is good for business," Johnny says and lifts his glass. "Congrats, buddy."

The food is terrific, and we go through an entire bottle of champagne, then order another with dessert. I'm feeling happy and frustrated that Johnny is so far away, and I can't touch him in here. Times like this where we're not hiding, and we're out doing things other couples do, I can see it. I can picture us doing this for real. But I don't know what that would look like with us a thousand miles apart.

He catches me staring at him and lifts a brow. "See something you like?"

"Maybe." I inch my chair closer.

He smirks. "Tsk. Tsk. Three feet."

"Two and a half," I say and slide my foot under the table so our legs touch. He drops a hand to my knee and grazes his fingers across my smooth skin.

I'm lost in his touch when Rhett clears his throat and Johnny's hand on my leg stills and then squeezes in warning. He rushes to get his phone and aims it across the table. I look up in time to see Rhett get down on one knee. Sienna brings both hands to her mouth in a gasp, her eyes full of tears.

Rhett's words are sweet, though I hear little of them because I'm too stuck in my own head thinking *I want that*. All of that. To date, fall in love, move in together, get engaged. We've done things all wrong, Johnny and me, and there's no taking it back. Can I really go back to Valley as his girlfriend after this summer? It all feels too messy.

"Yes!" Sienna shouts and frames his face with her hands. "Yes, I'll marry you." There's polite applause around the restaurant.

Rhett slides the big diamond on Sienna's finger, and then they go back to kissing. I run my thumb along the elastic on my finger. It isn't about the diamond. It's about the thought that went into it. Rhett probably spent weeks planning this moment. He was sure about his decision before he acted. It wasn't a drunken whim.

"Congratulations!" Johnny refills our glasses with champagne, and we toast to the happy couple. I feel sick to my stomach, but I plaster on a smile for my friends.

We leave soon after. Johnny invites them to hang out with us and continue the celebration, but when we get to the apartment, they're so lost in each other I'm not surprised when they decide to spend the rest of the night alone.

"Crazy night, right?" Johnny asks as we get ready for bed.

"You knew."

He nods. "Yeah, Rauthruss told me last night. It's why I didn't tell him about us."

"Right. Yeah, I'm so glad I didn't tell Sienna now."

"We can tell them in a week or two when their news has died down. I almost missed the whole thing with your sexy legs taunting me. Rauthruss would have been *piiissed*."

"It's sweet that you did all of that for them."

"It was nothing. I'm happy for them and happy to be a part of it."

"It made me realize that's what I want," I say, taking a seat next to him on the bed.

"Check." He traces an imaginary check mark in the air. "Wifey."

"I mean, all of it. I want to date someone, fall in love, then get engaged. We've done everything out of order."

"Yeah, but it was all pretty great." He shrugs.

"You're not hearing me, Johnny. I want that. This summer has been amazing, but it's ending, and maybe we should stick to the original plan and leave it at that."

"You want to break up?"

"Are we even together?" My laugh is brittle. "We decided to use each other for sex all summer, and then we got married in Vegas."

"I was there. I know what happened, Kota. Your description isn't accurate. It was never about using each other, and you know it. But whatever it was we did, I don't regret any of it. Do you?"

I don't regret it, not really, but if we hadn't gotten married in Vegas would he still be trying to make this work? And the real kicker, the thing I can't shake is the image of Johnny the first week in Minnesota when he got hurt. He begged me to stay because I was comfortable and familiar, a piece of Valley and his friendships that he'd made at college. When I leave, he'll go out more and make friends, meet new people. He'll start his new life here, and then will he still want this?

I don't answer, and he nods slowly. "Guess that's my answer."

He sits up. "We're good together. I've never had this with anyone. Ever. Maybe it doesn't fit into whatever box you're trying to force it in, but it doesn't make it any less."

"Johnny, I—" My voice cracks as I realize he's not just talking about me right now. I've done exactly what his dad does to him—

made him feel like he isn't good enough.

He holds up a hand and moves toward the door.

"Where are you going?"

"I'm going to take a walk. Believe it or not, sometimes I do know when to walk away."

I go to bed feeling like an ass, hoping he comes back. He does two hours later. The bed dips with his weight, and he lies beside me.

"I'm sorry," I whisper.

"Me too." His mouth slants over mine. And then there are no more words. We spend the rest of the night speaking our love language of kisses and touches that make promises and dreams neither of us dares to say out loud.

Chapter Thirty-Five

JOHNNY

Monday morning, I stare down at the picture I took of Dakota in Vegas draped all over me, and then I glance over at where she sleeps on the other side of the bed currently. Yesterday we spent the day with Sienna and Rhett, and last night instead of rehashing our shit, we fell into bed and had sex instead.

I want this to work. I'll give her whatever she wants. She wants a diamond ring and an elaborate proposal? I'm on it. She'll never even see it coming. In fact, I'm a little pissed at myself for not going bigger the first time. I was in the moment, a little drunk, and I just wanted her to be mine.

But, as soon as she goes to work, let the planning begin. The most epic of proposals. I'm thinking something big. I'll make a movie trailer starring our friends, rent out a theater, fly in everyone, and have five or six different rings for her to pick from. No, something even bigger. I'll work out the details later.

I have an email from Hugh asking what I want to do about the marriage—his way of nicely asking if I want to file the paperwork for an annulment. I don't respond. Not necessary, Hugh. I'm gonna fix this.

But first, I open up Instagram and post the picture of Dakota, cropped so it's just a sexy leg tangled in the sheet with one single word. *Mine.*

She's mine, and it's time to figure this out so I can tell the world.

I shower and make her morning smoothie. I can be an epic husband. I've already been an epic summer hookup, if I do say so myself. I just need to show her how serious I am about this. Big and bold gestures, baby, bring it.

I grab my phone and scroll through local jewelry stores while I wait for her to wake up. I'm anxious, foot tapping, mind racing with possibilities. Is she a round cut or square cut kind of girl? Regular diamond, or would she like a yellow or black or something totally different than a diamond?

"What the hell, Johnny?" I look up from my phone as she rushes out from the bedroom, still in the oversized T-shirt she slept in.

"Morning, baby. Sorry about the noise. I tried a new smoothie recipe. It sucked, so I had to start over."

"I'm not talking about the noise. I'm talking about this." She holds out her phone to show me my post of her leg on my Instagram.

"You should see the original. Your veil is covering your face, and your arm is around my chest—"

"Why would you post this?"

"I wanted everyone to know I'm taken. I'm in this. Not just for the summer, for real. And I didn't show your face or tag you."

She closes her eyes and blows out a breath. "They know, Johnny.

They know it's me."

"Who? Our friends?" I shrug. "They already know."

"No, my boss, your teammates, my coworkers."

I look at the picture again. "Your legs are memorable, but I doubt they're going to be able to tell from a grainy picture. I blurred it a little, so it's harder to tell." I wink. I thought of all of this already.

I get another sigh. "The shoes, Johnny. They know because of my shoes."

I bring it up again and see the red Converse at the bottom of the photo. They're such a staple in her wardrobe, I didn't even notice. "You said you wished you had white ones that night."

She places a hand on top of her head and paces. "Oh god. I'm going to be fired."

I come around the counter and stand in front of her. "They're not going to fire you."

"Why don't you understand how serious this is?" She raises her voice. "This is going to cost me my job."

"It won't. I'll take it down. Fuck. I just wanted to tell someone. I'm tired of keeping this to myself. I'm crazy about you. I'm in this."

"Someone? You told *everyone*."

Her phone pings, and she whimpers as she looks at it. "That's Blythe. She wants to meet with me first thing this morning."

Already? Damn. Panic makes my throat tight. "I'll talk to her."

"No." Her tone is stern. "You might as well tag me in it if you show up to talk to her."

"I know you don't want to tell people, but we are married, Kota. If you tell her, she can't fire you."

"You really think I want to pull the Johnny Maverick card

again to keep my job? I wanted to earn this job. I wanted to do things the right way."

"Fuck the right way, Kota. It's bullshit. Do whatever makes you happy."

"Like you?" She scoffs and then sighs. "I'm Johnny Maverick, and I do whatever I want on a whim. Fuck the consequences." She stops, eyes wide like she can't believe she said that out loud. "I didn't mean that."

"No, you did, and I guess I deserve that. I haven't done things the way I wanted with you, but I don't regret it because of where it brought us."

"I have to go to work," she says, voice small and broken. I'm gutted. I can't believe I screwed this up so epically.

"I'm sorry. I didn't mean to fuck this up for you. I just wanted you to know how much I want this." I hug her to my chest. I will fix this somehow. "Everything is going to be okay. You'll see."

Chapter Thirty-Six

DAKOTA

Everything is not okay.

I take a seat in Blythe's office, stomach clenching and acid rising in my throat. Reese and Quinn both texted, along with Reagan, Sienna, and Ginny. I'm blowing up. And Johnny thought no one would know? Seriously?

"Katherine will be here soon, but I wanted to talk to you first and get ahead of it. I can't tell you how much I despise prying into my intern's lives, but the news that Johnny Maverick is off the market is big news. Made bigger by the fact these red shoes look a lot like yours." She glances down. I wore them today because not wearing them made me feel too guilty.

"We're together," I confirm. "I'm sorry. I know I should have told you."

She gives me a sad smile. "Katherine will want you and Johnny to sign a form disclosing the relationship, and I can work with you both to draft a statement if you'd like, but I'm afraid I will have to reassign you to another department. I can make some calls, but it's the last week. What do you want to do?"

"I can't imagine working for anyone but you. This summer has been amazing."

"You're talented and hardworking. You'll be okay." But it doesn't feel okay. This was my chance to prove myself, and all I did was become an urban legend like Crissy before me.

I think about Johnny's advice, tell her we're married. The thing is, Blythe has become my role model. I respect her, and I can't bear to see the disappointment on her face that I would expect if I told her I got married in a hush-hush ceremony drunk off my ass. All I have to do is picture my dad's reaction, and I feel like the lowest human alive.

Besides, she'd probably still have to reassign me.

"I think I want to go home," I say and mean it. "Thank you for this opportunity."

She stands and hugs me. "It was my absolute pleasure. Stay in touch, Dakota."

I have to suffer through an awkward exit interview with Katherine, and then I walk out of the Wildcats office for good.

As I get on the elevator at the apartment building, I bite back angry tears, ready to unload on Johnny, but I know it isn't him I'm angry with. This is all on me. I should have told Blythe weeks ago.

I go up to the eleventh floor, and by the time I get there, I realize all I really want is for Johnny to hold me and tell me everything is going to be okay again. I don't believe it, but I still want to hear it. I want to live in our summer of fun just a little longer.

But he isn't home, and I can't bear to be here without him, so I get back in the elevator, not sure where I'm going but not wanting to be alone.

When the elevator stops, Declan and Leo are waiting inside. I wipe my tears and step into the small space.

"Hey, Dakota," Leo says in his soft, deep voice. Both guys give me a nervous once-over.

I wave, not trusting myself to speak.

I clench my jaw in the silence of the ride, willing myself not to cry. I almost make it too, but when the doors open on the first floor, I can't move.

"Everything okay?" Leo's voice is laced with hesitant concern.

"Yes. Fine," I say, but the words end on a sob, and I burst into tears.

He rests a big hand on my shoulder and lets me cry. The three of us ride the elevator together. Me crying harder with every passing second, Leo trying to comfort me, and Declan pressing the close button and barking "take the stairs" to anyone else trying to get on.

I fucked up. I fucked up so badly. Johnny may have dealt the final blow, but I put us in this position. Me and Johnny Maverick? We don't make any sense. We're too different.

When we get to the first floor a second time, neither guy gets off. I hold up my hand to stop the doors from closing. "Thank you. I'm good now."

They still don't make a move to get off the elevator. "Are you sure?" Leo asks. "Do you want me to call Johnny?"

"No," I say quickly and shake my head. "No. I'm okay. Thanks, guys."

With a nod, they exit. Just in time, too, because I start to cry all over again when the doors close between us.

I call Reagan, tears running down my face as my best friend's concerned gaze fills the screen.

"Oh, honey," she says, then her features harden. "Who do I

need to kill?"

"Me. I fucked everything up."

"I'm booking a flight." She stands from the bed. The familiarity of it all tugs at my emotions.

"No, don't. I'm coming home."

Her smile is tinged with sadness. "You're sure?"

"Positive."

"Okay," she says. "I'll be here."

Chapter Thirty-Seven

JOHNNY

Jack tries to take my empty glass from me to refill it, but I motion to the bottle in his hand. "Don't be stingy."

"Are you sure she left?" he asks after handing over the half-empty bottle of Don Julio.

"The only thing left in her room is the furniture," I say.

I was at the jewelry store trying to pick out a ring when Declan called to say that he and Leo had seen her in the elevator crying, and I just knew. By the time I got back to the apartment, she was gone. I came here, not really sure where to go or what to do. It's all my fucking fault.

"I couldn't keep it to myself for one more week," I say. I feel like someone reached in and ripped out my heart, stomped on it, and then tried to put it back.

"What did compel you to post a picture of her mostly naked except those little red shoes, obviously in bed with you."

"Stupidity. Maybe love."

"Hand in hand, my friend."

"Where do you think she went?"

"If I had to guess, Valley. Maybe Kansas to see her dad."

"Did you call her?"

"About a hundred times." I drink from the bottle, spilling a lot of it on my bare chest. No idea where my shirt went. I think I ripped it off and said something about not being able to contain my emotions. I'm a sad case. I can't believe she left. All I got was a Dear Johnny note that said *Thanks for a great summer*.

"Okay. Now you're not even making it in your mouth." He takes the bottle back from me. "I've got some Patron around here somewhere if you're just going to waste it."

"What do I do, captain?"

"You're asking me?"

"Couldn't hurt."

"Forget about her. Focus on hockey. Want me to call some girls?"

"Scratch that. Worst advice ever. Got any Mad Dog?"

"Yeah." He laughs. "I bought a couple of bottles."

"Really?" I hadn't expected him to say yes. "You really are a good captain, stocking your boys' favorite drinks."

He brings me a bottle of MD 20/20. "Never know when you're going to have to step in with words of wisdom and booze."

"So far, your words of wisdom are shit."

"Yeah, I do better when it's related to hockey. Hence the booze."

I unscrew the cap and take a long drink. It doesn't hit the same way, and I groan. "I've lost the ability to taste."

"Oh geez." Jack runs a hand through his hair. "I might need to call in reinforcements."

Ash and Leo show up next. They live in the neighborhood, just down the street. They show their support with sad smiles and drinking in solidarity. Ash offers to take me to the strip club. I accost Leo for every detail about his interaction with Dakota earlier.

By the time I've finished the bottle of Mad Dog, the party is huge. When girls start trying to cheer me up by sitting in my lap, I'm out.

Declan offers me a sober ride back to the apartment, and I accept it. He drives my SUV and says he'll come get his motorcycle tomorrow.

"You'll have your vehicle in case you decide to go after her," he says. "But promise me you'll wait twelve hours or so and let the alcohol ooze out of your system."

"Promise." I hold up my pinky, but he doesn't link his with mine like Heath would have. I miss him. I miss Dakota. I miss my life before I screwed everything up. What was so wrong with being her secret slam piece? At least then I had her to go home to.

Inside, I grab Charli and we lie on the god-awful pink couch. Charli jumps down with a whine and jogs around as if she's looking for Kota.

"We'll get her back," I promise her and pat my chest until she hops back up to keep me company. "Somehow."

I CALL HEATH FRIDAY AFTERNOON WHEN I STILL HAVEN'T HEARD from her. Yes, I've resorted to using our friends for information.

"She hasn't said a lot. At least not to me. Last night, they kicked Adam and me out to have girl time. Ginny is hungover as fuck today."

I hadn't really expected her to sit on the couch and recount the entire thing to our friends, but I wonder what she's told them. Do they know we got married? I'm guessing not, or Heath would be giving me so much shit right now.

"Did she get the flowers? And the balloons?"

"Yeah, man, their place is one flower arrangement away from looking like someone died in there."

"Someone did." I'm lying on the pink couch, my new favorite spot, arm thrown over my face.

I don't have to look at the screen of my phone to know Heath is holding back laughter. I can hear it in his voice. "Dude. No one died. You're going to be fine. You two will work this out. She just needs—"

He stops mid-sentence, and I hear Dakota and Ginny's voices in the background. I can't make out their words, but I can hear her, and everything inside of me lights up and then dies all over again. Fuck, I miss her.

Chapter Thirty-Eight

DAKOTA

There are three weeks before the fall semester starts. The apartment building is starting to fill up again, and most of the jocks are back for preseason training, which means there is no shortage of things to do and parties to attend. Not that I have any interest in any of it.

Ginny and Reagan have been great. I've never been the one that needed consoling, and they keep looking at me with big, sad eyes that I know are from a good place but make me feel worse because I know I must look as awful as I feel.

Two nights ago, we had a night in and watched sappy movies and ate ice cream and all of the queso in Valley. Not together, but it was still glorious.

But after too many days of feeling sorry for myself, it's time to do something. I lace up my shoes and go for a long run. Running has always been an outlet for me. I was a sporty kid, but I didn't start running competitively until after my mom died. It was one place where no one asked me if I was okay or questioned my silence. If you sit alone in the cafeteria at school, people whisper. But not when you run. I didn't realize at the time how much those runs allowed me to escape, but as I once again find myself searching for solitude, I realize this is where it's always been okay for me to not be okay.

When I get back to the apartment, I feel lighter than I have since returning to Valley. Reagan is in the kitchen, standing and eating a bowl of cereal.

"Another delivery came." She points to a box on our kitchen counter. All the lightness fades in an instant.

"Want me to open it?" Ginny asks from where she lies on the couch.

I pull my earbuds out and drop them next to the box. "No. Yes. *No.*"

"Come on. You don't want to know what's inside? I'm dying." Ginny hops up and comes to the kitchen. She runs a finger over the packing tape and looks at Reagan. "Back me up here."

"It has been interesting. Who could have predicted an entire box of hair ties?"

My already tight chest constricts a little more. A hundred hair ties to be exact. All red. I look down at the one I haven't been able to remove from my ring finger.

"Or the Pop Rocks. Do I even want to know?" Ginny asks.

"Open it," I say. As much as it hurts, I do want to know. Every single gift has been over the top in true Johnny form, but also more sentimental than I pegged him for.

Ginny tries to hide how giddy she is about it but fails spectacularly. She rips open the box and stills.

"What is it?" Reagan asks.

Instead of answering, Ginny holds out the box to me.

White Converse covered in rhinestones or crystals. Oh, god, they better not be crystals. Either way, they're custom and expensive. So very Johnny. I pull one from the box to show them both.

"Those are cute." Reagan smiles. "But why white?"

I shrug like I don't understand the significance, put it back in the box, and hand it to her. "Set it with the others. I can't deal with that right now."

"Do you think you'll ever forgive him?" Ginny asks.

"Of course, I'll forgive him." I'm mad, and I'm hurt. The second more than the first. I know he didn't do it maliciously, but he still did it. No thought beyond the moment and no consideration for how it might impact me. I know he's sorry and, yes, I know that I will forgive him, but right now, I can't forgive myself. I knew it was a bad idea to get involved in a summer fling and break the rules of my internship, but I gave in and let his carefree and wild attitude overturn my better judgment.

My phone rings, and I don't even have to look to know it's him. He calls every day, leaves rambling voice mails telling me about his day, and then signs off by apologizing and asking me to call him back.

"He messed up." Reagan reaches over and squeezes my hand.

"We never should have happened. We were two people in a new city clinging to each other out of loneliness and forced proximity. We're too different. It's better to cut things off now, and maybe someday we can be friends again."

I can't admit to Ginny and Reagan that I think we're beyond ever going back to friends. I know myself well enough to know that seeing him will break my heart all over again. Maybe with enough time.

"I'm going to shower."

Their gazes full of pity and sadness follow me into my bedroom where I shut the door and then lean against it to let out a shaky breath.

I miss him. There I've admitted it. Woo. Go me. What do I win? Another day filled with sad memories and heartbreak.

Because I've apparently turned into a masochist, I bring my phone to my ear to listen to his most recent voice mail.

"Hey, Kota. It's me. It's Johnny." His deep voice drives tiny daggers into my heart. "I'm out for a walk with Charli. Went to a Twins game last night with Jack. Thought of you. Saw Quinn and some of the other interns at Wild's. Thought of you. Oh, and get this, you know how there was a rumor that Jack hooked up with an intern who went all psycho on him and blasted it on social media? It wasn't Jack. It was Declan. Can you believe it? He told me himself. It's a crazy story." He pauses. "I wish you were here so I could tell you in person. I don't think it'd be the same over voice mail. I miss you. I'm sorry. I'm so sorry. Call me back." He's quiet, but I hear his sigh, and then the recording ends.

I head over to the Hall of Fame to talk to my boss and see if I can get on the schedule sooner rather than later. She's ecstatic to have me back, which makes me feel a tiny bit better about everything. Maybe I blew my dream job, but this one isn't so bad. And Blythe did say she'd write me a reference letter, so maybe the summer wasn't a total waste.

There are only so many ways to kill the day, and I end up back at the apartment, resigning myself to another night of watching my happy roommates text or hang out with their boyfriends.

I swear I saw Adam and Heath less when they lived across the breezeway from us. Now that we've moved into a three-bedroom a floor up, our apartment has become the new hang spot.

And I'm happy for my friends. I really am. Even more so after the amazing summer I had. I had a little piece of that this summer. I get it now.

Heath is in our living room by himself when I walk in.

"Hey," I say, dropping my keys on the counter. "Where is everyone?"

"Ginny is talking to her mom on the phone. Adam and Reagan are in her room."

I nod and grab a sparkling water from the fridge. Ginny comes out of her room, falling onto the cushion next to Heath. "Hey, you're back. Where'd you go all day?"

"I stopped by the Hall of Fame. Regina got me a few hours this week helping with events and doing office work. It's boring, but it's better than sitting around waiting for summer to end."

The days are long even as I try to fill them full of activities. When Sienna and Rhett group call us later, I wander out to the living room and plaster on a happy face. It's the first time since their engagement that they've come up for air, and we huddle around Ginny's laptop in the living room so everyone can hear all the details. I was there, of course, but I stay and listen to them retell the story.

"Maverick helped arrange everything," Rhett says. "Where is he anyway?"

"Might have been my bad," Heath says. "I wasn't sure if…" He glances at me, and I drop my gaze to the floor. "Let me text him to hop on."

A minute later, Johnny's face appears on the screen. He's got on a Wildcats hat pulled low on his eyes, but his smile is easy and light. "Hey, guys. What's up?"

Since the rest of us have already caught up, the questions turn to Maverick. I can tell by the background and noise that he's at Wild's—clinking glasses and people talking. Declan's big shoulder is in half the frame.

"How's Minnesota?" Adam asks him.

"Uhh, it's okay." Johnny briefly looks at me. "Most of the guys are still on vacation, but I'm working out hard every day, and they've got me doing a lot of press leading up to the season."

"Miss you, buddy," Heath says and makes a heart with his hands.

"Right back at ya."

The conversation bounces back around to Rhett and Sienna. When are they getting married? Where?

My stomach twists with sadness and a little guilt that I haven't shared with my friends the biggest thing that's ever happened to me.

When the call is over, I ask Reagan and Ginny to come into my room. Normally, Heath and Adam would whine and complain, and the fact they don't makes me feel like poor, pitiful Dakota. But whatever, right now, I don't care. I need to tell someone.

We sit on top of my bed. I can't figure out the right way to say the words. It still sounds so ridiculous in my head. I go back and forth on whether I should call Sienna. I don't want to steal any of her thunder from the engagement, but I don't want her to feel excluded either.

Screw it.

"I'm calling Sienna." I hold out the phone as Ginny and Reagan share a worried look.

"Are you okay?" Reagan asks. "Was that hard seeing Maverick?"

"Brutal," I say honestly. Sienna answers, and I angle the phone so that she can see everyone.

"What's going on?" she asks.

I swallow and look around at my best friends in the whole world.

"Johnny and I got married in Vegas."

It's so quiet I can hear the guys in the living room and the TV. They're watching the NBA playoffs, and something big must have happened because they are excited about it. I'm finding a million things to focus on, anything but the silence and disbelieving jaw-dropped faces of my favorite girls.

Sienna is the first to recover. "When you say married, you mean…"

I hold up my left hand. "Married."

Ginny starts giggling. She slaps a hand over her mouth and waves a hand. "I'm sorry," she gets out before erupting into laughter again. Soon Reagan joins her, and then Sienna and I do too.

"I know," I say, tears that are some weird mixture of happy and sad stream down my face. "It's absolutely ridiculous. I wanted to tell you guys but… I don't know. I was afraid that you'd tell me how wild it was. I mean, I know. I knew then, but some small part of me wanted to be happy about it too. And then this one went and got engaged." I motion to the phone. "I'm so happy for you, and I'm sorry that I'm dimming your excitement with my marriage disaster. You're getting married, and I'm getting an annulment."

"Wait." All the laughter dies as Reagan rests a hand on my leg. "You're going to get it annulled?"

"Well, yeah. It was a summer fling and an impulsive, drunken decision." I share a picture with Sienna and then show Ginny and Reagan. It's the only picture I took the night we got married. We didn't want to risk the chapel releasing photos and outing us, so we only took them with our phones. We were coherent enough not to make headlines with a Vegas wedding, but not for much else.

"You look beautiful and really happy." Ginny tilts her head and lays it on my shoulder. "Are you sure you two can't work it out?"

"And then what? He's there. I'm here."

"But you're married," Reagan whines.

"Oooooh. The white blinged-out Chucks make sense now!"

"And wait, this is your wedding ring?" Ginny touches the red hair tie.

"It was a whole thing," I say, blushing as I recall a hazy memory of him fucking me against the window of our Vegas suite, my wrists bound by the flimsy elastic.

"Do you love him?" Reagan asks.

I stare at my hands and nod. "I do. I really, really do."

Chapter Thirty-Nine

JOHNNY

If I had it my way, I would have left to win Dakota back days ago, but Blythe has filled my schedule with media and promotions, so instead, I spend the week fulfilling obligations, moving anything scheduled the following week, and planning. I've never planned so much in my life. I think I have a real knack for it, though.

So far, I've sent flowers, chocolates, balloons, gifts that somehow reminded me of her, and approximately one million photos of Charli and me with accompanying *I'm so sorry, please forgive me* texts.

Dakota hasn't responded to any of them, but I didn't expect her to. I fucked up bad. A few gifts aren't going to make her forget that. Besides, we need to hash this out in person. The gifts and texts are just to make sure she knows how sorry I am.

Saturday morning, I wake up to knocking on the door and someone yelling on the other side.

"Nobody's home," I yell and roll over. I've slept on this awful pink couch every night just to feel closer to her. I've probably jacked up my back permanently. It's so uncomfortable.

"Open the door, *Maverick*."

I still, the disdain and amusement drip off his deep baritone, and recognition dawns. My pulse races, and I sit up. Charli, the traitor, jogs to the door and actually looks happy as I open it for Dakota's dad.

"Hi, Jerry. Good to see you, sir." I run a hand over my bed head and sneak a glance back at the messy apartment.

"You're missing a shirt," he muses and steps inside.

"Uh, come in. Dakota's not here."

"No kidding." He looks around the place while I find my T-shirt and pull it on. He zeroes right in on the empty liquor bottles in the kitchen.

"I wasn't expecting anyone," I say.

"Clearly."

"What are you doing here?" I toss a bunch of empty take-out containers and bottles into the trash.

"I came to get her furniture."

"Oh." I nod. "I would have gotten it back to her."

He wastes no time finding her room and taking the nightstand out first. He's got old man, freaky-strong muscles, the kind that have been developed over a lot of years of constant use, but I remember how his back hurt him last time, and I jump in.

He lets me, wordlessly, and together we load up her furniture in the trailer attached to his truck. I step back on the curb, hands in my pocket. It feels so final now. I always knew she had to go back for school, but I guess maybe I hoped that was the temporary thing and not us.

"Dakota told me what you did," Jerry says, and my heart

drops to my stomach. "How you got her the internship and the endorsement contract."

"Oh." I guess of all the things she could have told her dad that I did, that's the safest one. "She deserved it. She's a hard worker and so smart."

"It's difficult not to be able to give your kid everything they want. Some things are just out of your control. Thank you for what you did." He stares at the ground as he delivers the words. It hits me—Jerry's uncomfortable thanking me. Somehow that makes me feel worse. I don't deserve his thanks, and he wouldn't be giving it if he knew how I ruined it for her.

"She did an incredible job." That much is true.

He watches me with those parental *I know things* eyes. "I'm hungry. Somewhere around here to get breakfast?"

"Yeah, there are quite a few places within walking distance."

He hits the lock on the key fob and starts down the sidewalk, stopping a few feet away. "Are you coming or what?"

I take Jerry to the café where Dakota and I came on several Sundays with Charli. He orders the same thing she always does, too, but I keep that to myself.

"So, you screwed up pretty good, huh?" he asks, catching me off guard again.

"You know?" Oh shit. Maybe he brought me here to kick my ass with an audience.

"No. She didn't tell me anything, but she's not here, and you look like shit. I'm old, but I'm not stupid."

Man, he doesn't hold back. So I decide not to either. I tell him everything. Okay, almost everything. I give him the short version of how I got her the job and then how I ruined it for her. I leave out how we decided to be slam buddies all summer. And truth, it was never just that. We both knew it. Keeping the focus on sex made it easy for us to give in. The traditional route was never going to work for us. We are different. She's right about that, and those differences would have kept us from seeing how alike we really are underneath.

"I love her, and I miss her something fierce. How is she?"

"She's back in Valley. Sounds okay. Sorry if you were hoping she was crying her eyes out over you every night."

"I don't hope that at all. I don't ever want her to feel like this." I wave a hand in front of me.

He chews his food, watching me carefully.

"I'm going to win her back. Or at least try. I would have already left, but I had a few commitments here I couldn't bail on."

With a thoughtful nod, he says, "Sometimes people need to come around on their own."

"Are you saying that I shouldn't go see her? Because I don't think I can stay here hoping she'll change her mind. I need her."

"No. I'm not saying that. But what she might need is time."

"I respect that, but I have to tell her how I feel." I drop my gaze to the table. "Tradition and family, I know they're important to Kota. She talks about you so fondly. And her mom. That awful pink couch."

He actually laughs, just a tiny bit.

"My parents… we're not close. But Kota, she's like family. That's how much I love and need her. I screwed up. I did. That's kind of my thing. Just ask my dad. I ruined her job, but I have to make it right somehow." The pit that's been in my stomach all week grows. "It was so dumb. I wanted everyone to know she was mine.

She asked me not to, but I did it anyway, and she paid the price."

I don't know why I'm telling Jerry this. He's never going to approve of me, so he might as well hear just how big of a fuckup I am.

"Have you ever been so excited about something you just couldn't keep it to yourself? You had to tell someone, or you'd burst?" I don't wait for his answer. "That's how I felt. I didn't think. I just wanted everyone to know how much she means to me." I shift in my chair, remembering that morning and wishing it had gone differently.

"If she'd have just told them we were married, they couldn't have fired her." My head snaps up. Oh shit.

Jerry's brows raise, and his fork clatters on his plate. "I'm gonna need you to repeat that. Start from the beginning and don't leave anything out this time, *Maverick*."

Chapter Forty

DAKOTA

On Sunday morning, otherwise known as the end of my sanity, I wake to Heath and Ginny in the kitchen making breakfast together. Well, Ginny is. She was so excited about moving out of the dorms and into an apartment where she could cook something besides noodles that taste like cardboard.

Her boyfriend sits on the counter next to her while she fries bacon in a pan.

"What are you making?" I ask, standing on the other side of the counter and flipping through yesterday's mail.

"Omelets. Want one?"

I shake my head as I pull out an envelope addressed to me from my high school. Looks like they finally found me. Not that I wasn't getting the mail they were sending my dad, but I felt like I could pretend I wasn't. I open it and read the letter inviting me to a Hall of Fame inductee ceremony at halftime of the homecoming football game in two months. "Anything else come?"

They exchange a look before Ginny says, "That's it."

Huh. The flowers and gifts from Johnny have stopped. Nothing new has come since Friday. Maybe he's finally given up. I wish I felt better about that outcome. I've started to call him so many times, but part of me needs to give him space to see if he really wants me or if he just fell into this thing because I was his little piece of home.

"Oh!" my friend exclaims, breaking me from my thoughts. "We're going to the movies tonight."

"To see what?"

Neither answers right away.

Heath clears his throat. "There's this new action movie."

"Pass," I say, and Ginny smacks her boyfriend on the arm.

"He meant a rom-com." She turns and gives me a pouty lip. "Please? You have to come. We're all going. It'll be fun."

"I'm not really in the mood for a big group date. Besides, I'm working at the Hall of Fame."

"*Tonight?*"

"Yeah, there's some sort of event for the basketball team. Anyway, thanks for the invite."

I take the letter to my room and put it on my desk. Maybe it's time to face the past and move on. That's the thing about having your heart blasted to smithereens—all the other cracks and fissures you've been walking around with seem a lot less significant.

When I arrive at the Hall of Fame, I'm able to jump right to work and put everything else out of mind. The Valley basketball team is having a fancy party for a promotion on the coaching staff. There's dinner and cocktails and lots of laughter.

I weave through the guests, making sure everyone is happy. I could have left already. I only needed to stay for setup, but my friends went to the movies tonight, and sitting home by myself sounds worse than working.

I smirk when I see the man of the hour hiding in a corner away from the people who came to celebrate him. I grab a beer from the bar and take it to Wes Reynolds, the new head coach of the men's basketball team. He's the youngest head coach in the history of the school.

"Thanks. Thought I was going to have to decide between abandoning my spot in the corner and grabbing a fresh drink."

"No problem. Any particular reason you're hiding? Is there something we can do?"

"No, this is great. I've never had a party dedicated to me. It's a little overwhelming. I wanted a few minutes to take it all in without having to talk to anyone." He stares out at the party. I can't read his expression—excitement, nerves, amazement?

"Congratulations, Coach."

My boss beckons me from across the room.

"Enjoy tonight," I tell him. "Don't hide out too long. A lot of people want to share this with you."

"Thanks." He doesn't move. "Maybe just five more minutes."

Laughing, I head over to my boss, Regina.

"I thought you'd already left," she says with a smile. She hasn't said a word about the extra hours I've been putting in or even asked why I'm back early.

"I decided to stick around. I timed out. Don't worry."

"No, I'm glad you're here. We need to preview a new video for the hype room, and I'm all tied up."

"Tonight?"

She hesitates. "We have an early tour in the morning, and I'm hoping to use it."

"Okay. Sure. I can do that." Really, what is my other option, go home and sulk? Pass.

"Thank you, Dakota." She hands me a tablet. "I labeled it Dakota Preview."

"Should be easy to find," I say with a small laugh.

I punch in the code to get in the hype room, and the door slides open. It's a little weird being in here by myself. I've done it before when we were testing something or working out kinks, but usually, we just preview the videos on the computer. Or maybe Regina does this, and I've just never had to.

Whatever. I select the Dakota Preview video. I didn't even ask her which sport it was for. They're all pretty great. These hype videos could make a sports fan out of just about anyone.

The music comes on first. It's a slower beat than the others, but with the heavy bass. I'm digging it. Also, it's familiar, but I can't put my finger on it.

When the first image fills the wall of screens, I gasp. It's me. I've never seen the photo before, but it's from the summer. I'm sitting on the pink couch with a playful smirk aimed at the person taking the photo. *Oh Johnny, what did you do?*

Photos from our summer together, so many that I'm shocked by how many he took, display before me. They're more than just random images of two people over eight weeks of their lives. They're a montage of two people falling in love. It hits me seeing it like this that I never stood a chance. I would do it all again, even knowing the heartbreak that was coming. I'd risk everything for him. No, I *did* risk everything. And sure, I can blame him for the way it ended, but I knew what I was doing, and I decided he was worth it. Why was that so hard to remember when everything I feared would happen did?

Three minutes and twelve seconds. That's how long it takes for me to fall in love all over again. Tears in my eyes and a smile on my face, I have to punch in the code twice because my fingers are trembling.

I already have my phone to my ear to call him as I exit. I come up short when I spot him. I don't know why it didn't occur to me that he might be here, but I'm so glad he is. Johnny stands alone in dark jeans and a white T-shirt, hair combed and styled. His jaw is tight, and brows slanted with nerves as he watches me.

I spent a summer seeing him in so many different ways—dressed up, casual, shirtless, at home, at work, out with friends, playing with Charli, and just the two of us. I've seen him mad, sad, happy, serious, content, playful, tired, hurt, and a million others. He gave me all of him, always. He never holds back.

So neither do I. I run to him and throw my arms around his neck, breathing him in. "Johnny."

"Kota." His arms wrap around my back, and his mouth covers mine. He apologizes over and over again as he kisses me softly, hands roaming over my back and my hair, and then framing my face. "I am so in love with you. Tell me I didn't blow my only chance. I need you too much."

I need him too. I need him despite his ridiculousness and because of it.

"I love you too. Like a really crazy, wild, ridiculous amount."

He grins. "And all the rest?"

I don't have the answers, but I know I'm not giving up on us without a fight. "We'll figure it out, but right now, take me home, Johnny Maverick."

We don't come up for air until the following afternoon.

"I'm sorry," I say quietly, tracing the outline of a new tattoo on his chest. A pink sofa and my name in cursive along the edge. His first colored ink.

"For what?" He threads his fingers through my hair.

"I shouldn't have left. It wasn't just because of everything with the Wildcats. I was scared. It all felt too fast, and I wasn't sure how much was real and how much was this Maverick-induced, crazy, fun lifestyle."

His deep laughter shakes his chest. "I know. I'm a lot."

I lift up so I can stare into his hazel eyes. "I love you. I'm sorry I didn't give you more credit. You might be a lot to handle, but you're also the most genuine and reliable person I know."

He places a hand on my forehead as if he's checking my temperature. "Do you have Maverick fever? Did we have sex so much you've overdosed on the D?"

"I'm serious," I say when he pulls me down onto him and cinches his arms tighter around my waist. "The things you do for people, the way you make them feel, it's big, and it's important. You are a good man. The best, actually."

I angle my face to his, and he kisses my already swollen lips.

Eventually, I fall back on his chest, head resting over his heart. "When do you have to go back?"

"Tomorrow."

"Let's stay here all day then."

He kisses the top of my head. "Can't. We have a lot to figure out."

I groan.

"Look at you, avoiding planning. Never thought I'd see the day."

"Can't we just enjoy today without talking about how I'm never going to see you again?"

"Reagan is the drama queen, babe."

I sit up. "I'm serious. I've seen your schedule. It's nuts."

"Yeah. So?"

"So?" I laugh. "We'll never see each other."

"Phone sex. Remote vibrators. Weekend trips. Dirty letters. Sexting. The possibilities, babe. We've barely scratched the surface." He looks so genuinely excited about all of it that I can't help but smile.

"Aren't you looking forward to life as a big-shot NHL star? Traveling and puck bunnies and, I don't know, threesomes galore?"

He barks a laugh.

I straddle him. "What if you start to resent having a ball and chain a thousand miles away?"

"I won't."

"We could do what we did this summer."

"Fuck like bunnies in spring?"

"When we're together, yes, but all the rest of the time you'd be free to do what you want." I'm slammed with visuals of social media capturing his hookups and I have to hold on to my resolve.

"And you'd get to do the same here in Valley?"

"Yeah." I shrug. Where does one go after Johnny Maverick? Who could possibly compare to him?

"Fuck, no. I don't have the kind of money I'd need to bail me out of jail every time a guy hit on you. And truth be told, I don't want to be free to do whatever I want on the road. I want you. It's only a year. Then you can be my trophy wife."

I raise a brow.

"Or girlfriend. Whatever you decide."

"I want to work."

"Fine." He sighs. "I was really looking forward to a 1950s type housewife that answers the door in high heels and an apron with a beer in her hand to ask me about my day."

I pinch him, and he laughs. "Kidding. Though, maybe we could do some role-playing because the visual that just gave me was pretty spectacular."

He holds me, and I stare down at the new ink. I still can't believe this man tattooed my name on his body.

"I'm always going to support your dreams. Hopefully, some of them are naked dreams, but I digress. My contract is two years. After that, we'll make decisions together. You want to be a big-shot boss lady, then I'll stay home and be a househusband. Maybe I'll wear the apron and high heels."

"Now there's an idea."

"Just say you'll be mine, Kota. I'm flexible on all the rest."

I nod.

"Yeah?" One side of his mouth pulls into a boyish smirk.

"How could I say no to having a househusband?"

"Husband? Did you say husband?"

"Legally, that's still what you are."

He leans over the edge of the bed and grabs his jeans. "Your response to that is to get dressed? Really?"

I admire the view of his tight ass and the muscles of his back.

When his head pops back up, he cradles a black box in one hand, and all the air is sucked from my lungs.

"I was going to wait. Take you out on a bunch of really baller dates first. Wine and dine you, impress you with all sorts of really romantic shit. I was going to do it the right way this time, but it's the quiet moments like this that I feel the closest to you." He opens the box and a beautiful ring sparkles back at me. "Marry me, Dakota. Today. Tomorrow. In a year from now or five. Whatever you want. I promise I'll never stop showing you how much you mean to me. Over the top, big and wild love."

"I wouldn't have you any other way, Johnny Maverick." I stare at the ring again. "It's gorgeous."

He plucks it from the box and slides it down my ring finger. "Your dad helped me pick it out."

"He did?"

"After I accidentally told him we eloped."

I gasp. "You didn't?"

"I did. Sorry." He winces.

Oh no. "But you're still in one piece."

"It was touch and go for a few minutes, but I told him what you mean to me and promised that I'd spend my entire life making you happy."

"What do I do with this?" I twist the red elastic around my finger. I haven't removed it since the night in Vegas.

He lifts it over the diamond ring and then wraps his lips around my finger, gliding the elastic up my finger. He holds the red hair tie with his teeth as he covers my body with his.

"Hands above your head, baby."

Chapter Forty-One

DAKOTA

Two months later

Johnny's handsome face stares back at me through the phone. "Are you wearing it?"

"Yes." I roll my eyes but lower my phone to show him I'm wearing the Wildcats jersey he sent me. His.

"Maybe you should wear the shirt from the Frozen Four instead. The one I made with the Valley colors."

"Already thought of that." I lift the jersey to show him it's underneath. "You've got this."

He blows out a breath that puffs out his cheeks. His dark hair is slicked back, and he's in his pads and jersey for their first game.

"I wish you were here."

"Me too."

"Phone sex later?"

"Yes, and I'm sending you a little something right now." I send the text and wait for him to get it.

He chuckles. "My two favorite girls."

I pat Charli's head, and Johnny coos at her, slipping into the sweet voice he only uses for his dog. We decided since he's traveling so much, it would be easier for Charli to stay with me for a few months. She and I get along great, but she misses her guy. Me too.

"Now go crush it. I want to brag about my superhot, super talented husband to all my friends. They're coming over to watch, and we're doing a Zoom call with Rhett and Sienna. My dad's even watching. We're all so proud of you."

"I knew I'd win Jerry over." He smirks, and then it falls. "Okay. Love you. I'll call you later."

We gather in the living room for the game. Sienna and Rhett are watching in Minnesota, but Ginny pulls them up on her laptop, so it's almost like we're all together to watch Johnny's pro debut.

All his nerves were completely unwarranted. The Wildcats get off to an early lead. Johnny gets an assist in the first period, and seconds before the end of the game, he fires a shot that sneaks by the goalie and lights up the goalpost.

Heath jumps to his feet and screams. He does a lap around the living room and rips off his T-shirt and swings it around his head. While our friends celebrate, I stare at the TV with tears in my eyes. I'm so proud of him.

He calls me as soon as he's done with interviews and headed to the airport with the team.

"Congratulations!"

He grins. "You're my lucky charm."

"You have to call Heath. He was out of his mind when you scored that goal."

"I will. First, check your email."

"My email?"

"Mhmm. I just sent something to you."

"Okay." I move to my desk and find the email from Johnny. It's a forward, and I skim quickly, stopping when I get to the bottom and see the photo of him in the shower from the photo shoot we did this summer.

"I don't understand."

"My dad called me after the launch. Apparently, it didn't do as well as they expected."

I bite my tongue. I'm still pissed about the way his dad handled that. Not about the photos. I can handle my work being critiqued, but I cannot handle my man being shit on by someone who is supposed to love him unconditionally.

"He wanted to renegotiate, and I told him the only way I was going to be the face of Maverick Corporation's new line was if they used your ideas. All of them."

I scroll up and read more carefully as he speaks.

"They created a new scent called Rebel. Johnny Maverick wears Rebel. It goes live tomorrow. They're using all of your content, the image you selected, the behind-the-scenes videos, everything. Your check is in the mail."

"My check?"

"A little bonus to show JM Holdings' appreciation."

"Johnny," I admonish. I know we're married, but I'm not sure I'll ever get used to his money being our money.

"If you're opposed to buying something for yourself, then use it to come see me next weekend. Invite the whole gang."

And there it is. I'd wager just about anything that when that check arrives, it'll be for the exact amount to fly me, and all our friends, to Minnesota.

"I love you."

"Love you too, babe. I'll call you as soon as I get home. Be naked."

And that's how the first few months apart go. We talk every day. I cheer him on from afar, and in the Wildcats arena that I spent so much time at this summer, I hang out with my friends, work at the Hall of Fame, study, and countdown the minutes between every visit and call.

On a crisp fall weekend, Johnny has two days off, and we travel to Kansas together. The ceremony is held during halftime of the homecoming game. Dad and Johnny watch from the sidelines. I'm nervous as I walk out onto the football field with the other former athletes being inducted into the school's Hall of Fame.

Mr. Hote, my old track coach, is probably here somewhere in the stands, but I specifically requested that he not be the one to give me the award. I keep my eyes trained on Johnny and my father standing and clapping. They both look so proud. It's a silly award, but it means everything that they're here. Maybe life is less about accepting the award and more about the people who are there for you when you receive it.

It's over in minutes, and it feels a little childish that I waited all these years to come back.

"Do you want to stay for the rest of the game?" Dad asks me when I make my way back to our seats.

"No. I think I'm good. Thank you both for coming."

Dad hugs me tight against his chest. "Your mother would be so proud."

Johnny takes my hand as we walk out to the truck.

"Dakota!"

I turn at my name and find Coach Hote jogging after us. He really is a handsome guy. Age has been kind to him. His hair is a dusty blond, and his blue eyes are bright, only the faintest wrinkles giving away he's now in his forties.

"Coach," I say, squeezing Johnny's hand tighter.

My husband takes a step, so he's standing in front of me. I avoid looking at my dad. If he knew that this man—a man that used to frequently pick me up and drop me off at home—tried to have sex with me, he'd kill him and maybe me for keeping it from him.

Coach Hote must understand the situation isn't altogether friendly. He holds up both hands. "I just wanted to offer my congratulations. You were a great runner. I was sad to hear you gave it up. I hope it wasn't because of our misunderstanding." He looks to my dad. "Sometimes crushes like this happen. The teenage years can be very confusing for kids, especially girls." His gaze sweeps back over me, and I'm frozen. Oh my god, is he trying to play this off like I was crushing on him, and he turned *me* down? I'm so angry I can't breathe. "You look good. How long are you in town? Maybe we could catch up."

Johnny's hold is a vise, and I squeeze back equally as tight to keep him at my side. I do not need him to get in a fight and get suspended or fined.

"You son of a bitch." Dad takes a step and throws a punch that none of us see coming. Least of all Coach Hote. He winces and shakes his hand. "Stay away from my family, or I'll borrow my new son's hockey stick and let him show me how to use it on your kidneys."

Coach wipes at the corner of his mouth where his lip is split.

I'm speechless as I stare at my dad.

Holy shit. Johnny tugs me away, and Dad wraps his arm around my shoulders as if nothing happened. "Who wants pizza?"

Epilogue

JOHNNY

On a beautiful July weekend, I throw a party. A very big, very over-the-top party. Mr. and Mrs. Maverick style.

"You have really outdone yourself this time," Heath says, sitting next to me at a table covered in white linens and colorful floral arrangements. So many floral arrangements. Roses in every color. Candles, fairy lights, music, dancing, food, and a four-tier cake.

All of it for her.

Dakota meets my gaze from the dance floor. She and the girls are in a circle, moving to the beat and belting out the lyrics. I can't hear her from here, but I feel the place she's belting it out from. Bliss. Home. I've found my person.

One year after our Vegas wedding, we're celebrating our anniversary with the wedding I should have given her the first time. I have regrets, but it's hard to add that one to the list. Still, I wouldn't be me if I didn't try to give her everything she missed out on.

"What about you and Ginny?" I ask my buddy. "You buy a ring

yet?"

"Without your help?" He laughs and tips back the beer in his hand. After he's drained it, he stands. "Soon. I just want to finish school first and get my signing bonus so I can buy a huge diamond." He moves his hands apart wider than his body.

Without warning, Ginny throws herself between his arms and wraps her arms around his chest. "Come dance with me."

He tosses his empty bottle and sweeps her off her feet. "Great idea, baby doll."

I find Adam and Rhett standing shoulder to shoulder on the edge of the dance floor watching their girls.

"Gentleman," I say, stepping between them.

"The man of the night." Adam holds up his drink. "Congratulations."

"Thank you. I appreciate you guys coming."

"Are you kidding? We wouldn't miss it." Rhett rocks back on his heels. "Who would have thought you'd be the first to get married?"

"What can I say? I'm more worldly and mature than the rest of you fools." I bust up laughing. Yeah, that isn't it. "I'm a lucky guy. Got the girl, got great friends, and I look damn good in a tux."

"You clean up nice," Rhett confirms. "You'll have another chance to wear it next month."

"Can't wait," I say. He and Sienna are up next. They're getting married in a church in Sienna's hometown. It's the summer of love. The second of many. I might just keep right on throwing an anniversary party every year. "I'm going in. Meet you guys in five like we planned?"

I don't wait for an answer, I know they've got my back, before I move toward my wife. Now that she's graduated and moved to

Minnesota, I see her every day. I wake up with her, come home to her, and still she takes my breath away.

"Wifey," I say as I circle an arm around her waist and pull her to me. She's wearing a white dress and the Chucks I bought her.

"Yes, handsome husband of mine?"

"I have a surprise for you."

Her eyes light up with excitement and humor. "Of course you do."

I lead her away from the dance floor. Her hand takes mine, and I interlace our fingers.

"Because the car and the jewelry, and—"

I silence her with a kiss. Her sweet laughter spills into my mouth. Okay, so I bought a *few* things for our anniversary. Sue me, I like to spoil my girl.

"This one is different."

Some of my teammates are hanging outside of the tent with their dates.

Jack juts his chin as we approach. "Congratulations."

"Thanks, man."

Declan shakes my hand and then hugs Dakota.

Leo, Ash, and Tyler offer fist bumps.

Quinn and Reese made it, too. Together. That's a pair I didn't see coming.

"We'll be back, guys." I squeeze Dakota's hand. "Enjoy the booze."

Inside our house, yeah, that's right, we're homeowners, I pause in the entryway and kiss my wife. We bought a place not far from Jack's. I can walk to half my teammate's houses.

"Johnny Maverick, did you pull me away from our party to

have sex? Is the surprise your penis? Because I've seen it." She leans in and lowers her voice. "*A lot.*"

"Baby, my dick is always a gift, but no." I tug her into the office on the first floor. We just moved in last week and have a few projects going to make this our dream home.

Dakota wanted a workout room and a killer kitchen, and I wanted, nay, *needed*, a living room to hold the biggest TV you can buy and enough seats for all my friends and teammates. And one more thing.

On the bookcase, there's a framed picture of Kota and me from one night years ago at Valley playing sardines. I push on the back of the shelf directly behind the picture, and the entire bookcase moves.

Dakota jumps back as it swings open, revealing the secret room behind it.

"Johnny," she gasps, walking in slowly.

I follow her, raise my hands and look at her through a window I make with my thumbs and pointer fingers. Perfect.

"This is incredible." She turns in a circle with a grin that makes it all worth it.

"We finally have the best hiding spot. Got about five minutes before they start looking for us."

"You did this for a silly game?"

"Nothing silly about it," I say. "A lot of great memories from the nights I spent hiding in the dark with you."

She wraps her arms around my neck. "And a lot more to come."

ABOUT THE AUTHOR

Rebecca Jenshak is a *USA Today* bestselling author of new adult and sports romance. She lives in Arizona with her family. When she isn't writing, you can find her attending local sporting events, hanging out with family and friends, or with her nose buried in a book.

Sign up for her newsletter for book sales and release news.

Made in the USA
Las Vegas, NV
01 August 2023